NIGHT
FLIGHT

TRUTH SEEKERS SERIES

NIGHT
FLIGHT

DIANE & DAVID MUNSON

Micah
House
media

ISBN-13: 978-0-9835590-2-3
ISBN-10:   0-9835590-2-3

Scripture quotations, unless otherwise indicated, are taken from the HOLY BIBLE, NEW
INTERNATIONAL VERSION®. NIV®. Copyright ©1973, 1978, 1984 by International Bible
Society. Used by permission of Zondervan. All rights reserved.

This is a work of fiction. Names, characters, places, and incidents either are the prod-
uct of the authors' imaginations or are used fictitiously. The authors and publishers
intend that all persons, organizations, events and locales portrayed in the work be
considered as fictitious. Any resemblance to any person, living or dead, is coincidental.

Authors' photo © 2010 Diane and David Munson

Printed in the United States of America
17 16 15 14 13 12   7 6 5 4 3 2 1

Dedication

Annelise, Kira, Leah, Sarah, Steven.
You light up our lives.

Jesus said,
"My command is this: Love each other as I have loved you."
(John 15:12)
and
"Love your neighbor as your self."
(Matthew 19:19)

Acknowledgments

Many thanks to those of you who support and inspire us: Ginny McFadden, Pam Guerrieri, Dave Rogers, the search dog Kahlua, and the readers who encourage us to keep writing about the real Federal and Intelligence agents. Thanks to our colleagues who remain on the front lines in government. You know who you are.

About the Authors

David and Diane Munson are ExFeds and a husband and wife team who craft suspense stories based on their exciting careers. David tracked down criminals as a Special Agent for NCIS, just like the TV show. He also traveled the world, facing danger as a Special Agent, working undercover for DEA (Drug Enforcement Administration). He likes to kayak, photograph wildlife in places like Yellowstone National Park, and ride a tandem bike with Diane. Diane is an attorney and former Federal prosecutor in Washington, D.C. She served in the U.S. Department of Justice and in her law practice helped people to solve legal problems, sometimes using mediation. She likes photographing animals and birds, taking long walks early in the morning, and cooking new recipes.

Diane and David thank the Lord for the blessings of family and friends as they cloister to write and travel, looking for inspiring stories. Read more about these ExFeds on their website at www.DianeAndDavidMunson.com. Also on the website you will find their ExFeds News Wrap blog where they comment on justice news and critique NCIS episodes.

www.DianeAndDavidMunson.com

Glenna Rider clutched the wheel of her parents' van, training her eyes on the dangerous curve ahead. Her dad's erratic breathing made it hard to focus. Gusty wind shoved the van across her lane to the right. Fear stuck in her throat.

"Dad!" she cried. "The wind's strong. Am I too close to the edge?"

"Nope."

He leaned over to check the speedometer.

"You're doing fine," he assured her.

She stole a glance at him in the passenger seat. His voice had sounded calm, but his face seemed tense. Could he be afraid too? This was only her second time driving since she received her learner's permit. She had overestimated her driving ability in offering to buy groceries for Mom, but it was too late now.

Glenna navigated the curve, chewing her bottom lip. Snow flurries swirled across the windshield. With each wind gust fear bolted through her. Hoping to make it home before the roads became slippery, she turned up the heat. Her eyes locked onto the rearview mirror.

A yellow Hummer roared up behind her, the driver's beady eyes threatening her to get out of his way. She pressed down on the gas pedal.

"Slow down, Earnhart," Dad cautioned.

"But a crazy guy is hugging my bumper."

"That doesn't matter. The speed limit is for him too. He'll have to slow down."

Glenna lifted her foot, easing off the gas. The van slowed and thankfully, the SUV dropped back. Following another sharp curve, Glenna's eyes flew to the mirror to check the SUV. The yellow beast nearly smacked her bumper. Adrenaline pulsed through her veins.

"He's almost in our backseat!" she cried.

Anger radiated from the man's eyes. She was frantic to pull off the road. But she had nowhere to go. A dangerous drop-off lurked by the edge of her lane. The shoulder was nothing but a strip of gravel.

"He is egging you on to speed. Don't be rattled. Keep your foot steady on the gas."

Without thinking, her foot lifted off the pedal.

"Glenna, don't slow down," Dad said, his tone prickly. "Maintain a safe speed."

He whipped his head around before resting a firm hand on her shoulder. "He can't pass you. There's a double yellow line."

"But a car is coming in the other lane!"

She gripped the wheel so tightly, her nails dug into her palms. Headlights from the SUV shone in her mirror. As Glenna pressed her foot on the accelerator to go faster, the driver blasted his horn. He swerved around her. Would he hit the oncoming car? Glenna's heart banged against her ribs.

"Wow, Dad! What should I do?"

"Stay calm. Let him pass and he'll go on by."

The SUV tore past the van like a speeding bullet. The maniac driver hit his brakes and screeched to a stop. Glenna jammed the brake pedal with both feet. Dad lurched forward against the seat belt.

Oh God, help me!

She tried not to shut her eyes and stopped with inches to spare. The driver leapt from his SUV, swinging a baseball bat. Glenna screamed. Dad poked her right arm.

"Drive on the shoulder. Be quick."

He whipped out his cell phone. Glenna fought panic. The man coming straight at them looked crazy with his unshaven face and eyes sparking like a savage storm lived in his heart.

I can do this!

Her legs quaked, but she sped past his SUV, the van's tires bumping over the loose stones. Dad punched in numbers on his phone. Glenna bit down her bottom lip. Her eyes roamed to the mirror again. The angry dude ran to his vehicle, swinging the bat.

"Dad! He's coming after me."

"It's Bo Rider," Dad shouted into the phone. "My fifteen-year-old daughter is driving our blue van. A driver is in road rage." He paused. "We're on Waterford Road near Wheatland. Middle-aged man in yellow Hummer forced my daughter to stop. He came at us with a ball bat."

Glenna's foot bore down on the gas as she fled away. Her instructor never covered dangerous psychos in driver's training. Then she recalled the jet exploding above her head in Israel. But shouldn't life be safer in Virginia? She looked for a place to turn off.

Seeing none, she asked in a wobbly voice, "Dad, will you drive?"

"You're okay. Dad is here."

He spoke into the phone again, "No, I don't have the license number."

"The police will swing into action any second," he told Glenna after ending the call.

She clung to the steering wheel, her insides shaking. Then help arrived. At least she hoped so. She heard a siren blaring in the distance, coming closer. Then from behind the SUV, red and blue lights flashed.

"The police are behind you," Dad said. "What should you do?"

Her heart thumped hard before she pulled the van off the road, onto the skimpy shoulder.

"Good job. Let's see what the Hummer does."

The Hummer thundered past, the wind shaking the van. As the police car shot by them, the siren blasted Glenna's ears. Her arms trembled. She checked her side mirror before pulling onto the road.

"There's a gas station past this curve. Turn in there. You're doing real well."

Glenna followed his directions and came to an abrupt stop. Tears burst from her eyes.

"I can't drive home, Daddy. I can't!"

He wrapped an arm around her shoulder and said firmly, "Don't quit on me."

"My legs feel limp like wet spaghetti."

Her words sounded like defeat. Dad must have thought so too. He folded his arms.

"You *can* do it, Glenna. Gather your courage. In Israel you made heaps of progress. Remember the tunnels you and Gregg explored beneath the Old City?"

"Those men came after my brother with a stick," she said, lifting her chin.

"Lesson is you survived. Ready to drive home? Mom's waiting for the chicken."

In Israel, she'd started "building a backbone," as he said. Up ahead, she saw police lights.

"He's still out there," she said. "You drive, *please*."

"Nope. I'd like you to drive us home. Just keep your eyes on the road."

Glenna forced out a sigh before putting the van into drive. "Okay, but don't tell Mom."

"I won't. She has enough on her mind with the twins cutting their teeth."

"Thanks, Dad," Glenna said with a sigh. "She already thinks I'm too young to drive."

She circled around the gas pumps. Before driving out, she saw him staring at his phone.

"What is it, Daddy?"

"I'll tell you when we get home."

Glenna's heart lurched. Had something else happened?

Glenna shut off the engine in the driveway and blew out an exhausted breath. She should feel safe, but fear pricked her heart. Though she grabbed the keys, she did not slide out.

"Dad, what if the wild driver finds me?"

He held out his hand for the keys.

"That nut is gone. Can you manage the groceries? I have to talk to Mom."

"Don't tell her how scared I was. Since the twins were born, she cries if I stub my toe."

"Nope. It's between you and me."

Dad dashed off with the keys, dipping his head against the stiff breeze. Glenna wanted to hear *exactly* what he would tell Mom. She scooped up the fabric bags and breezed in the back door. Her parents were talking. Glenna stopped before her boots made squeaking sounds.

"Bo, you'll be gone over Christmas *again*? It is so unfair."

"I'll be at Camp David a few weeks. Julia, national security is involved."

Her parents were discussing Dad's job, which had nothing to do with her. She shouldn't eavesdrop. Glenna flitted outside, the wind blowing down her neck. She shivered and opened the door once more.

"Mom, here's the roasted chicken," she said brightly. "I bought stuffing and mashed potatoes. Dinner is hot and ready."

Her parents were whispering eye-to-eye near the table. Glenna hummed a Christmas tune and shoved a half-gallon of fudge ice cream into the freezer. Mom laid a hand on her arm.

"Your dad's going out. We'll eat when he returns. Scoot downstairs and search for our ornaments and the baby box."

Not the basement!

Rather than admit to being scared, Glenna slowly folded the fabric bags.

"Um, it's dark down there," she mumbled.

Dad treated her to a huge smile.

"Hey, the Glenna I know isn't afraid of trouble."

Then he winked. Dad took out his cell phone and sauntered away. He hadn't told Mom about her scary time on the road. Still, Glenna's shoulders sagged. The old farmhouse gave her the creeps with its loud, screeching sounds. Wind howled like wolves were living beyond the door. Besides, the basement smelled funny, like old newspapers.

"Hurry up, Glenna. The twins are down for their nap."

Mom's voice sounded tired so she relented. Maybe Blaze would like to visit the basement. She adored their new yellow Labrador. Well, he was part Lab, part golden retriever.

"Say no more," Glenna said. "I agreed if you let us adopt Blaze that I'd look after him."

She opened his crate, patting his cold nose.

"Good boy. Come on and keep me safe downstairs."

Blaze gazed back. His big brown eyes suggested he understood he was to protect her. She opened the unpainted door to the basement.

"Blaze, I hope no strange critters are lurking down there. Last week Mason found a skunk in his basement and was sprayed. Yuck!"

She herded Blaze to the first step. He refused to budge any further. Glenna had to pull the reluctant dog behind her. Blaze's nails made scratching noises on the wooden steps. As she crept down, the lightbulb cast her shadow on the white stairway wall. She looked ten feet tall.

They finally reached the bottom. Glenna glimpsed a large shadow and her heart leapt wildly. She whirled around.

"Gregg! You scared me!"

"Ha, ha. You're easy pickings."

Glenna resisted sticking her tongue out at him. At nearly sixteen, she wasn't as clever as her thirteen-year-old brother who loved teasing and joking. Blaze lifted his nose in the air and Glenna wanted to plug hers against the musty smell.

"Help me find a box marked Christmas so we can get out of here," she exclaimed.

Gregg grunted, "So?"

She pointed to a string hanging from the rafters. Was a spider spinning a web? A shudder ripped through her and she dropped her hand.

"Turn on the light, would you?"

"Get your own box. I need Blaze. I'm taking him with Dad to the Storage Vault."

A quick movement from the dark corner made Glenna jump.

"Look out!" she screamed.

She scrambled onto the bottom step. Gregg pulled the string, flooding the basement with more light. Blaze wagged his tail, making a soft shadow against the wall.

"What a baby," Gregg said, jerking his head. "There's your Christmas box."

"Grab it and let's go. I'm coming with you and Dad."

Gregg leaned over to lift up the box, but then stopped.

"Wait. I see something shiny."

"There's nothing valuable in this dump."

His back disappeared behind a sewing machine. Curious, Glenna stepped closer. Blaze smelled the floor. Gregg pulled out something heavy and let loose a sharp whistle.

"Sweet! It's an old sword. I mean *really* old."

"How do you know?"

"Because Grandpa Crockett sends me Civil War stuff. You hate it when I know something."

Glenna crossed her arms. "You are wrong."

"Ah, forget it. This is my find. Don't tell Dad until I clean her up."

"You could destroy its value. I read too, you know."

Gregg shoved his sword back under the sewing machine.

"Hey, here's a plastic box marked 'Baby Things.' Mom wants it, right?"

He picked up the decorations and snapped off the light, tearing up the stairs with Blaze after him. The darkness of the cellar closed in on her. Glenna grabbed the baby box. She flew up the stairs before a spider landed on her head.

She set the box on the mudroom bench. Her arms covered in gooseflesh, she put on her coat, dashing out the back door before Mom gave her something else to do.

OUTSIDE, GLENNA JOINED GREGG, who was holding Blaze's collar and talking to Mason. Glenna liked the neighbor kid they'd met a few weeks ago. He always waved at her, even though he was a freshman at Wheatland High School.

Because they moved here after school started, Glenna and Gregg were being homeschooled by Mom. Mason flashed Glenna a wide smile.

"When did you get a dog?" he asked her.

"We wanted a pup but adopted Blaze a few days ago. His owner couldn't keep him."

Mason scuffed the toe of his shoe in the gravel. "I asked for a dog for my birthday next month, but I might get a boogie board instead."

Glenna thought he looked stressed.

"We're nowhere near water," Gregg objected, letting the collar drop from of his hand.

"My uncle owns a crabbing boat in Norfolk," Mason said, smiling. "It's near the ocean."

Blaze sniffed around Mason's big athletic shoes.

"Our dog likes your shoes," Glenna kidded. "You know what? Our grandparents live in Hampton not far from Norfolk. Our other grandparents live in Florida."

"Cool. You can try my board, *if* I get one. Things are pretty tight on our farm. Dad sold two horses to pay the taxes. He is relieved you have rented Grandfather's old farmhouse."

Mason's eyes looked sad. Glenna understood money was getting scarce.

"Mom bakes our bread to save money," she said casually. "I help by adding flour in the machine."

Gregg nodded. "Yeah, I wanted to mow lawns, but then we moved out here. I'm trying to save up for a used video game, *Call of Duty, Black Ops.*"

"I play that game all the time."

The strapping football player squatted down. With both hands, he ruffled the dog's ears and looked him straight in the eye.

"Nice dog, Blaze. Do you like your new home?"

Blaze licked Mason's face with his pink tongue. Mason laughed, but stood quickly. He brushed his cheek with the back of his sleeve.

"Blaze likes Mason. He never licks me." Gregg stepped back as if offended.

"Don't mind my brother. He's always making jokes."

Mason scratched Blaze's silky head. "Maybe Blaze wants to come live with my family."

"No way!"

Glenna snatched his collar, jealousy stealing into her heart. She hadn't gone two feet when Dad raced out the back door, keys bunched in his hand.

He stopped to ask Mason, "How did your game go yesterday?"

"We won, Mr. Rider. I sat it out on the bench and never had a chance to kick."

"Rightly so," Dad replied with a grin. "The juniors and seniors on your team spent their first year on the bench. You should be proud—you made the varsity team as a freshman."

Mason kept his hand on Blaze's head. "I wanted to kick a field goal and help my team win. I'll consider what you said. If you travel, your dog may stay with us instead of a kennel."

"I'll keep your offer in mind," Dad replied. "Let's go, Gregg. We're leaving."

"Can I bring Blaze?" Glenna asked, reaching for his collar.

Dad thrust his legs behind the driver's seat. "Okay, but he stays on a leash."

Mason's lonely stare gave Glenna pause for feeling jealous. He had no brothers or sisters.

"See you later, Mason," she chirped.

"I better feed the horses."

"That sounds like fun."

"It is hard work caring for horses. But come by and bring Blaze anytime."

He waved good-bye and Glenna watched him zigzag across the brown field to his neighboring farm. Instead of seeing his game yesterday, she had finished her math homework.

Dad started the van and Glenna dashed into the house. She grabbed the leash. At the last second she swiped her knitted bag. Running up to the driver's door, she waved her driver's permit in the air.

"Oh no!" Gregg protested. "You're not letting *her* drive, are you, Dad?"

Dad tossed her the keys and made a beeline around the front of the van. He slid into the passenger seat, pointing a finger at Gregg.

"You hunker down with Blaze in the backseat. Be sure you keep him on the leash."

Glenna drove down the long driveway, glancing both ways when she reached the road.

"No cars coming from your right," Dad announced.

She looked left. "Ah ... you don't think we'll see the yellow Hummer, do you?"

"Who is Yellow Hummer? Some new boyfriend?" Gregg piped from behind her shoulder.

"Never mind," she shot back before pulling out.

Glenna glanced at Dad. He seemed tense. Driving again so soon scared her too. Anything might happen with Gregg in the backseat, forever pulling tricks. Of course Dad would come down on him heavy if he veered out of line.

She kept checking the mirrors. As she rounded the curve, she had visions of the crazy driver waiting to pounce. She kept her foot steady on the gas pedal.

"Watch it!" Gregg shouted.

Blaze barked, *Woof!*

Glenna's heart thumped and her head swung left. The van's wheel dropped over the shoulder. What had she done?

Dad tapped her arm. "You are fine. Ease back on the road, but slowly."

"I didn't see anything," she gulped.

"Nah," Gregg snickered. "I saw a dog running at you. Blaze did too, I guess."

Dad whirled his head around.

"Son, trick your sister again while she's driving and you won't get your license until you're eighteen. Don't think for one minute I am kidding."

"Thanks, Dad." Glenna's heart rate returned to normal.

She turned into the storage place, but coasted past the gate's decoder.

"You need more training," Gregg grumbled under his breath.

Glenna pursed her lips, shoving the van into reverse.

"When I drive, I won't miss."

Frustration building against her brother, she snapped, "Dad won't let you behind the wheel."

"Maybe you need glasses."

"Gregg, it is five long years until you're eighteen."

Glenna backed up and tried to snug close to the keypad. *Rats!* She stretched her hand out farther. Electricity shot down her neck. Finally, her finger touched the cold steel.

Dad rattled off numbers and barked, "Hit the pound symbol." The heavy metal gate rolled open and she pulled forward. Dad pointed at the third long building.

"Stop right by that door."

Her heart soaring with adventure, she maneuvered between a white truck and a building.

Dad's hand flew to the handle. "When you approach a vehicle like this, watch underneath for feet walking around in front. Expect someone to step from behind cars you are passing."

"Okay. I don't see any possible victims."

"What about me!" Gregg howled. "My stomach's ready to hurl from your backing up."

Glenna slowly pulled to a stop and Dad jumped down.

"Good job, kiddo. This shouldn't take long, so don't go anywhere."

Gregg bounded out with Blaze. She killed the engine, pocketing the keys. Driving was a big responsibility, as Mom kept telling her every day. Dad lifted the storage compartment door. The metal monster banged and rattled into a coil above the opening.

Glenna stared at the stack of boxes. All those used to be stuffed in their basement before they moved to the farmhouse. She sighed. Living in the country was the pits. Besides the school and the Storage Vault, all Wheatland had was an antique store and a gas station flying an American flag. At least Sam, who owned the gas station, had a cute boxer puppy named Piper. Glenna kicked at a box.

So what if I don't have a puppy? I can become used to Blaze.

She reached for his long silky ears, but Blaze lit out the Vault door like his tail was on fire. Before she could react, Dad rolled a soapbox derby racer around the boxes.

"Have Gregg move his racer out of our way," he ordered.

Glenna turned to fetch her brother. Her hand flew to her mouth. She couldn't believe her eyes.

"Gregg, look!"

Blaze loped past the truck, his leash trailing behind.

"Where's he going?" Gregg demanded.

"You're supposed to watch him. Good thing Dad's inside the storage unit."

"Right!"

Gregg rushed off, hot on Blaze's trail.

She chased after them, calling, "Gregg Rider! Dad told you to keep him on the leash."

Gregg stopped in his tracks. She nearly crashed into his back. After catching her breath, she saw what was wrong. Two men carried large plastic pails out of an open storage locker.

Blaze stood rigidly staring at them, his fur puffed up. He started whining. One of the men, a tall guy in a jean jacket and ponytail, glared at Glenna. His wild eyes reminded her of the driver wielding the bat. Fear sizzled through her like a hot current. She grabbed Gregg's arm.

"Ow!" He shook off her hand.

The mean-looking man scurried into the stall. So did the shorter man, his black hair slicked with gobs of hair gel. Blaze lunged after them, but then he stopped. His whining sounded like he was in pain. Gregg snapped Blaze's leash backward. Mr. Mean stomped out of the stall, his eyes shooting darts.

"I warn you kids. Get yer mutt outta here!"

Glenna flinched at the threat. She stumbled backwards.

"Gregg, let's go."

"I'm trying." He tugged on the leash. "Blaze won't obey me."

Blaze strained and a deep rumble escaped from his throat. *Grrr! Grrr!*

Mr. Mean threw a pail, hitting Blaze in the head.

Yelp! Blaze jumped backwards.

"Get that mangy mutt out of here or you'll be sorry."

The man's black eyes burned like hot charcoals. Blaze shot for the van, his leash wrapping around Gregg's leg. He lunged after the dog and nearly fell. Glenna ran to catch up, not sure what was happening with Blaze. Had their sweet dog gone crazy?

BE CAREFUL, BOY. DON'T LOOK DIRECTLY AT GRAMMA'S TEETH. SHE JUST GOT BACK FROM THE DENTAL HYGIENIST!
CRANE
© 2004 Brian Crane

IT'S TIME FOR YOUR
DENTAL CHECK-UP AND CLEANING

☐ Please call today for an appointment

☑ Your appointment is

BREANNA,

___THUE DEC 15TH 10:50AM___
Day   Date   Time

If you are unable to keep this appointment, please call us today.

Tradewinds Dental Centre

Dr. Daryl D. A. Chin, Inc.

57 Lonsdale Avenue

North Vancouver, B.C. V7M 2E5

Telephone: (604) 987-8802

Glenna rushed up to her dad huffing. "Blaze scared some men. They hit him with a pail!"

"Where did you go?" He pushed a box into the hatch of the van. "I needed your help."

Gregg crouched next to Blaze, wiping a small cut on the dog's nose.

"Blaze growled at two guys by the stall around the corner."

"Your dog should be on the leash."

Glenna hugged Blaze, pleading, "He got loose and sneaked over there."

Dad stepped out of their storage stall and looked around.

"The white truck is gone. Secure Blaze in the van while I close up."

"I'll do it." Glenna grabbed the leash from Gregg and brought Blaze to the side door.

Instead of climbing in the van, he sped around the corner pulling Glenna behind.

"Dad! Help!" she screamed. "He's doing it again."

Blaze stopped at the men's storage shed. Glenna blinked. The door had been rolled down. No one was around. Blaze whined like crazy and Glenna had no clue what to do. Haul him back to the van by dragging his leash? She might hurt him.

"Hey, Glenna," Dad said, jogging up. "I said to put Blaze in the van."

"He insists on coming over here."

"Mom's waiting dinner for us. We're heading home."

He took the leash and started toward the van. Blaze stopped again. Pulling against the leash, he bristled and barked. Dad seemed to lose patience. He grabbed Blaze by the collar and hauled him to the van. He pushed the dog in the side door before rolling it shut with a thud.

"I'll drive," he said.

Glenna thumped into the front passenger seat. During the ride home, Gregg sat in the backseat wiping Blaze's bloodied nose with a napkin.

"Gregg, you never listen," Dad said. "Didn't I tell you to keep hold of Blaze's leash?"

Glenna saw him glance in the rearview mirror as if waiting for Gregg's reply.

Ha, ha.

Gregg had to be stewing in the hot seat. After the razzing he'd dished her, maybe he'd lose video privileges for a week. Or maybe he'd have to take out the garbage on her night.

"Ah ... you did, Dad," Gregg stammered. "I had the leash on him."

At the stop sign, Dad turned his head around. "But did you have a grip on it?"

"Blaze broke free. He blasted straight toward those men before I could stop him."

Glenna interrupted, "Blaze can't stand those men. He stared and growled."

Dad faced the road and went through the intersection.

"Has Blaze growled at anybody before?" he asked.

Uh oh.

His caustic tone and the way he'd shoved Blaze in the van put Glenn on high alert. Dad might be ready to send Blaze from the house. She saw Gregg pull Blaze closer.

Glenna swallowed. "No, Blaze likes us. He wags his tail and licked Mason's face."

"Yeah." Gregg patted Blaze's nose with a tissue. "He's a great dog."

Dad removed his cell phone from his belt clip. At the next stop sign, he selected a name from the contact list and raised the phone to his ear.

"Eva, it's Bo. We had an incident with the dog you convinced us to adopt. He has an ugly streak."

He put the phone on his belt and Glenna gathered her arguments.

"Blaze is a good dog. He is *not* mean. We are going to keep him, aren't we?"

"We can take him to obedience training," Gregg said, a plea in his voice.

Dad's phone rang. He answered before turning the corner. No cars were behind them.

"This is Bo."

Glenna leaned toward Dad. The sound was scratchy, but she could hear the caller's voice.

"It's Eva Montanna. What happened with Blaze?"

"He challenged and growled at strangers."

"Remember what I said when you adopted him. He was a working dog for Homeland Security. When his handler Anthony retired on disability, they retired Blaze too. I don't think he's an attack dog. I'll call Anthony and find out."

"Okay. We'll wait to hear from you."

Gregg slid forward against his seat belt.

"Dad, you can't send Blaze back!"

He sounded as concerned as Glenna. For all their bickering, she loved her brother. She joined in making the case to keep their dog.

"You didn't see Blaze and those men. Don't assume he's vicious."

Dad drove home in silence. Glenna hunched toward the door, chilling toward him, her mind whirling. There was one thing she could do. She prayed for God to help them.

He's our only friend out here in the boonies, except for Mason.

She wouldn't tell Gregg about her prayer. He wasn't convinced prayer worked in his life. Though Glenna had seen prayer answered in her life, she was uneasy sharing personal feelings with her brother.

Glenna saw Mason running along the road near their driveway. She waved.

"Gregg, see how hard Mason works to stay fit for football?" Dad said. "If you want to play, you might as well start running."

As they turned in the drive, tires crunching on the stones, Glenna heard Dad's phone buzz. He reached for his belt and pressed the phone to his left ear.

"Bo here."

Glenna tried in vain to hear the person on the other end.

"What time?" Dad asked. "Okay, thanks, Eva. We'll decide then."

The van rolled to a stop in front of the garage. Gregg opened the side door.

"I'm packing my bag and taking Blaze," he hissed. "We're leaving together."

"Don't be hasty, Gregg. You may have no need to escape."

Dad lifted the rear door of the van and reached in for the Christmas tree box. Glenna helped Blaze out. Then Dad asked her to hold open the mudroom door. She fought panic.

Eva's coming for Blaze!

Dad wrestled the box into the house, followed by Blaze pulling Gregg behind. Glenna stepped inside, the kitchen smelling of wonderful cinnamon. Mom wiped her hands on a towel.

"Christmas is almost here," she said, smiling.

Dad frowned at Gregg. "Did you give Blaze a potty break?"

"Um," was all Gregg mustered.

"I didn't think so," Dad said with a grunt. "Take him outside. We have to put up the tree in a hurry. Company is coming right after we eat."

Mom's shoulders slumped. "Who is coming?"

"Blaze barked at people and they hit him with a bucket. Eva is bringing Anthony, Blaze's retired partner, to see if he is dangerous."

Glenna hustled forward. "Dad makes it sound worse than it is. Blaze protected us from two angry men at the storage place. He didn't show his teeth or bite anyone."

"Dinner is ready." Mom peeked into the oven. "Thanks for picking up what we needed so we can have an early dinner. Glenna, I am proud of you."

"You're preparing me for a letdown, aren't you?" Glenna asked, her heart in her throat.

"Blaze is here on trial. Because he used to be a working dog, he might not adopt us."

"But, Mom—"

Her mother held up a large hot mitt. "Get busy tidying up and wash your hands."

Glenna sighed and trudged to the mudroom.

Please, God, I know you hear my prayers and brought Blaze to me. I'm lonely out here.

Glenna ate a hurried dinner, with Dad and Mom talking about Grandpa Crockett buying a boat at a government auction sale.

"Buck says she was used by smugglers or pirates." Dad grinned at Gregg. "He wants to take you out on *Pollywog* if we head to Florida during Easter break."

"I'm ready to find some treasure."

Gregg bit into a chicken leg, but Glenna's heart wasn't in eating or going to Florida. After pushing the chicken and potatoes around on her plate, she asked to be excused. Mom shook her head.

"Eat two bites and drink your milk."

Glenna stuffed two forkfuls in her mouth, washing down potatoes with milk.

"All right, but finish dusting," Mom said. "Then help your brother with the tree."

Glenna dashed to the sink where she plunked down her plate. Then she hauled the baby stuff upstairs, furious with Gregg for letting Blaze confront those men. After depositing the box on the floor of her room, she ran back downstairs. She vowed to protect Blaze at all costs.

Her brother crouched on his knees, building the tree from the bottom up. She zipped a blue dust cloth over the coffee table.

"Ouch!" Gregg howled. "The fake branch stabbed me in the ribs."

"Quiet. We have bigger issues to decide."

He waved a branch in her direction. "Like what? Your Christmas list?"

"Have you forgotten Blaze is on the chopping block?"

"It's my fault." Gregg looked sad kneeling by the drooping tree.

Her anger forgotten, she almost burst out laughing. Rather than rile him, she looked out the window. No one was out there. That gave her time to hide Blaze in the barn. Then Glenna had a change of heart; it might freeze overnight.

"I have an idea," Gregg announced, twisting in the final branch.

"Tell me."

She scooted closer. Her heart wasn't in Christmas, not with Blaze about to be banished.

"When Mom and Dad go to bed, we'll hide Blaze in Mason's cellar."

"I don't know ..."

Car headlights swept across the windows, making Glenna jump. She ran to the window. A lime green VW shuddered to a stop in the driveway.

"Some kid is driving," she said, counting several people piling out of the tiny car.

A whole crew was on the march, coming for Blaze. She dropped the dust cloth as if it singed her hand, and crossed into the kitchen with a heavy heart.

"Dad!" she called. "They're here."

"Don't forget. You promised to be open-minded about Blaze," Gregg added, rushing up.

Mom bustled toward the laundry room carrying a basket of soiled towels, her hair drooping in her eyes.

"Bo, I hope there's a logical explanation for his behavior. After all the kids went through in Israel and then moving out here to be safe, I don't want to cause them anguish."

"Mom, you're great," Glenna trilled. "It will cause me anxiety to send Blaze away."

Dad took the laundry basket and kissed Mom's cheek.

"This is too heavy for the mother of new twins," he said.

Her mom's cheeks blushed like summer peaches. Glenna chuckled and formed an idea.

"Let me do the wash."

By offering to help, Glenna hoped Dad would be easier on Blaze. She heaved the basket on her hip and shot toward the laundry room where Blaze also had his doggie bed. He laid on his side, unaware of his plight.

A car door slammed, which sent her racing to the living room. Dad opened the door and she took cover by Gregg near the piano.

Her brother pressed a finger to his lips. "I put Blaze's toys and brush in the barn."

Glenna's eyes darted around like bees. She spotted two kids on the porch by a tall blonde lady she recognized. Mrs. Montanna wore jeans and an icy-blue parka that matched her eyes. Having spent time with her in Israel, Glenna told herself to be more trusting. For a Federal agent, Mrs. Montanna was pretty cool.

Dad invited them inside. Mrs. Montanna walked in and gave Mom a hug.

"Julia, it's great to see you again. How are Ricky and Annie?"

"Gaining weight since you saw them last," Mom replied, a lilt in her voice.

A man ambled up the steps, leaning on a cane. Two teens lingered behind his back looking glum. Mrs. Montanna introduced the older man.

"Anthony DeNozzo is retired from Homeland Security. And meet two of my three children."

Mrs. Montanna touched the shoulder of a pretty teen with blond hair. "Kaley is my oldest." She nodded toward a boy about Gregg's age. "Andy is my son. They know Blaze."

Mom urged everyone to sit in the living room.

"Mr. DeNozzo, please take the recliner," she said.

"Call me Anthony. Mr. DeNozzo is my father, who is doing great at ninety-three."

Glenna put out her hand. "It's good to see you again, Mrs. Montanna."

"Yes it is and, Glenna, it's okay to call me Eva."

She took a seat between her kids on the sofa while Glenna perched on the piano bench. Gregg stood in the corner, his arms crossed.

Dad cleared his throat. "What can you tell us about Blaze's behavior?"

The dog must have heard his name. His toenails started clicking on the kitchen linoleum and Glenna pictured him hurrying from his bed in the laundry room. Under the living room arch, Blaze stopped. His eyes fixed on the recliner.

Suddenly he rushed at Anthony, tail wagging. He plunged his front paws into Anthony's lap and licked the retired agent's face. The man folded his arms around Blaze's head.

"I miss you, buddy."

Anthony massaged Blaze's shoulders before pushing his paws to the floor. He cupped his hands around Blaze's broad head and gazed into his eyes.

"Good to see you again."

Glenna's heart lurched. She saw love for Blaze in Anthony's eyes. *He must be here to take him back home.* Anthony swiped tears from his eyes and turned to her dad.

"Bo, it gives me joy to see Blaze adapting to your home. He is well cared for and happy. Thanks for calling Eva to bring me over."

At the sound of his name, Blaze jumped up with his paws on the chair. He forced his massive head against Anthony's chest.

"Enough." He pushed Blaze down. "I miss my former partner. He's an award-winning dog. When my first hip was redone, my doctor urged me to retire."

He picked up his cane and shook it. Blaze looked at the man with something like awe in his eyes. Anthony continued with his tale.

"Recently, my second hip was replaced. Eva has seen me work with Blaze over the years. She and I are well acquainted. We're members of the same big church in Vienna."

Anthony patted Blaze's side as if sorry to be apart from him. Glenna toyed with her hair, not knowing what to do or say.

"Blaze developed some quirks and I let him violate a few protocols of a search dog. He can't be introduced to a new partner, so he retired with me."

"Whew. I am glad he was a search dog." Dad inched forward on the chair. "I was afraid he'd been trained to attack."

"He is a friendly dog."

Anthony tapped Blaze on his hind end. "Get around here and sit like a gentleman."

The dog turned his body around and sat by Anthony's chair, facing everyone in the room. His eyes stayed fixed on his former partner. Glenna caught her breath. Blaze never looked at her with such devotion. She glanced at Gregg. His cheeks sported red blotches. No doubt he'd caught Blaze's look and was plotting his getaway.

But how can we help our dog with Anthony here? Blaze is glued to his side.

Glenna forced her mind to stay positive. She folded her sweaty hands.

"We were doing well in retirement," Anthony said. "Until Bonnie and I got married last month. She knew my deceased wife and lost her husband a year earlier."

He fumbled with his cane. "Sorry to say, but Blaze came between us. Bonnie is allergic to dog dander. I asked Eva if she wanted Blaze to live with her."

Kaley Montanna dropped to her knees, stroking Blaze's side. "I want him."

"No," Eva replied, shaking her head. "That wouldn't be fair to Zak. Our kitty has been our good friend for years. You wouldn't want him hiding under the bed, would you?"

Glenna narrowed her eyes, wanting to tell Kaley that she had no right to Blaze.

"So that's how we became Blaze's fortunate owners," Mom said, grinning. "Eva told Bo and me some aspects of Blaze's professional background, but we didn't tell the kids."

Dad scowled as if not enjoying the meeting. "After Blaze accosted two men at a storage facility," he said, "I called Eva seeking assurance Blaze isn't an attack dog."

"Yes, and I asked to stop by." Anthony smoothed Blaze's fur. "He's never growled before. Such a willful act can't be tolerated. Rather than assume he has become dangerous, I'd like to test his behavior."

Mom stood. "Now? I wanted to serve you all apple pie and ice cream."

"I noticed your pole barn out back." Anthony boosted himself to his feet. "I'd like to take Blaze out there and see if he still knows his job."

Blaze quickly rose from the floor.

"Let's do it, Dad!" Glenna could hardly contain her excitement.

Everyone else leapt to their feet, but Gregg tossed her a skeptical look as if she'd ruined his escape plan.

Anthony pointed his cane at Gregg. "Young man, come with me to the car."

They all barreled out the front door. On the porch, Gregg grabbed Glenna's arm.

"Did you hear what he said? Blaze's growling is willful."

"What does he mean?" she asked, feeling confused. Wouldn't the test clear Blaze?

"If Blaze growls in front of Anthony, he's a goner."

Her heart twisted. "We have to save him, Gregg."

He nodded. It felt odd, but with this unfolding crisis, Glenna suddenly felt that she and her brother were one.

6

Glenna trudged behind Anthony toward Eva's green VW. Her mind buzzed with the test he'd concocted. What if Blaze failed? Before she could think of how to smuggle Blaze over to Mason's, she noticed Anthony's cane had a dog's head carved on top. In the dim light, she couldn't be sure, but it looked like a replica of Blaze.

Tears stung her eyes. Deep in her heart she knew Anthony could never part with Blaze.

She and Anthony joined Eva by her VW.

"Your daughter drove well," he said. "I wasn't even afraid."

Eva's face lit into a smile. "You were brave, Anthony. Kaley still needs more hours for her license."

Glenna eyed Kaley who was hovering near Blaze. The teen girl seemed nice, but Glenna refused to give her Blaze, no matter what Eva had said about her cat. The world was stacked against her, but Glenna knew God had a plan for her good.

In the driveway she lifted up a prayer while Eva opened the trunk of her car. Anthony dug in a satchel, pulling out a man's sock stuffed full of something. Only Glenna didn't know what that "something" was. She narrowed her eyes, ready for some trick to take Blaze away.

Anthony handed Gregg the sock folded over at the top and wrapped with rubber bands.

"Hide this in the barn." He shook his cane toward Gregg. "Make sure it's out of sight, but no higher than four feet from the floor."

Gregg fled to the barn. Anthony pulled a harness and leash from his satchel.

"Let's prepare Blaze for his work."

Torn, Glenna wanted to check on Gregg in the barn, but decided to stick with Blaze. She watched Anthony secure the harness, and the beautiful Lab pranced in circles, no doubt eager to be working again. Glenna's heart flipped at the thought of losing him.

Mom motioned her up to the porch.

"I'm serving up the pie. You may scoop the ice cream."

Glenna's hands flew to her hips.

"Can I *please* watch Blaze find the package?"

"Go ahead." Mom wiped her hands on her apron. "I thought you were done with the experiment."

Glenna raced toward the barn hoping she hadn't missed Blaze in action. Anthony, Eva, and her kids were still talking outside with Dad. Glenna snuck past them, joining Gregg inside. She closed the heavy sliding door behind her.

Under the subdued lights, Gregg paced by a dented pickup truck left by Mason's grandpa.

"Let's make it hard," he said tossing the sock in the air. "So when Blaze doesn't find the sock, they can't take him away from us."

"Good idea. How about the truck?"

Gregg shook his head. He inspected the tailpipe and tried pushing the sock in the end.

"It doesn't fit," he griped.

Giving up that idea, he strode around the barn until Dad's voice echoed from outside.

"What's the holdup? Blaze is antsy to work."

"Just a minute," Glenna called back.

How hard could it be to hide a sock? She spun around. A large snowblower sat in the corner with a large auger that spit snow out of its shoot.

"Gregg, look!" she pointed. "The stack on the top sends snow along the side of the driveway. It's the right height."

Gregg's eyebrows shot up. He crammed the sock down the pipe and stepped back.

"Can you see it?" he asked.

"No."

"Okay, it's time to test Blaze. We better hope the results are in our favor."

He rolled open the barn door. Glenna hung by the opening. Her heart leapt at Blaze sitting obediently next to Anthony. He used the leash to pull Blaze toward his legs.

"You are welcome to watch from the doorway," he instructed. "But Blaze needs room to smell the barn. Glenna and Gregg, I may ask you to come closer, depending on what Blaze does. If so, approach quietly."

Kaley giggled softly. Andy pushed his way to stand next to Gregg. Glenna breathed deeply as Anthony leaned over and spoke softly to Blaze.

"Okay, fella. Are you ready to work again?"

He patted Blaze on the side before walking him inside. Blaze whiffed the pickup and then trotted to a cabinet with doors. His eyes examined countertops loaded with tools and boxes. Blaze roamed to the back of the truck, where Anthony stopped, letting the slackened leash drop to the ground. Blaze kept his nose low, swinging his head from side to side.

Glenna wandered over and stuck an elbow in Gregg's side.

"He's sniffing for the sock," she whispered.

Blaze walked along one side of the barn. Then he turned back to search by the old truck. He reached the tailpipe, tilting his head. This time Gregg elbowed Glenna, but neither spoke.

The dog smelled along the other side of the truck and then passed the snowblower. He stopped and lumbered back to it, distracted from the truck. Glenna felt something tickling her neck. She slapped away whatever it was, hoping it wasn't a spider. That would be gross, but she wouldn't disturb Blaze's hunt.

Her heart swelled with anticipation. Blaze's nose went straight for the auger. Without warning he sat down and stared at the shoot, right where Gregg had hidden the sock.

Anthony asked Blaze, "Where is it?" He beckoned with his hand for Glenna and Gregg to come near. They stepped softly behind the retired agent where Glenna heard Blaze whining.

"Show me. Show me where it is," Anthony urged.

Grrrr. Grrrr. Blaze strained at the end of the leash.

Anthony leaned on his cane, motioning for Glenna and Gregg to leave. He pulled Blaze away from the snowblower and followed them outside.

"Did Blaze growl like that at the storage place?"

Gregg was already nodding. "Yeah, just like that."

Words stuck in Glenna's throat. She might be pronouncing Blaze guilty.

Anthony threw up his hands at Eva and Dad. "That cinches it. Blaze's growl was willful."

Glenna's knees wobbled. There was no hope for poor Blaze. Anthony had other ideas.

"Okay, the game is over," he said. "Is the sock hidden in the snow-blower?"

"Yes! He's smart and we want to keep him!" Glenna cried, bouncing on her tiptoes.

"Good boy," Anthony praised Blaze. "Gregg, can you get a d-o-g-g-i-e-b-o-n-e and sneak it to me?"

Gregg hustled off to the house and Glenna wondered why Anthony spelled out doggie bone. Blaze must know the words as well as his name.

Anthony leaned on his cane. "I trained Blaze to sit and stare at his find. He shouldn't whine or growl. But over time, he grew impatient if I didn't seize what he found. He tried tricks to gain my attention."

Dad rubbed his chin. "Did Blaze growl because the men at the Vault have hidden drugs?"

"No. Blaze isn't trained to sniff out drugs."

Gregg sped over, slipping Anthony the doggie bone. Yet Blaze, the star of the show, seemed oblivious to the treat. He stared up at Anthony, which made Glenna all the more uneasy about losing their special dog. She didn't know how to react. But Gregg, ever the impatient one, pointed at the barn.

"Let him show us what he found."

Woof!

Blaze looked at Anthony as if asking for permission. The retired agent turned on his cane and Blaze led the parade of onlookers inside the barn. Glenna chewed on her lip. Would Blaze come through? And if he did, would that mean he'd be gone forever?

Blaze strutted over to the snowblower, where he sat, glaring at the machine.

"Show me, Blaze. Show me," Anthony urged.

Blaze whined loudly, wagging the very tip of his tail.

"Where is it? Show me."

Blaze reared upwards, his nose sniffing by the shoot of the snowblower. Anthony reached inside the shoot and yanked out the sock.

"Good boy, Blaze!"

Anthony gave Glenna the find before dramatically presenting Blaze with a doggie bone. He seized the snack with his sharp teeth and munched his bone at Anthony's feet. He seemed so content that Glenna did a double take. Could he ever bond with her family like that?

Anthony motioned for her to stand under the light behind the truck.

"Glenna, come see what Blaze discovered."

She blinked her eyes, wondering if she should.

7

Had Glenna heard correctly? "You want me to open the sock?"

Anthony nodded his balding head. As she jerked off the rubber bands, one thwacked her wrist. She ignored the stinging sensation and reached inside, pulling out a stack of cash.

Her jaw dropped in amazement.

"Wow! Blaze smells money!"

She thumbed through the stack.

Meanwhile Kaley complained, "How dumb. It's only dollar bills."

"Good boy, Blaze," Anthony said, ruffling Blaze's head. "You know your job."

Glenna handed Anthony the money.

"You are smart, young lady. Blaze is a search dog trained to find currency."

Glenna didn't know how to take his compliment. Was he buttering her up to pull the rug out from under her? Gregg pocketed his hands and lifted his jaw.

"Why does Blaze find money and not illegal drugs or bombs?"

"There is a good reason, son," Dad said.

He held out his hand and Anthony gave him the wad.

"Your dad is right. Criminals and terrorists use money to buy and sell drugs, which pays for their acts of terror. Our government trains dogs like Blaze to find currency so we can stop them."

"But how does Blaze know who to go after?" Glenna asked.

Eva looped an arm around Andy's shoulders. "Drug cartels sell dangerous drugs like marijuana and cocaine in our country. They smuggle money, in mostly one hundred dollar bills, back to Mexico, Colombia, or Afghanistan where the drugs came from. Dogs like Blaze help us stop the money from leaving the country, which is illegal."

Glenna's feet felt numb. She stamped them on the cement floor of the barn, and turning slightly, she noticed Mason watching. His green eyes gleamed.

She walked up to him. "What's up?"

The muscular football player strode into the barn and handed a disc to Gregg.

"I'm returning the video I borrowed."

"You won't believe what we discov—"

"Mason!" Glenna cut off her brother so she could tell. "Blaze is a search dog. Dad, show Mason the money *our* dog just found."

Bo opened his hand and Mason drew near.

Glenna hugged Blaze, asking Anthony, "How does Blaze know it's money and not drugs or even dog food?"

"Other dogs are conditioned to sniff out drugs or explosives. Blaze received top-notch training to find one thing—currency. He's highly decorated."

"If my kids had known what a special dog Blaze is, they might have made me put Zak up for adoption." Eva dropped her arm from Andy's shoulders.

Glenna shot Gregg a "Dad better let us keep our dog" look.

"But Marty, my youngest son, is allergic to dogs," Eva added. "He detests needles. So Blaze is safe with you, Glenna."

Hooray! Glenna started humming but stopped the second she saw a strange look pass over Dad's face. Anthony didn't seem to notice; he just praised Blaze some more.

"Blaze knows the distinct smell of the ink used in printing U.S. currency. He doesn't find drugs or explosives. Likewise, drug dogs can't smell currency. Each has their own job."

"I flew to England with my parents last year," Mason said. "A German shepherd smelled our suitcases in the airport line."

"The dog you saw was either searching for explosives or people sneaking money out of the country," Eva explained.

Anthony rested a hand on Blaze's head. "This good boy sniffed out record amounts of hidden cash. He and I found millions of dollars while partners. If the government had let us claim the moiety, we'd be rich."

He looked proud, like a father might after his son made a touchdown. Glenna stroked Blaze's back, loving him more every minute.

"What's moiety?" Mason sounded very interested.

As if he hadn't heard Mason's question, Anthony faced Eva.

"Perhaps Blaze detected illegal cash at the storage facility."

Blaze ambled to his feet and smelled Anthony's pocket. Eva traded glances with Dad.

"Then I should investigate," she said. "A drug cartel might be storing currency at the Vault until they can smuggle cash to South

America. Glenna could take us to the storage locker where she saw the two men."

Dad shook his head. "My kids are not getting entangled in a dangerous escapade. Do your thing without their help."

Glenna straightened her back, eager to show what Blaze could do. "Dad, you always remind us to live right. Should we let criminals break the law? Those men bloodied Blaze's nose."

Gregg whizzed over. "Yeah! It's no big deal pointing out the door where Blaze growled."

"We'll stay in the van," Glenna said, hope rising in her heart that the men would be caught.

Dad ran a hand through his hair. "Anthony, what could we safely do?"

Glenna needled Gregg's side, certain victory was within reach.

"We drive to the storage facility. I walk Blaze past the door Glenna points out. I test if he is alerting to currency. Since no one else will be there, Eva decides the next step."

"I can take Blaze," Dad replied. "My kids don't need to go along."

Eva tossed her keys into her other hand. "Only the kids know which door to check."

Glenna could have thrown her arms around Eva's neck, but then Dad burst her balloon.

"Nope. I saw the open door."

"The exact door?" Anthony probed.

Dad paused. "Well … close to it."

"Won't work," Eva declared. "We need the *exact* door for the judge to sign a warrant."

Glenna could almost hear Dad's mental gears working. He puffed out a sigh.

"Okay. But you kids stay in the van and point out the door from inside."

Glenna's heart flipped. She felt like she was back in Jerusalem, about to be part of a new adventure.

"Hey, Mason, want to come?" Gregg slugged their friend on the arm.

Dad pocketed his hands. "Only if he stays in the van and his parents agree."

Mason raced away. Anthony walked out barely using his cane. Gregg snatched up Blaze's leash and took off. Kaley walked with Andy to their VW.

Glenna stayed behind to hear Dad ask Eva, "What if Blaze alerts to currency at the Vault?"

"You hightail it home with him and the kids. I'll find out who rented the storage stall. If I obtain a search warrant, we enter it."

"Why do people keep money in a storage place?" Glenna asked Eva.

"Does your family keep money in a storage facility?"

"We use a bank."

"Why doesn't your dad use the Vault?"

Glenna thought hard, coming up with, "Because our money isn't safe there."

"True. If someone gets money illegally, they don't take it to a bank. They risk hiding it in a storage place. A judge may think so too and give us a search warrant to find out."

Eva closed the heavy door and walked with Glenna to the van. Mason ran up, wearing a lopsided grin. He steered Glenna and Gregg to the steps. Blaze tagged along.

"My father is okay with me going if your dad stays with us. I turned on my smartphone's locator so we can remember where we have gone."

"What do you think will happen?" Gregg's eyes bulged.

Mason rubbed his hands together. "By morning, we might be on TV."

As Glenna helped Blaze into the van, she wondered if Blaze should be involved in another test. What if this time he failed?

8

Glenna walked away from the van where the boys joked noisily with Kaley. She wanted to find out what the agents had in mind for Blaze. Eva talked to Anthony in hushed tones.

"FBI agents and officers will meet us," she said.

Anthony leaned on his cane. "I wish I knew if Blaze really alerted at the Vault."

Glenna leaned forward, straining to hear Eva's reply.

"We'll find out soon enough if Bo's kids are overeager or if Blaze did his job."

Glenna wanted to shout, "We're not making this up!" But instead, she slunk away, on to their game. They were testing Blaze's smelling abilities. She climbed into the van next to Blaze on the middle bench. He sat proudly, his black nose sniffing the air. Gregg hunched beside Mason in the third seat.

"The agents don't believe us," she whispered. "Will Blaze growl again, do you think?"

Mason wasted no time passing his smartphone to Glenna.

"Look what I found about moiety."

Glenna squinted at the small screen and tried to wrap her mind around the meaning.

Moiety. A noun. 1. A half. 2. An indefinite portion part or share.

It was all so peculiar. She felt overwhelmed by Mason's knowledge.

"I don't understand your gobbledegook." She thrust the phone back at him.

"Glenna, it's moiety. Did you hear what Anthony said?"

She should have, but no, she hadn't. She'd been too worried about losing Blaze. If Mason thought it was important, it must be, so she turned around in her seat, opening her mind.

"What did Anthony say?"

"If the government would have let him and Blaze claim moiety for all the money they had seized, he'd be rich."

"Let me see."

Gregg snatched the phone and stared at the lighted screen. "Why should we care if Anthony is rich?"

Her brother sounded as confused as Glenna. Mason retrieved his phone and pointed to the screen.

"I should be your English teacher. Moiety is a reward, a part of what is seized. Consider this. You own Blaze and you don't work for the government."

Gregg pounded the seat and Blaze barked.

"Quiet, boy, or Dad will nix the deal," Gregg said, lowering his voice.

"Mason, I still—"

Mason rolled his eyes. "You get the reward. If the storage facility is loaded with cash, you and Glenna will receive part of it. Maybe even half of the loot."

"Wow!" Gregg hollered. "That's why Eva thinks we're not on the level. She doesn't want to pay us."

"Sshh! They're coming," Glenna hissed, her heart pounding like a jackhammer.

If the guys who hit Blaze had that much money hidden at the Vault, they could be real trouble. Blaze stuck his head under her hand as if needing reassurance. She patted his side as she'd seen Anthony do.

Gregg gave Mason a high-five. "And because you're our special friend, we'll buy you the most expensive electronic game."

"Yeah, and …"

His voice ebbed away and the driver's door flew open. Dad slid behind the wheel. With the ceiling light still lit, he gazed in the mirror.

"Mason, do your parents know we might be gone for some time?"

"Yes, Mr. Rider. They are fine with it, sir."

"Fasten your seat belts. We're off."

Dad slammed the door and started the engine. The interior light faded to black. Glenna's pulse fluttered as she clicked on her belt. She watched Kaley climb into Eva's Bug, noting she wasn't driving either. Glenna had no desire to take the wheel, not with her quivering knees.

But she was determined to prove Blaze was the real deal. He sniffed out something wrong at the Vault *before* she and Gregg knew he possessed special smelling powers. Besides, if she earned moiety, she'd have enough money to buy Blaze dog food for life. Plus she could buy him a new doggie bed, a better leash, and squeaky toys.

As they trailed behind the green car zooming down the driveway, Glenna put her arms around Blaze's neck. He nuzzled his wet nose against her cheek. She couldn't help it, but a giggle erupted from her lips. She clamped a hand over her mouth too late.

"What's so funny?" Gregg demanded. "If you're getting all scared again, stay home."

So what if she was nervous? Glenna refused to be made fun of by her know-it-all younger brother. He was always raining on her parade. Rather than argue, she closed her lips. After all, Dad was along and wouldn't let anything happen to her or Blaze.

Mason tapped Glenna's shoulder. She glanced around and saw his brilliant smile. His happy face was like a light in the darkness. She giggled again, stroking Blaze's soft fur, caught up in the moment. Then her joy popped like a balloon. What if those men returned to the storage shed and had guns?

9

Glenna stared out the van window as Dad zoomed past Eva's little car, pulling into the Vault ahead of her. He stopped at the gate. Garish lights reflecting off the keypad reminded Glenna that she'd typed in that code herself. So much had happened it seemed like days had passed and not just a few hours.

The metal gate ground open and a shiver ran down Glenna's spine. Buttoning her jacket around her neck, an idea came to her. She told God about her fears. He cared about her. After praying, a funny thing happened. Courage began filling her heart.

Eva tailgated them through the gate just before it closed. Dad turned the van down the aisle near their stall.

"Oh oh!" he exclaimed.

Glenna jerked her eyes to the window. She saw a bright yellow Hummer. Fear roared through her like a flood.

"Dad … is the man here who had the baseball bat?"

"It might not be the same vehicle," he replied. "I never saw the license number."

Dad put the van in park and stepped out, walking to Eva's VW. His hands flew in all directions and he pointed at the Hummer.

"Dad thinks we're in danger." Glenna looked behind her. "Killers might be watching us."

Gregg flipped off his seat belt, making a snapping sound.

"Who says they're killers? You're exaggerating again."

"They could be killers. If you saw the guy who came at me, you'd shiver in your boots."

"Maybe these dudes are spies." Mason stared out the van window. "I wish I had my binoculars."

Blaze lifted his head to see too. Dad slipped back behind the wheel.

"Glenna, keep Blaze quiet. We are going to hide around the corner. Eva is phoning in the Hummer's license number."

Glenna talked softly in Blaze's ear, "Stay quiet or we're all toast."

He nuzzled her shoulder and seemed to know he shouldn't bark or growl.

Dad drove to the next corner in the complex, turning *away* from the Hummer. Eva followed with her VW's lights out. Both vehicles went past the closed doors of other storage compartments. At an intersecting aisle, Dad cut the engine. He tried opening his door, but Eva already stood by it.

She leaned in, telling Dad, "Stay here with the kids. I'll walk through the passageway and eyeball the Hummer. I'll see if anyone is around."

"Want me to go with you?"

"No." Eva opened her purse. "My seventeen friends are with me."

Glenna's eye grew huge at the gun she saw inside. As Eva strode away, Mason leaned forward.

"Man alive! Did you see inside her purse? What kind of mother is she?"

"She's a Federal ICE agent," Gregg shot back.

"What's that?"

Glenna had to chuckle. "Mason, I thought you knew everything. She arrests people."

Dad slumped down in the driver's seat as if he was used to stake-outs. How could he be? He worked in an office. Glenna watched everything going on outside the windows, curiosity building to a fever pitch. She didn't forget to pet Blaze. He was such a good boy.

Meanwhile, Mason's fingers flew along the tiny keypad on his cell phone. Glenna released her seat belt. She flipped her head around and saw him type the letters, "ICE." Just then, Eva charged toward the van from between the buildings. Dad perked up, lowering his window.

"No one's around. The Hummer's plate was swiped off a car in Springfield."

"Then it's probably not the same one from this afternoon," Dad said, sounding relieved.

Eva nodded keenly. "Why risk being caught wielding a ball bat?"

"Still, I wonder where the men are from the white truck. Maybe they left in another car."

Eva snuggled her purse to her side. "Anthony and Glenna will walk Blaze by the door that was open earlier this afternoon."

"Let me go." Gregg slid open the door and climbed out.

"Send me, Dad," Glenna objected. "I'm more responsible. We don't want mistakes made."

Dad spoke softly with Eva and motioned Gregg back into the van. "Gregg, stay with Mason and Blaze. Eva and I are going with Glenna."

Eva held up her hand. "No parade. Three's already too many."

"Will Glenna be safe with you?"

"If she is quiet, we can pull this off." Eva pointed at her VW. "Bo, I'd like you to protect my kids."

Dad helped Glenna out and wrapped an arm around her shoulder. "You have your orders. Make no sounds."

"Sure, Dad. Like when the choir sings, I try not to cough."

"Good girl."

Glenna had an odd feeling of being watched.

"Pray for me, Dad."

"I always do."

GLENNA WALKED WARILY behind Eva to the VW. Anthony scrambled out using his cane. Kaley and Andy glared at Glenna from the backseat. Well, they'd have to sit there out of the loop while Glenna fingered the bad guys. The trio took a few steps toward the building.

Anthony stooped toward her ear. "Show me the door where Blaze growled."

Glenna didn't have to think. She knew the door by heart.

"It's the second one from the end on the left side."

Eva held up a finger. "We head through the passageway, then you point to the correct door. Walk lightly, so your feet don't scuff the pavement. Understand?"

"Yes, ma'am."

Eva spun on her boot heels and headed for the passageway just beyond the van. She looked back, motioning for Glenna and Anthony to follow. Glenna glided on tiptoe, glad for those tiring days in ballet class. She'd also worn her soft leather shoes.

They walked in silence. Lights on the side of the building sent weird shadows on the red metal walls. Glenna tuned her ears for strange sounds. Her eyes searched for the road-rage man. Hearing nothing and seeing no one, she hoped the cold didn't make her sneeze.

Eva led them across the asphalt driveway between rows of garage doors. In the quiet, a hot current sizzled along Glenna's head, prickling her scalp. They entered another passageway. Then she saw *the* door ahead and pointed. Eva motioned her past.

Glenna heard someone cough. She glanced at Anthony, only he hadn't covered his mouth. Was someone inside the stall? Once they navigated the last passageway and turned down the next driveway, Eva angled them out of sight behind a building.

"Glenna, are you sure that's the right door?"

"Yes. The door was rolled open, but Blaze scared two men before I could see inside."

Anthony raised his eyebrows. "Eva, someone coughed from behind the door."

"I heard it too!" Glenna was ready to be safe in the van.

"Not me," Eva replied, looking puzzled.

With a shake of his cane, Anthony said, "Take off your cap. We'll stroll by again."

Eva folded her knit cap into her pocket, letting loose her long blond hair that flowed to her shoulders. Anthony led the way, lifting his cane like a sword. Glenna grinned in spite of her fears. The retired agent was getting stronger just being on this mission.

They made it through the covered passageway, but Glenna hardly dared to breathe. At the mouth of the second passage, Anthony slowed. He took a few more steps before stopping right by the second door. It was closed. He cupped a hand around his right ear.

Glenna heard more than two voices behind the door. They were muffled at first, but grew louder. Her heart thumped. What if they opened the door and saw her? If they flew out with the baseball bat, Eva might use her gun!

Eva flexed her two fingers like someone walking. Anthony took the hint and turned away. Glenna grabbed his arm. Together, they stole back to the van. When Dad climbed out of the front seat, she finally breathed.

Eva's orders came fast.

"Glenna, hop in. Anthony, you ready Blaze. Let's take him to the stall before the men spot us."

Dad hustled Glenna into the van with a hand on her back.

"How many men are there?" he asked.

"At least three," Eva replied. "We must act quickly."

As soon as Anthony fitted Blaze with the halter, the dog pranced, ready for action. He and his former handler disappeared down the spooky passageway. Eva removed a gun from her purse, pointing it at the ground before slipping into the darkness.

"Did you see that?" Mason whispered. "She's taking her seventeen friends with her."

"Where? I don't see anybody." Gregg plastered his nose against the side window.

Mason erupted in laughter. He held up his phone. "It says Immigration Customs Enforcement special agents carry nine millimeter Glock pistols. They hold seventeen bullets, which are Eva's seventeen friends. I am impressed."

Dad opened the driver's door and poked his head inside. "Glenna, come with me."

He led her cautiously to the corner of the nearby storage building. Dad pressed his back against the building, waving for her to stay behind him and do the same. After peeking around the corner, he nudged her to walk past him.

"Glenna, are the agents at the correct door?"

She peered down the dark passageway. Blaze sat by the suspect door staring intently.

"Yes! He's alerting just how Anthony trained him. Is their stall loaded with money?"

Dad popped his head around the corner.

"Quick!" he cried. "Here they come. Scoot back to the van."

Blaze came tearing around the corner, pulling Anthony. Eva hurried up, out of breath. The retired agent gave Blaze a doggie bone.

He turned to Eva. "My dog says currency is in that storage unit. Did you see him alert?"

"Oh, definitely," Eva replied, her voice low. "I heard him whining too."

"Yes, but I yanked him away before he growled. I think you have enough for your search warrant, but hurry. Those men are shouting in there."

Eva snatched a cell phone from her purse. "I should take Kaley and Andy home, but I have no time. Bo, can they sit in your van? I'll get help out here pronto."

Glenna swallowed, going over every word she'd just heard. Eva was getting a warrant to search the storage locker. Blaze had done his job perfectly. But what did Anthony mean that Blaze was *his* dog?

10

Glenna dove into the third seat, letting Kaley and Andy jump into the middle one with Blaze. They fit; however, over the next hour, one problem arose. Blaze didn't like being crowded. He kept turning around to get comfortable. Finally Glenna took matters into her own hands.

"Hey, Gregg, I'm moving up front. You and Andy sit back here with Mason."

Changes were made. In the front seat, Glenna lowered the sun visor, watching behind her in the mirror. She was shocked to see Blaze plop his head onto Kaley's lap. His friendliness to a stranger didn't sit well with Glenna. If Eva's daughter planned to get her mitts on Blaze, what could Glenna do?

She put her ear close to the opening of the window where Eva was telling Dad, "I'll drive my VW to the gate and park it sideways so the Hummer can't leave."

"I thought your team would be here by now," Dad said.

"The agents are bringing the search warrant and should arrive any minute."

Dad nodded and paced by Anthony. Eva kept raising her cell phone to her ear. Glenna checked the mirror. There was Kaley, petting Blaze nonstop.

"It must be exciting living with an ICE special agent," Mason said. "Can you guys tell us any good stories?"

Kaley shrugged. "It's no big deal. Mom fixes dinner. If she's late, my dad cooks."

"My dad won't let Kaley touch the stove," Andy said. "Last week, she burned up a whole chicken."

Glenna's distrust of Kaley changed. She felt for the girl, who also had to put up with a smart-mouthed younger brother.

She was about to tell Kaley about a movie she liked when Mason asked, "Do you ever get to play with her seventeen friends?"

Kaley stroked Blaze. "What you mean?"

"You know. She carries a gun with seventeen bullets."

Mason held up his phone. "You are looking at a Glock. You know, what your mom has."

"Mom taught me and Kaley to shoot her gun once," Andy said. "We were out in the pasture at our Grandpa Marty's house in Michigan. But only once."

"Does she keep a gun at your house?" Mason pressed.

Andy took Mason's phone, holding the image closer to his eyes. "Sure, but we can't touch it. Maybe I'll ask my mom to take me to a gun safety class."

"Forget it, Andy. You're too young," Kaley cautioned.

Mason took back his phone. "I finished gun safety class. But this is too cool, being at a real crime scene and in a car with special agents and spies."

"What?" Kaley cried. "My mom isn't a spy."

"Maybe not. But," he jerked his thumb over at Gregg, "his dad is. My father said so."

"Mason, our dad is *not* a spy," Glenna declared.

She turned and glared at him. Mason leaned forward. "Have you guys ever asked him?"

"My dad is a diplomat," Gregg fired back. "He recruits for the State Department. His last assignment was in Israel and we went along."

"Sorry to burst your bubble," Mason insisted. "My father knows."

This is ridiculous. Why does Mason say hurtful things in front of strangers?

Frustration at her friend rolled in Glenna's stomach.

"Please stop," she commanded. "You don't know what you're talking about."

"Glenna, I'm not trying to make you upset. My father said a Federal agent came to see him. The agent wanted to rent my grandparents' farmhouse, the one you are in. Because they're no longer living, the agent spoke with my father."

"So?" Gregg asked.

"I overheard my father tell my mother it was hush-hush. Something about you guys moving from your house near D.C. because it's no longer safe for you to live there." Mason looked outside. "My father said your family is being hidden in our rental house."

Glenna felt someone's hot breath on her neck. She brushed it away thinking her hair was tickling her neck. Only it wasn't. Blaze was poking his nose in her hair.

She reached back and patted his head, happy he hadn't abandoned her for Kaley. Strange things had happened in Israel, causing them to move. But Mom and Dad had insisted Glenna tell no one, not even Gregg or their grandparents. She sure wasn't going to discuss secret matters with Mason or the Montanna kids.

"You watch too much TV," she told Mason. "We live next door because Mom wants us to live in the country. It's part of our home-schooling."

Glenna watched Gregg in the mirror. He nodded furiously.

"Yeah," he piped. "We're getting two cows next week. Glenna will get up every day at five to feed and water 'em."

Mason smiled. "I'll be happy to teach you what I know, Glenna."

"Don't believe Gregg. My brother's nose is growing as long as Pinocchio's."

"I looked up the CIA," Mason said, tapping his phone. "CIA agents working in our embassies only *pose* as State Department employees."

Andy leaned against the window. "What's the CIA?"

"It means Central Intelligence Agency. Our spies work for them."

Andy swiveled his head from Gregg to Glenna in the front seat, his mouth hanging open.

"Wow! That's who your dad works for?"

Before Glenna could defend Dad, she saw him punching in the code to the front gate. A flashing red light lit the corner of her eye. A parade of black SUVs and cars turned into the Vault. Each one turned off its flashing lights the moment they entered the drive.

By driving her VW a few feet to the side, Eva allowed the vehicles to pass through the gate. They rolled to a stop next to the Riders' van. Federal agents, men and women wearing different jackets with big letters, flooded the drive. Mason clamped a hand on the seat in front of him.

"Wow! FBI, ICE, DEA, Secret Service, IRS. And look! They all have seventeen friends on their belts!"

Five human pairs of eyes and one set of canine eyes watched from the van. An FBI agent wearing cargo pants hefted a large pry bar from the back of a SUV. Eva talked to the whole group. She gave Dad a walkie-talkie. Because he stood right outside the van, Glenna heard their conversation.

"Bo, you and Anthony stay with the kids, but monitor the radio in case of trouble."

Dad nodded. "Is it safe here or should we move further away?"

"We have you covered." She tapped her purse.

Glenna gulped down anxiety. With Eva patting the Glock in her purse, the guys in the storage locker must be toting guns. Federal agents scurried behind one another down the passageway. An FBI agent backed up one SUV, turning it toward the Hummer.

Dad and Anthony stood talking behind the van. No one in the van said a word. Glenna's heart started racing. Everything was so exciting and scary at the same time.

A voice yelled in the distance, "Federal agents! Search warrant! Open up!"

Loud banging split the air and Glenna flinched. Andy covered his ears. Blaze whined.

Glenna heard, "Don't move. Show your hands. You're under arrest!"

At total silence, she shoved her ear against the window.

"I can't hear anything."

Mason whispered, "But this is so cool."

"Sshh!" Gregg hissed. "I'm listening."

"Halt! Stop him!" Eva shouted.

A man bolted from between the buildings. Eva chased him, yelling, "I said halt!"

He ran toward the gate. Glenna hugged the passenger door. When he veered straight for the driver's door, she screamed. Her mind whirled. What should she do?

He reached for the handle and she pressed the door lock, *click*. He hit the driver's door with a thud and yanked on the handle. Glenna ducked down. The door held.

Eva slammed her body against him. Glenna peeked up, amazed to see Eva battling the large man with such force. The fearless agent crashed his head against the windshield. His nose smashed against the glass and his mouth plastered open. His evil eye stared straight at Glenna, steam from his mouth fogging the glass. She'd seen that eye before.

Dad appeared out of nowhere. Anthony ran too, without his cane.

"Let me help," Dad said, reaching out his arms.

"I've got him." Eva clicked handcuffs on his wrists.

She yanked the man to a standing position. "You have the right to remain silent."

Eva pushed him toward the storage locker, still talking to him.

Dad looked concerned. Glenna unlocked the doors to the van and Dad cracked opened the driver's door.

"Wow, that was exciting. *All* you kids stay here. We're making sure Eva is all right. We'll will be right back."

Dad and Anthony just disappeared down the corridor when Mason slid open the door. He jumped down. Gregg and Andy followed.

"Hey," Glenna protested. "Dad said to stay in the van."

Mason waved for her to come. "He said we had to stay *here*. We won't go far."

Kaley dashed out, leaving Glenna alone in the front seat. When she saw them lined up peering around the corner, she thought of Eva, the super-agent, and her heroics.

Glenna patted Blaze's head. "Stay here."

She joined the others. Beyond the dimly lit corridor, she spotted several agents lingering outside the stall where Blaze had alerted.

"I don't see drugs or explosives," Glenna whispered to Mason.

The agents seemed relaxed while Eva spoke to the handcuffed man. Glenna had acted so quickly, she hadn't been sure before. She nudged her brother's back.

"Gregg, do you see who Eva arrested? He's the guy who tried to run me off the road!"

Gregg let loose a whistle. Glenna rammed him with her elbow.

"Be quiet. He's a lunatic. He lunged at me with a baseball bat."

"He didn't look tough when Eva grabbed him," Mason said softly.

"Gregg, your whistle alerted Dad that we've left the van," Glenna needled. "If he finds us here, you're toast. No video games for a week."

"Sorry," Gregg gulped. "The whistle just flew from my lips."

Glenna looked around the corner. An agent led another man, the one with slick-backed hair, out from the storage stall. The third man came out last, the one who had hit Blaze in the nose with a pail.

"They're all handcuffed." Kaley sounded in awe of her mom's work.

The men were hauled to a black SUV. Eva's prisoner turned and gaped at Glenna. The kids all jumped back, banging into each other. Mason had the guts to peer around the corner.

"The three guys are locked in the SUV," he said. "But your dad's coming with Eva."

"Scram!" Glenna darted off first.

All five kids sprinted away. By the time Dad approached, Blaze was surrounded by five obedient teens, all watching out through the van windows. If Dad could have listened to her heart, its rapid beat would have given Glenna away.

The black SUV passed through the gate, then Dad opened the driver's door.

"The men are under arrest. Come see what Blaze found. Stay outside the storage locker and don't touch anything. Bring Blaze too."

A herd of teens slammed the van doors and Blaze galloped behind Glenna. Several agents hotly discussed the case in the corridor, stepping aside for them to pass. The overhead door had been raised. A single lightbulb hung from the ceiling.

Glenna stared at loads of money crammed inside, too much to count.

"Blaze did great," Dad said, waving his arm. "Look at all these one hundred dollar bills. Millions of them."

Gregg pumped his fist in the air, whistling again, louder than before. Mason spun around. He held out his hands, palms up.

"Give me five," he said, grinning.

Gregg slapped his hands and Glenna danced around Blaze.

"This is my greatest day ever. Whoowee!"

Blaze thumped his tail against Glenna's legs. Eva shook Anthony's hand.

"Your dog hasn't lost his touch," she told the retired agent. "You should be proud."

"I am and thank you. But he is no longer *my* dog."

Anthony stared at Glenna without a smile. She tried swallowing the ache in her throat.

Poor Anthony. He's sorry he gave up Blaze. What's going to happen?

Mason dropped his hand. "Mrs. Montanna, will you pay Glenna and Gregg the moiety?"

"Moiety?" Eva scowled. "I don't think so. Why would we?"

Mason pushed forward. "The law provides a reward for anyone who finds the money. You know, moiety."

Eva crooked her finger at Gregg and Glenna. They walked over to her side.

"Mason is correct. The law does permit moiety for recovering of illegal currency, or currency that has not been taxed."

"So, Gregg and Glenna should be paid, maybe millions." Mason smiled.

"There's just one problem."

"What?" Glenna glanced at Dad, his eyes giving away nothing.

Mason shoved his hands in his pockets, waiting for some terrible news.

"The money is counterfeit," Eva said. "It's worthless."

Glenna's heart sank to her toes. She looked down at Blaze. His brown eyes searched her face. Though he seemed to realize something was wrong, Glenna refused to believe he'd failed.

"You mean Blaze didn't find real money?" she asked, puzzled by what it all meant.

Dad slung an arm around her shoulder. She leaned against him, absorbing his strength.

"Sorry, honey. Blaze did his job well. He sniffed out the unique ink used on currency. The ink was real. Unfortunately this paper seems like real money, only it isn't."

"No moiety," Eva said, shaking her long blond hair.

"But," Gregg squared his jaw, looking stern, "Blaze caught three criminals."

Dad dropped his arm from Glenna's shoulders. "You should all take pride. The counterfeiters are under arrest."

Glenna reached for Blaze, nestling her face in his silky coat.

"Can we take him home? He's exhausted and I am too."

11

A week later, Glenna brushed Blaze to a brilliant shine in the mudroom. She should be upstairs finishing a paper on threats posed by North Korea, but instead, she gave her dog's coat a final touch. When she heard someone talking in the kitchen, she stopped brushing to listen. "Julia, my boss isn't inviting me to Camp David for fun. He ordered me to go. I'm not *choosing* to be gone again over Christmas. My boss insists it must be me."

Glenna heard Dad's tortured sigh. Everything grew quiet. Was Mom crying softly or did Glenna imagine it? She had to quit eavesdropping. Guilt overwhelmed her and she vowed not to listen when she shouldn't. At least she would try.

She slipped on a jacket and headed out with Blaze for a walk. He sniffed the gravel drive, lunging after a blue jay. Glenna tugged on his leash. Even her dog needed something to do.

"You have an amazing nose, smelling ink. Too bad it wasn't real."

She shuffled down the drive. Eva had said the case would take time to resolve. The men dealing in fake money had posted bond, meaning they were out of jail.

"I hope that nut job with the ball bat is sent away for life."

Blaze bounded to some weeds, his last job long forgotten. A horse browsed along the fence line, but Mason wasn't outside feeding the animals. His words at the Vault peppered her mind: "Your dad is a spy for our government."

Could he be right? She leaned down to ruffle Blaze's fur.

"What do you think, boy? Is my daddy a hero, spying for our government?"

Blaze stared at her. Did he blink his left eye?

Glenna shook her head. Maybe she was seeing things?

"Okay, is that why he's going away on Christmas?"

Woof!

Did Blaze have special senses besides smelling ink? Her new best friend had stayed right by Glenna's side when she had popped corn to string on the tree, lifting her spirits. He'd lain by her feet last night as she drank cocoa and sang carols while Mom played the piano.

Even the twins had stopped crying. It seemed the babies were finally growing up.

Glenna wished she knew "dog talk." But she didn't. She crunched the gravel with her toe, haunted by sounds of Mom weeping.

"Why is Mom crying, Blaze?"

He pulled her up the drive, straining against the leash as if trying to tell her something. Okay, she could fix nachos, which Mom loved. Glenna had experience dicing jalapenos.

"Let's make supper," she announced.

Woof! Blaze ran along, keeping close to her fast-moving feet.

She swung open the back door and mustered a lively, "We're back."

Mom stood with one hand on the gingham curtains. Glenna unhooked Blaze from his leash and washed her hands. She checked the refrigerator. Good, she had tons of salsa, shredded cheese, and diced onion. Glenna had no desire to drive to the store, not with Mr. Ball-bat on the loose.

She shut the fridge and faced her mom who stared out the window. She touched her arm.

"Mom, is something wrong?"

"Grandpa Buck and Grandy just invited us to Treasure Island for Christmas."

"We already put up the tree. I'll miss being here, but if we're *all* together, who cares where we celebrate Christmas. It's Jesus' day."

"Dad will be working. He can't come." Mom's voice sounded flat.

Glenna stepped closer. "But he'll fly down when he can, right?"

Mom wiped her eyes and adjusted her smile.

"Of course, sweetie. Glenna, you're growing up so fast."

Mom enveloped her into a warm hug. Glenna had no heart to admit she'd heard her parents talking. Maybe she would later, after she cooked supper and everyone else was upstairs.

THE NEXT MORNING GLENNA shoved clothes into her suitcase, frustration building. She loved dolphins and wiggling her toes in the sand. But going to her grandparents' in Treasure Island without her dad made her unhappy.

And Mason was becoming a good friend to her and Gregg. If she left him behind, wouldn't he forget their fun times together? Christmas wouldn't be the same without Dad. All because he had to go camping.

She tugged her soft carry-on bag, stubbing her toe on the box of baby things Mom had wanted. Maybe Glenna should take out light clothes for Ricky and Annie to have in Florida. She tore off the lid and lifted clothes out of a sealed plastic bag. The tiny clothes inside made her wonder.

Gregg waltzed in demanding to know, "What is that stuff? Your doll clothes?"

"I haven't played with dolls since you were six. These clothes look ancient, like they're from another century."

Gregg sat on the floor, holding up a little sailor costume.

"Did Dad wear this? Grandpa Popeye served in the Navy, you know."

"I know that. Look at these tiny white shoes."

She removed a baby book from the box.

"Hey, that's mine," Gregg said, snatching it from her and flipping open the cover.

Glenna peered over his shoulder. Something wasn't right.

"No, that baby has black hair. When you were born, your hair was wavy and brown like Dad's."

Gregg turned the page. "It says here this kid is Jasper Mason Lockridge—"

"Born ninety years ago," Glenna interrupted. "This belongs to Mason's family."

"Even I figured that out."

"What about these?" She held up a stack of letters tied in a red ribbon.

"Some mystery we don't have time to solve. I'm looking for my sandals."

"They're stuffed in the back hall cubbyhole. I'm taking these letters to Mason. Want to come?"

"Nah, Dad and I are gonna play a video game."

Sadness rang in his voice and Gregg stomped off. She turned to the mystery box. Rather than open crackly yellow papers and risk damaging old letters, she'd bring Mason the entire box. She wanted to tell him good-bye anyway.

Glenna put everything in order, lifted the box, and skipped downstairs. In the back hall, she slipped on her jacket. The cold wind taunting her, she barreled across the drive and through the yard.

Near Mason's barn, loud bellowing sounds nearly scared her out of her wits.

She lugged the box and hurried past, running up to Mason's front door. After she knocked, he opened the door, holding a laptop.

She cradled the box in both hands.

"One of your cows sounded sick, like it has pneumonia."

"Hmm," Mason's eyebrows shot up on his forehead. "The large animal vet came this morning. All of our critters checked out in good shape."

"That animal was so loud I freaked out."

"Oh," he said, laughing. "You probably heard Stormy, our guard donkey."

"Not a guard *dog*?"

He smiled. "A donkey guards our cattle. My research revealed donkeys bite and kick predators like coyotes. So my father bought one. This morning Stormy brayed at a wild fox, which took off, causing no trouble."

Glenna juggled the box, prompting Mason to ask her, "What did you bring me?"

"I found this old box in our basement. Since your grandparents used to live in our farmhouse, I think these clothes and ancient letters belong to your family."

Pushing the door open wider with his foot, Mason struggled to balance his computer.

"Come in before you freeze. My folks are in town. They'll look it over later."

Glenna set the box on a table before joining Mason in the living room. A thought came into her mind.

"Does Stormy have a cross on her back?"

Mason flashed a puzzled look. She smiled at the idea of teaching Mason something new.

"Jesus rode a donkey just before he was crucified. I read an article about every donkey having a cross on its shoulders and back."

Mason looked up from his computer. "I did notice that Stormy's fur crosses on her upper back."

That said, his eyes returned to his computer screen. Glenna wasn't content to let the subject drop. She was curious to see if Mason shared her interest in the Bible.

"I believe donkeys have the cross because Jesus rode one to his crucifixion."

Mason navigated his keyboard.

"If you are doing homework ..." Her voice trailed off.

If he was too busy to talk, she'd forget telling him about their trip to Florida. She walked toward the door. Then Mason slid his laptop onto a side table and came over.

"Sorry, but I'm researching colleges with good football teams. I just found one highly rated in scholastics."

"What's your hurry?" Glenna asked. "You're not even a junior."

"I know. My future concerns me."

A cloud darted through Glenna's mind. She hadn't thought much about the far-off future. Instead, she worried about Dad going on a camping trip instead of coming to Florida. Why did he have such a demanding boss?

Glenna noticed Mason peering at her closely.

"Did I say something wrong?" he asked. "Your face turned gray."

"I also came to tell you we're leaving. Not moving, but visiting my grandparents in Florida."

"A family vacation on the beach sounds terrific. Me? I'll be feeding cattle and working on an independent study paper about how social media changes our lives."

"Christmas is weird without snow." Glenna forced a sigh. "We spent last Christmas in Florida. Grandy's tree is the size of that box, with no lights."

"Glenna, I'd love to ride big Atlantic waves on my new Mischief boogie board."

"Fine for you. I have no boogie board and we'll be in Treasure Island on the Gulf side."

"Too bad. Surf is way better on the Atlantic."

Glenna struggled with telling Mason about Camp David. Maybe he knew where it was.

"There's more," she confided. "My mom is coming, but Dad's going camping."

Mason spun around. "Camping in this cold? Is he nuts?"

"I don't know. Mom said he is going to Camp David."

He stared with his bright green eyes and burst out laughing. "There's your proof, Glenna."

"Proof?"

"Your dad *is* a spy. At Camp David you don't sit around campfires making s'mores. It's a highly protected military installation where the president has vital meetings."

Mason walked over to his computer, fingers flying over his keyboard. He pointed.

"Our president just hosted Russia's president at Camp David."

Glenna zipped up her jacket. She really needed to finish packing.

"That's news to me. I thought it was like soldiers sleeping in sleeping bags."

"Not so. I think your dad, Bo Rider, is a big-shot with the president. So if he hasn't told you what he does, then he probably is a secret spy."

Glenna's cheeks flamed. How did Mason know more about her dad than she did? Upset that she'd told him anything, she changed the subject.

"I'll ask Mom if you can visit us over your break. Bring your Mischief board."

A slow smile crept to Mason's face. He closed his computer.

"That would be cool."

Glenna smiled. "I'll let you know what she says before we leave for the airport."

"Your grandparents' tree will be bigger than ours," Mason said, opening the front door. "My father doesn't believe in Christmas."

She looked around. Mason was right. They didn't even have a tree.

"Wait for my call," she said.

On the way home confusion flooded her heart.

Mason would share Christmas with his father who didn't believe in Jesus' birthday. Glenna had to leave her father who did believe in Christmas. Plus, Mr. Lockridge said Dad was a spy. Mason just said presidents met with world leaders at Camp David, where Dad was going.

When she reached Stormy, the guard donkey brayed. Only this time Glenna didn't jump. The donkey with the soft gray coat trotted over to investigate. Glenna put out the back of her hand as she'd learned to do with horses. Stormy sniffed with her nose, showing her teeth.

"It's okay, girl. I'm no threat to you or your livestock."

Stormy seemed to spread her lips apart in a smile and Glenna waved.

"See you in a few weeks."

She rushed home, feeling better about her beliefs. They would get her through this time of change. Jesus had come to earth as a baby. He gave his life for her and lived in her heart, guiding her and helping her. Glenna also trusted her dad, no matter what he did for a job.

As she crossed the gravel drive, Dad loaded suitcases into the van. A sick feeling lodged in her stomach. Her life was growing more complex by the minute.

12

Gregg Rider adored Treasure Island. He felt certain that at any second he'd find what he was looking for. It sure was hot though. How could Christmas be days away?

Sweat dripped into his eyes. He swiped off his headset and then his ball cap. After running an arm across his forehead, he pulled his cap lower to shade his eyes. After clamping the headset over his ears, he trudged among the weeds in the vacant lot across from Grandpa Crockett's house. Treasure waited to be found.

His metal detector in one hand, Gregg kicked aside empty food wrappers. He struck a rubber ball with his foot, sending it high in the air. Boy, the ground was tangled with thorns. His bare ankles were all scratched. Gregg pulled up his white socks, streaked with dirt.

Forget thistles; he had a job to do. He aimed the detector over a mound, waiting for the magic beep.

"Wait and see, Glenna," he muttered. "I'll find something valuable yet."

Even a banged up penny would quiet her criticism over his new hobby. So far the day was a bust. He'd found one rusty nail. How could that be? Grandpa Crockett had found a whole wall of uniform buttons.

Unwilling to give up, Gregg waved the sensor back and forth, trying to cover every inch of the property. Grandpa had found the antique buttons with his metal detector in a Civil War battlefield in Mississippi near a place called Vicksburg.

Two days ago, Grandpa had surprised Gregg with his very own metal detector. Ever since, Gregg and the detector he called Klondike had been inseparable.

This morning over pancakes, Grandpa had whispered to Gregg, "Mark my words. They named this place Treasure Island because there's buried treasure around here."

So here he was with Klondike trying to find something so he could afford *Bounty Hunters*, a new video game. A high-pitched whining in his earphones made him stop. He backed up, putting the wand over the spot where the tone sounded the loudest.

Gregg bent down, and with Grandpa's recovery scoop, he dug furiously. Sand disappeared through the tiny holes, and in seconds, he saw his priceless find: another nail. At least this one had no rust.

They had no value, but Gregg did what he'd seen Grandpa do. He shoved the nail in his pocket so people wouldn't step on them. Then he swung Klondike back into action, hovering the wand inches above the ground. He concentrated hard to hear the tone.

Two hands grabbed his shoulders and squeezed.

"Agghh!!" he hollered.

His heart beat wildly. Gregg spun around, facing his attacker. Glenna stood with her mouth wide open, exposing her retainer. Gregg ripped off his headset.

"What are you doing? Are you crazy? I could've killed you with my karate kick!"

Glenna laughed. "You don't know karate."

"I might have tried, if it wasn't you. What do you want?"

She picked up his cap that had tumbled to the ground.

"I came to see if we're getting rich from treasures."

Gregg held up his one good nail, keeping mum about the rusty one.

"Grandpa says we can sell these for scrap, but it will take a whole truck of them."

"When you found this," Glenna said, taking the nail, "did the detector whine in your ears?"

"Yeah, like it does for Grandpa."

She handed him the nail and grinned.

"I was riding to the bank with Grandy when it came to me."

"What did?"

Glenna tossed her brown tresses over her shoulder. "I devised a way to use the whine of the detector to find non-metal treasure."

"Nope. It has to be metal. Some metals won't even make it whine."

"You astonish me with your brain. I really came to find you, Mr. Smarty-pants, because Mom says dinner is served. You can try my fish tacos and then we'll test out my idea."

"Fish tacos sound gross, but searching in this heat is too much."

Gregg set off to show Grandpa his good nail. Glenna followed hot on his heels.

AFTER DINNER, GREGG LOADED the dishwasher, his mind fixed on finding treasure. He let Glenna scrape goop off the dishes. Grandpa was reading the paper in the living room. Grandy visited with Mom and the twins on the porch. Glenna washed her hands and hung up the towel.

"You ready to see if my treasure detector works?" she asked, her eyes sparkling.

"Sure, but ask Grandpa first. He gave me special lessons on how to use my detector."

"I'm not using Grandpa's detector. I have my own detector."

"Do not."

"Do too."

Glenna nodded toward the den where Blaze was sleeping in his bed.

"Blaze, can you hear me? Come here, boy."

Nothing happened. She opened the cupboard beneath the kitchen sink and took out the box of doggie bones. She rattled it.

"Come here, Blaze."

Canine nails screeching across the tile floor hurt Gregg's ears. He covered them. Seconds later, Blaze rounded the corner. Gregg dropped his hands, folding his arms across his chest.

"Glenna, it's not time for his treat. You'll make him fat."

She raised her finger to her lips. "Sshh."

Blaze stood at attention, his tail wagging. Glenna placed a bone in the pocket of her jeans. Blaze tilted his head, his eyes searching her face. The poor dog looked confused.

"Don't be mean," Gregg insisted.

"You just watch."

Taking Blaze's leash from the kitchen door handle, she fastened it to his collar.

"Blaze, you're going to work for this bone."

She took his head in her hands, looking him in the eyes. "Show me. Can you do that?"

Gregg elbowed his way into their huddle. "What are you doing? Quit teasing him."

"You saw Blaze work in our barn and at the Vault," Glenna snapped. "If you want to stay, be quiet."

With the leash, she nudged Blaze over to the refrigerator and pointed underneath it.

"Where is it, Blaze? Where is it?"

When Blaze simply looked up at Gregg, he patted the dog's head. His sister was trying something neither he nor Blaze understood.

"See, Glenna, you are confusing him."

She shook her head. "This is what Anthony did. Where is it, Blaze?" The dog lowered his head toward the front of the fridge as if smelling odors beyond the black void. Glenna nudged Blaze toward the stove and he kept sniffing.

"Good boy, Blaze. Keep going."

Next she led him into the living room. Gregg was skeptical, but curious. He trailed behind, hands in his pockets so his sister wouldn't think he was too interested. By a cabinet, Glenna pointed to an opening near the bottom.

"Show me, Blaze. Where is it?"

Gregg thought Glenna was tricking Blaze, but she'd already warned him to keep quiet, so he zipped his lips. Let her fall flat on her face. Then she'd see he had a better idea for finding treasure with Klondike. It was simply a matter of time before the best Rider won.

He toyed with the nail in his pocket, watching Glenna bring Blaze to Grandy's empty chair. The yellow Lab put his nose everywhere she took him.

"Good boy, Blaze. Where is it?"

She guided him to the sofa, where Grandpa stretched his legs out reading. Blaze stepped over them and sniffed. Back and forth his nose stayed busy at work. Glenna pulled him toward the TV cabinet, but Blaze strained at the end of the leash, returning to Grandpa's legs. This time he shoved his head under Grandpa's legs, pushing his nose beneath the sofa skirt.

"Hey," Grandpa protested. "Can't a man enjoy his paper?"

Blaze sat and stared at the sofa beneath Grandpa's legs.

"Show me, boy," Glenna said, her voice lilting. "Where is it?"

Blaze whined softly before thrusting his nose beneath the skirt. He whined some more.

Glenna spoke softly, "Is it there, Blaze? Show me."

Grrr. Grrr. Blaze sat staring at Grandpa.

Grandpa jumped up, the newspaper in his hands.

"What's wrong with that dog? Is he safe to be around?"

Gregg snickered. No one had told Grandpa how Blaze growled at the Vault guys. Glenna reached under the sofa, yanking out a sock. Blaze's eyes remained glued to the sock.

Glenna handed the sock to Gregg.

"What's in here?" he asked.

His sister gave Blaze the doggie bone saying, "Good boy, Blaze."

Grandpa folded his paper with a snap.

"Whose sock is that? Why should Blaze growl at it?"

"At the bank Grandy and I got a pack of crisp bills," Glenna replied. "Open the sock."

Gregg unrolled the black ball and removed a stack of money.

"Sweet," he chimed, staring at the cash.

Grandpa raised his eyebrows. "I never liked dogs."

"Don't hurt his feelings. Blaze is trained to find currency. He smells ink," Glenna said.

"But one that finds money," Grandpa said, taking the money from Gregg. "Well, that is another kettle of fish."

Glenna beamed a smile. "Gregg, I told you my detector could find treasure by whining, just like Klondike. Only Blaze finds real money."

Not wanting to be outdone by his sister, Gregg tossed Blaze the sock. The dog dove for it, and Grandpa stroked his chin. Gregg couldn't wait to find out what Grandpa had in mind for their Christmas break. Would it be as interesting as finding treasure?

13

Christmas was two days away. As the sun peeked above the horizon, Glenna bolted into the kitchen. She assembled breakfast things, whipping eggs in a bowl. After turning up the heat under the pan, she dropped in butter.

This morning she meant to surprise Dad and Mom with a hot breakfast. But in moments, Glenna received the surprise. Mom swung around the corner, dressed in jeans and a pink top.

"I'm making Dad's favorite eggs with ham." A smile stretched across Glenna's face. "Is he still asleep?"

"Ah … Glenna, he's not here. After you went to bed, I popped corn and strung it on Grandy's miniature tree."

Mom plucked a container of orange juice from the fridge and started pouring juice.

"Grandpa strung twinkle lights around the back porch. Be sure to thank him."

Glenna stopped stirring the eggs. Mom never glanced up from the glasses.

"Mother, where is Dad?"

"A snowstorm delayed his flight. He should be in the air in a few hours."

Glenna's appetite shriveled like a popped balloon. She turned off the heat and sat on a chair. Mom came over to rub her shoulders.

"Last night I filled all your stockings. They're hanging over the fireplace."

"You mean the fake one?"

"Dad promised to be here this evening for your play."

Glenna wrinkled her nose. "If more snow falls he won't see me in the Christmas play."

"I know you want Dad here. Meanwhile, finish making breakfast. Doing a kind deed—"

"I know," she interrupted. "Helping others brings happiness. Nothing is the same here."

Mom stopped rubbing her shoulders and strode to the fridge. She pulled out a loaf of homemade bread.

"Yes, it is different. But that doesn't mean it can't be better. I bought you special red tins for your brownies. I love your idea of making homemade gifts for Christmas."

Mom started humming as she spread thick jam on the bread.

Glenna took a chance and asked, "Is Dad a spy?"

The knife clattered to the floor. Mom stared.

"What gives you that idea?"

"Mason's father told him so."

"What exactly did Mason say?"

"That some government men came asking questions about Dad before we moved in."

Mom wiped the floor with a paper towel before picking up the knife.

"That sounds probable. Sometimes he is a diplomat at the State Department."

"You mean he is a spymaster, controlling spies he recruits around the world?"

"Mason's imagination is on overdrive. Don't let him influence you," Mom warned, taking out a clean knife.

Glenna refused to be deterred.

"Mason says Camp David is a military fort used *only* by the president for world meetings. So Dad isn't going camping?"

"Honey, your dad meets with government officials to learn of their recruiting needs."

"I'd rather believe Dad is a spy. That would be awesome."

Her mom tapped her shoulder.

"Finish the eggs. And please don't share your concerns with Gregg."

"Okay." Glenna looked squarely into her mother's eyes.

Did they shift a fraction? Glenna lifted her chin. Perhaps Mason had a point after all.

THAT NIGHT GLENNA STOOD in the side door of Calvary Community Church, gripping her shepherd's staff. She looked outside, hoping for a glimpse of Dad. When she'd left her grandparent's house, he had not arrived.

She adjusted the headdress of her shepherd costume, trying not to feel hurt. Dad had promised to be here. Her eyes took in the manger scene. Its wood hut covered in palm fronds looked ancient, like a scene from the first century. Except the tiny white lights sparkling around the stage and manger gave the set a modern feel. Bright floodlights shone up into the palm trees.

The play was about to begin, but Glenna felt empty, a stranger to herself. She guessed she was lonely, missing home. Battling an urge to check the audience again, she turned toward the kitchen. What if Dad wasn't there, sitting next to Mom?

If she were home, she could walk the long driveway with him and watch the stars. Dad liked to make his breath swirl in the cold air. She hadn't appreciated their together times so much as this moment.

Glenna pictured his goofy smile when he swiped mushrooms off her plate. He'd been trying that trick ever since she could remember. With him at Camp David, confusion had taken root. Mom still refused to shed much light on the president's compound.

Dad always said he recruited the best talent. Glenna didn't like Mason presuming him to be a spy. Thoughts of Dad sneaking around to save the country sounded heroic, but such feats meant danger. She'd seen a movie about a superspy; enemies tried killing him in every scene.

"Please get here, Dad," she whispered.

She also changed her mind. Dad shouldn't be a spy, no matter how cool spymasters sounded to Mason. While her dad had been away in the past for his job, the older she became, the more she needed him.

Gregg had Grandpa for a new buddy. Grandy and Mom had the twins, leaving Glenna feeling alone. Then she remembered Blaze. A smile crept to her lips. He followed her everywhere, hoping for one of her homemade treats.

A noise, like a falling tray, startled her. Glenna whirled around. Her heart sped like she was on a racetrack. Out in the dim lights, she glimpsed a shadow. She raised her staff, ready to defend herself. She listened, but heard nothing. Her pulse and breathing returned to normal.

Where's my cue?

This thought had just entered Glenna's mind when the choir director peered in the door from outside. Wire glasses perched on her nose.

"Are you ready, Glenna? The other shepherds are all outside."

"Mrs. Hernandez, is my dad sitting by my mom?"

"Not that I saw. I was busy retrieving a wandering lamb."

Music drifted through the open door. Glenna wrapped her fingers around her staff. What if Dad's plane was late again? This year the holy day held new meaning for her. Then why didn't the true meaning of Christmas—celebrating Jesus' birthday—fill her aching heart?

She wished the confusion about Dad's job would be over and that her family would be together this Christmas.

"I'll be right along, Mrs. Hernandez. There's something I need to do first."

"You look fine. Come along."

The door closed behind the director. Glenna shut her eyes and lifted up a prayer for God to keep Dad safe and for him to be out there.

She joined Gregg and the other shepherds on the lawn. The odor of lambs from the nearby pen drifted to her nose. An angel dressed in a white robe and a glittering headdress stepped toward her. Bright lights flashed, representing the glory of the Lord, as written in the Bible.

Intense lights blinded her eyes. All she could see were white dots. She was supposed to be terrified and in a way she was. Glenna fell to her knees.

"Do not be afraid!" the angel boomed. "I bring you good news. Today in the town of David a Savior has been born. He is Christ, the Lord."

Gregg nudged her elbow. "Get up now."

"Not yet," Glenna said in hushed tones. "We wait."

The angel told the shepherds, "This will be your sign. Go and find a baby wrapped in cloths, lying in a manger."

Glenna's mind whirled. What was she supposed to say? It was like those lights had blasted out all her thoughts. It was almost her turn.

More angels dressed in white robes flooded the lawn to the right of the stage, saying in unison, "Glory to God in the highest and on earth peace to all on whom his favor rests."

The angels disappeared as if they had gone to heaven. Glenna rose to her feet and faced the other shepherds.

She raised her arms excitedly, declaring, "Let's go to Bethlehem and see this thing that has happened, which the Lord has told us about."

"Follow me!" Gregg lifted his staff high in the air.

Glenna hurried after him. As she reached the stage, the actress playing Mary picked up her little baby, who was really Ricky. Under the twinkle lights, she saw her baby brother sleeping. Mrs. Hernandez turned on a CD. Sounds of a baby crying filled the air.

What would it have been like to be a shepherd and to really have seen Jesus? Awestruck, Glenna's heart filled with a firm belief that Jesus would be with her always. And Dad would be okay, even if he wasn't out there sitting next to Mom.

The lights dimmed. She focused her eyes on her mom. Was Dad at her side? Or was that Grandpa and her eyes were playing tricks? She stared. It was Dad and he wore a terrific smile. As Joseph the actor sang to Ricky, Dad's real son, Glenna grinned. Dad had made it after all.

The song ended and the audience clapped. They took their bows, with Gregg muscling his way to the front. Glenna waved to Dad and ran to change from her costume. As she burst through the side door, she passed a scrawny girl dressed in a dirty coat much too big for her. The girl, who looked about ten, carried a bag. She pushed past Glenna.

Mrs. Hernandez stomped up to Glenna. "Do you know her?"

"That girl?" Glenna tossed her head. "I've never seen her before."

"The cookies for the reception are gone. She must have swiped them during the play."

"She looked hungry."

"Oh, dear. We should connect her to our food pantry. I'll see about that."

"Dad could drive me home to get the extra cookies and brownies I made," she offered.

Glenna had a secret reason for wanting to go home. She was excited to tell Dad that her idea for Blaze finding money had succeeded. He'd be pleased by her creativity. Plus, she'd show him how Blaze could find money, without Gregg nosing in.

14

After spending the private time with Dad, Glenna's joyous reunion with her family around the fake fireplace lasted a mere thirty minutes.

"You and Gregg were fine shepherds," Dad said, smiling. "You both knew your parts."

His words gave Glenna a warm glow inside.

"I saw a young girl—"

The phone ringing in the den interrupted her tale about the girl in the old coat. Dad hurried to answer it and Glenna heaved a sigh. It was probably his boss calling, forcing him back to Camp David.

A few seconds later, he called, "Julia, bring Glenna and Gregg into the den."

"What did you kids do?" Grandpa asked with a smirk.

Glenna looked at her brother, who shrugged. They followed Mom in silence, but as Glenna shut the door, she sensed something was wrong.

"Eva is on the phone. She has a few questions."

Dad pressed a button, turning the cordless into a speakerphone. Mom backed against the door, her arms folded across her chest like a sentry. Dad held the phone out in front of him.

"Okay, Eva, we're here in the den and can all hear you."

"Hi, Eva. This is Glenna."

"I'm here too," Gregg piped as if not wanting to be outdone by his sister.

"Sorry to interrupt your fun," Eva said. "Lawyers for the men arrested at the Vault are demanding we identify the confidential informant mentioned in our search warrant."

Gregg's eyes widened. Alarm shot through Glenna like an arrow.

"What will happen to us?" she whispered, taking a seat next to Dad.

Eva cleared her throat. "Normally it's no problem, but the attorneys want more info about the person they believe is our informant. They have Gregg Rider's name."

Gregg's mouth dropped open.

"Ah …" Glenna stammered. "At the Vault, we stayed in the van, like Dad told us—"

Gregg shook his head furiously.

"No! Dad, it's Glenna's fault. I know what happened."

"Don't blame me!" Glenna popped out of the chair.

When she paused for a breath, Gregg wasted no time pointing a finger at her.

"She's wrong, Dad."

Glenna had no clue where her brother was going. With his arms folded, he looked like a twin to their mom.

"Blaze ran over to those men and growled. I wasn't holding the leash," Gregg admitted.

"You're off subject, Gregg," Dad said with a sigh. "What were you saying, Glenna?"

Before she could speak, Gregg shot her a "be quiet" glare.

He dropped his arms. "Right before the men smashed Blaze with the pail, Glenna yelled super loud, 'Gregg Rider, Dad told you to keep him on the leash.'"

"You called out your brother's name?" Dad's eyebrows creased.

"Yeah, she did. Those men heard her say it too. They must remember my name."

Eva interrupted the back-and-forth.

"Bo, that could be how they found out. The lawyers claim it's the name of a dog or a boy with a dog. Sometimes we refer to our search dogs as confidential sources, keeping defense attorneys confused."

"Whew," Glenna gushed, wiping her forehead. "They think Blaze is the informant."

Dad put the phone closer to his mouth. "Because Julia home-schools our kids, our new address isn't listed in any public schools in Virginia. It should be difficult for them to find Gregg."

Eva was silent a moment. "Your ace crime fighters can avoid being subpoenaed to court by staying in Florida until the case is resolved."

Mom and Dad traded looks, which Glenna couldn't decipher. Staying in Florida sounded okay, especially with Mason arriving soon. Dad pushed out his bottom lip.

"I'll talk to my in-laws," he said, "but they love their grandkids and want what's best."

"Great. I'll inform the court and attorneys that our confidential source is a Homeland Security dog. That is true, even if Blaze is retired."

"Eva, will they believe you have thirteen-year-old dog handlers?" Dad asked.

"Don't know that, do we?" Eva replied. "There's another reason you kids should remain in Florida. One of the counterfeiters, Clancy Graham, was cited earlier that day for road rage. I convinced the local police to drop that charge since he was looking at twenty years for counterfeiting. I did not want you, Bo, or Glenna to be disclosed as witnesses."

Glenna chewed on her bottom lip. Anxiety rose in her throat as she remembered his evil eye on the van's windshield. It didn't help when Dad and Mom kept exchanging glances.

Mom finally nodded at Dad and he told Eva, "Good thinking. I head to Virginia the day after Christmas. Julia will stay in Florida with the kids until you give the okay."

"Bo, can you stay on the line? You and I have other details to discuss."

Mom motioned for Gregg and Glenna to leave. Glenna planned to listen at the door in hopes of discovering any spy talk. Mom thwarted her, escorting them to the kitchen.

Glenna faced her. "Why is Dad leaving so soon?"

"His work is tricky, I'm afraid."

"That stinks." Gregg rolled his eyes. "I wanted to go fishing like we did last Christmas."

"What about tomorrow morning? The early bird catches the worm," Mom said.

The wistful look on her face made Glenna offer an idea. She wouldn't cause Mom trouble.

"I'll put the twins to bed if Gregg makes root beer floats. Then we can watch a movie."

Mom's eyes brightened. "I would like that."

She slipped out of the kitchen, probably to see what else Eva had to tell Dad.

Gregg smashed Glenna in the ribs with his elbow.

"You blamed me in there. Now you've got me making floats. Which glasses do I use?"

"Life is not all about you, Gregg Rider. It won't hurt you to learn how to cook. What if you have to live on your own?"

Glenna swung open a cupboard. She pointed to glasses and left him to sort out his own problems. She joined her grandparents in the living room and took Annie into her arms.

"Grandy, will you bring Ricky? I'm putting them to bed. Dad's leaving right after Christmas."

Out of the corner of her eye, she saw Grandpa lift his chin.

All he said was, "That's too bad."

"But we're staying longer."

Grandpa nodded. "Good. We're not done exploring."

Annie started crying and Glenna hurried to change her diaper. She felt like crying too.

15

On Christmas Eve, Gregg and Grandpa stopped their bicycles in the bike lane, smack in the middle of the drawbridge at John's Pass. They looked east into Boca Ciega Bay. The water churned from behind an expensive-looking yacht steering for the Gulf of Mexico.

"I wish Dad had come with us," Gregg said, watching the waves. "He'd like it here."

"Don't you think he and your mom deserve time alone?"

"I guess so."

A brown truck roared by, nearly knocking over Gregg's bike. Grandpa pointed to shore.

"Let's hustle off the bridge and grab a snack before buying our frozen bait. We don't want it to thaw while we're enjoying our time on the town."

Gregg focused on two kids paddling on kayaks close to the pier. They bobbed and rocked from the wake of the big boat.

"I spotted two kayaks hanging on hooks in your garage. Can Glenna and I use them?"

Grandpa nodded, but jabbed a knobby finger at the kids in the kayaks.

"Avoid this busy waterway. See the risk those kids are in? Boat captains can't always see canoes or kayaks. Besides, after Christmas, you might have another idea."

"What do you have planned?"

"You'll see. Come on, let's eat."

They hiked off the bridge and down to the boardwalk where Grandpa locked their bikes in a rack. Gregg stopped by some fishermen tending poles on the seawall long enough for Grandpa to peer into a cooler.

"Caught yourself a sheepshead, huh?" he asked.

The man's cigarette bobbed on his bottom lip. He nodded to emphasize his grunt.

Grandpa straightened his back. "You might catch a convict fish. Plenty swim by my dock."

"Why are they called convict fish?" Gregg asked. "Because you catch them?"

"I like your logic, but no. See the wide black-and-white stripes? Many years ago convicts wore black-and-white uniforms in jails."

"Yeah, I see. That's cool."

They headed down to a café with seating on the dock. Gregg read a sign carved into the side of an old boat.

"Smuggler's Cove," he said with enthusiasm. "Maybe we'll see a pirate."

"You know modern brigands might use the easy water access for their crimes. Take that table."

Grandpa plopped in a wooden chair and Gregg sat across from him. He poured over a menu that looked like an old treasure map. The burger with cheese sounded good. A server wearing a purple t-shirt with a smiling dolphin came to their table.

"What'll it be, gentlemen?" She held a tiny pencil and pad of paper.

"We'd like two orders of fried clams and hushpuppies. And bring me sweet tea."

"What do you want to drink?" she asked Gregg.

He shrugged, gazing around at other tables for ideas.

"Do you have lemonade?"

"Is that what you want?"

Gregg's stomach growled. He nodded, hoping she didn't take too long to bring their food. As she left, Grandpa wagged a finger at Gregg.

"Your Grandy doesn't know we're here." He held his stomach. "So if she's made lunch when we get back, you'd better eat again."

"It's our secret, right?"

"Correct."

An older man wearing a red vest sauntered in. He sat at the adjoining picnic table. Gregg saw he had a small animal on a leash, which bared its sharp teeth.

"Wow!" Gregg shot forward. "That man has a rat with a stand-up tail on a leash."

Grandpa swiveled his head to look, then said, "Careful. You don't want to hurt that teeny dog's feelings. It's a Chihuahua."

The man leaned close as if he'd heard Grandpa's warning.

"Cujo is a trained attack dog. You get on his wrong side and he'll jump you."

The man gave an exaggerated tug on the leash, saying, "No, Cujo." Those words did the trick. Cujo snarled and snapped his teeth like Gregg was his lunch. Gregg reared back, noticing the dog's vest proclaimed, *Service Dog. Ask Before Petting.*

"Hey, Grandpa, he really is an attack dog."

The older guy's wrinkled face erupted in a lopsided grin. "He isn't. He scares people when I give him the 'No, Cujo' command." The mutt snarled again, showing his needle-like teeth. Gregg slid farther away. "I read a book about a big dog named Cujo. He had rabies and tried to kill people."

Cujo's owner chuckled, patting the rat-like dog. The server brought their drinks, placing them on the wooden table with a thud.

"Hey, Kingman," she said. "How's your baby today?"

While she took the guy's order, she bent down. Cujo sniffed her face.

She left and Grandpa muttered, "He'd be more convincing if he weighed ninety pounds."

"You're really my wife's dog, aren't you, Cujo?"

The old-timer lifted the tiny dog to his lap. "Before this little guy became our service dog, my wife refused to leave New Jersey. She couldn't bear him flying inside a cage."

"He really is a service dog?" Grandpa took a swig of his sweet tea and waited.

Gregg wondered how a service dog was different from a working dog like Blaze. He tried the tart lemonade. When he smacked his lips, Cujo snarled. The old man winked.

He said in a low voice, "If Cujo wasn't a service dog, I couldn't bring him into the restaurant, could I? But he is, and Ned, the owner of this joint, can't keep him out. The airlines have to let this cute boy sit on my wife's lap."

Gregg was astonished that the small, ugly dog could help anyone. "What does he do for service—attack people?"

"No." Kingman waved. "My wife found a website where you train your own service dog. You sign up for their certificate and a nifty dog vest. She paid less than a hundred bucks."

"What does he do for service?" Gregg insisted, his mind buzzing with the possibilities.

"Companionship."

Grandpa shifted his eyes to Gregg and Kingman shifted his weight under the little beast.

"My wife certified she has anxiety attacks. Cujo senses them coming on. He gives her reassurance." Kingman snapped his fingers. "Her anxiety vanishes, making him a therapy dog. I tell fellows like you that he's a service dog."

Grandpa's jaw fell. "Sounds like a scam."

"It's the law. My wife couldn't fly with Cujo on her lap if he weighed ninety pounds."

Gregg snickered as the server placed their clams on the table.

"You gents let me know if you need anything else."

Grandpa dug into his clams, but Gregg hesitated. He bowed his head, saying a silent prayer. When he lifted his head, Grandpa squeezed his arm.

"Sorry, buddy. I forgot your dad's been teaching you to bless your food."

Then Grandpa plunged a fork into a fried clam, dipping it into red sauce.

"This here's cocktail sauce. You dip in your clam and it tastes even better."

He was right. Gregg liked the clams and the sauce. He dipped in more clams.

"That puny dog can't be a service dog," he whispered.

Grandpa shrugged. "Who knows? The Washington crowd specializes in passing laws most of us don't want. Maybe any dog can be a service dog, even Blaze."

Could Grandpa be right? Gregg guzzled his lemonade.

"We'll check the Internet when we get home," Grandpa said.

"Yeah. If Blaze is certified as a service dog, he can come to restaurants with us."

Grandpa bobbed his head, eating his meal. Then he brushed a napkin across his mouth.

"Let's buy our cut bait and head home. We have research to do."

Gregg munched a hush puppy, taking a last look at the mini-attack dog. Blaze would make a better service dog any day. But Gregg couldn't wait to find out what Grandpa had revolving in his mind.

16

Glenna awoke Christmas morning to loud thunder. She ran to the window, gaping at the dark sky. The clouds hovered so low it seemed they were touching Grandpa's roof. She threw on her robe and hurried to the den. She flipped on the TV and tuned to the local news channel.

"Oh no!"

The radar showed a tornado watch. Her heart thumped.

The reporter, standing in the rain wearing a blue slicker, said into the microphone, "Conditions are ripe for a tornado. Be alert."

Glenna dashed to her bedroom. She pulled on jeans and a short-sleeved top. With tornadoes on the prowl, she geared up to run and shoved her feet into tennis shoes. Or was she supposed to hide in an inner room? Grandpa's house had no basement.

She tore out to the porch. Gregg was asleep on the pull-out couch. He'd tossed his pillow on the floor.

"Get up!" She shook his shoulder. "There's a tornado watch."

"Big deal," he grumbled.

He flipped over, pulling the sheet to his chin.

"Okay, but did you see those tornadoes rip through Alabama and Georgia? Houses were smashed to smithereens. People died. I'm waking up Dad."

Glenna flew to the den and raised the volume on the set.

The reporter yelled, "Folks near Fort De Soto, take cover. A tornado will hit Treasure Island in five minutes."

"Dad!" she called, racing down the hall.

She banged on her parents' door. "A tornado is coming!"

Glenna pivoted, turning to knock on her grandparents' door. Grandpa opened the door, nearly colliding with her.

"Hunker down in the tub in the blue bathroom," he ordered. "I'll grab your brother."

Dad rushed out into the hall carrying Ricky.

"Get in the tub!" Dad barked.

Mom cradled Annie, who was balling her head off.

"Dad and I are already praying," Mom said, shooting past with Dad.

They ducked in the gold bathroom holding the twins. Grandy followed right behind them. Glenna plunged down the hall and dove into the blue tub, pressing her hands over her head. Her heart pummeled her chest. She didn't dare open her eyes. Grandpa and Gregg joined her in the tub. She felt something soft brush against her head.

"Kids, put the pillows on your heads. We should be safe here."

"Grandpa! Blaze is in his crate!" Glenna cried.

"I let him out in the—"

Bang! Terrible booming battered the house. Glenna screamed. Grandpa tucked her in his arms. *Bang!* Ripping and screeching sounds filled the air. Glenna thought she was going to die.

"Dear God, please save us!" she wailed.

She bit down on her lip, tasting blood. Then a horrible silence reached her ears.

"Is it over?" she squeaked, lifting the pillow off her head. "Are Mom and Dad okay? What about the twins? And Blaze?"

Gregg started out of the tub, but Grandpa pulled him back.

"Wait," he hissed.

"I want to find Dad," Glenna said. She couldn't help it, but she started whimpering.

"Sshh." Grandpa patted her arm. "I need to hear."

Glenna sniffled and tried to listen. She heard one of the twins crying.

"Oh no!" she cried. "They might be hurt."

"Okay, you kids stay here. I'll go see."

Grandpa scrambled out of the tub, leaving her alone with Gregg. He poked her back.

"Your scream blasted my eardrums. I'll never hear again."

"Sorry. I'm more afraid of tornadoes than anything, Gregg."

"Aw, that's all right. I'll protect ya."

Grandpa returned, heaving a sigh.

"Everyone's safe, even the dog. Let's go see what happened."

Glenna checked on Blaze. He seemed okay in the mudroom, cowering on his pillow. She patted his side and fled to the den, where Dad gave her a squeeze. Mom tried calming Annie who was still crying. Gregg dropped to the floor and rolled a ball to where Ricky was sitting. Their baby brother clapped his hands and gurgled.

"Glenna, you did some quick thinking." Dad kissed the top of her head. "I'm proud of you."

Despite the scare, Glenna had seen danger and acted to save everyone. Dad had been trying to toughen her up. His encouragement seemed to be working. Maybe one day she *could* become a Federal agent like Eva.

Grandpa opened the slider doors and shook his head. "Shingles blown off. Tree is down. We should canvass the house and the neighborhood."

Glenna and Gregg piled out behind him. They helped pick up litter scattered everywhere. A live oak tree had collapsed in the neighbor's yard, smashing in his roof.

As Grandpa took off for the garage, Glenna heard the distant hum of a chainsaw. Soon Grandpa brought his chainsaw over to the neighbor's house. Dad helped him assess the damaged roof and missing wall. A huge hole exposed their kitchen to the weather and vandals. Grandpa buzzed up the fallen tree and Gregg dragged branches toward the curb.

Glenna wheeled the garden caddy, filling it with fragments of roof tiles and fallen palm tree fronds. It was long, hard work.

Covered in sweat and feeling tired, she thumped into the back hall, her damp hair hanging in wet strands. She slipped out of her tennis shoes. In her room she found photos had fallen to the floor. After adjusting the curtain, she darted into her parents' room.

Dad's suitcase had been thrown open. She straightened the bag and his Bible came tumbling out. When she put the leather Bible into his suitcase, she was shocked to see a stack of currency, like none she'd ever seen. For a split second, Glenna froze.

What was that stuff? Then, she forged a plan. Back to her room she ran, and grabbing her cell phone, she snapped some photos before laying his Bible back on the clothes. With an idea to look later on the Internet, she went to find her mom.

She found her in the living room putting a silver bow on a red package. Soft music playing on the stereo sounded like "Silent Night." Mom set the present under the little tree.

"Where's the rest of our tribe?" she asked, pushing her long hair behind her ears.

"Dad is helping the neighbor. Grandpa and Gregg are buzzing everything. I picked up the yard. It's a miracle no one was hurt."

"Tornadoes make you realize how precious life is."

Glenna fidgeted with her hair. "Is Dad still leaving tomorrow?"

"Yes." Mom briefly shut her eyes. "Let's make this a day to remember."

"I'll never forget hiding in the tub and then bathing in sweat while doing all the pickup."

Mom flashed a tired smile. "Grandy and I have been busy cooking. You gather our clan. The turkey is golden and the potatoes can be mashed. Tell Dad that Grandy wants him to carve."

"I wish I'd brought my camera so I could take pictures of the whole family."

"In that case, you can open this present first."

Her mother tapped a finger on the silver bow. A weird thought pierced Glenna's mind. Should she ask about the money she'd photographed? No, not until she knew what it was.

Glenna wet her dry lips. "Can't Dad tell his boss we need him more than the president?"

Annie started crying so Mom hurried away. It was a crazy Christmas, but Glenna had better get used to life being topsy-turvy. She zipped past Grandy who was arranging the plates.

"Your table looks just like Christmas. I love you, Grandy."

Glenna hugged her grandmother and as she pulled away, she had to wonder. Were those tears of sadness or joy in Grandy's eyes?

17

Christmas was over. Dad had flown home yesterday and here Glenna was back at Tampa's airport. The place bustled with holiday travelers. Hordes of people pushed their way off the monorail, but she didn't see Mason. She gazed out a large window, watching passengers rush away. Had she mixed up his time?

Unsure what to do, she joined Grandpa and Gregg by the arrival board.

"Mason and his folks aren't here," she said, pocketing her hands.

"Since I've never seen him, you and your brother keep a sharp eye." Grandpa pointed up at the digital board. "His flight landed early, fifteen minutes ago."

"That's where I'd be." Gregg jerked his head toward a burger place in the corner.

Grandpa gave him a "right on" look. Glenna scurried over to the BK ahead of Gregg. She found Mason sitting with his head back, squeezing a napkin on his nose. Glenna rushed to him.

"Mason, are you okay?"

He tipped his head forward still plugging his nose with the napkin. "Sorry. My nose started bleeding while I was waiting for you. I think it's stopped now."

Gregg joined them, blurting, "Hey, what are you doing?"

Mason quickly pulled away the napkin and dabbed another one against his nose. When he pulled it off clean, he stood.

"That was strange. Good to see you both. My parents went downstairs for the rental car. They're driving to Sarasota for a few days to see the Lipizzaner stallions."

Glenna took Grandpa's arm and pulled him closer.

"Mason, meet our Grandpa Crockett."

"Call me Buck if you like," Grandpa said, sticking out his hand.

"Why do Dad and your friends call you Buck?" Gregg asked.

He laughed. "With the name Crockett, people called me Davy, but I don't look like a Davy. He was known as the Buckskin Buccaneer, so I adopted the name Buckskin. My gramps shortened it to Buck when I was sixteen. Works for me."

Glenna sported a grin. She'd rarely heard Grandpa string together so many words. Mason bent over to pick up his backpack, but Grandpa stopped him.

"I'll grab your gear. Keep your head up."

"Are you sure, sir?"

"Yes, and call me Buck."

"Thanks for picking me up at the airport, sir. I mean Buck."

Mason tossed soiled napkins into the trash bin. Gregg marched to the elevators, but passing an escalator, he stepped on. Mason and Grandpa followed despite Glenna's protests.

"Gregg, we take the *elevators* up to the garage."

He shook his head, so she hopped aboard. At the bottom, Gregg nodded at a uniformed officer leading a search dog with a leash.

"I spotted that beagle," he quipped, "and wanted to see him work."

Mason clapped him on the shoulder. "Good thinking. I almost forgot my boogie board."

"I can't wait to try your board," Gregg said, herding Mason down another escalator to the baggage carousel.

Not wanting to be left out, Glenna trailed along.

"There's my Mischief board." Mason pointed.

Gregg plucked his covered board and another bag from the belt, hooking the strap over his shoulder. Soon they were all up on the next level, where passengers stood in line to check baggage or get boarding passes. The uniformed officer directed his beagle in a criss-cross pattern through the luggage.

Glenna was amazed how the beagle focused. The cute tan and white dog wandered among the suitcases, his nose checking out a soft duffle bag. Every passenger stepped aside and permitted the dog to smell around their bags. No one said a word.

The dog and his handler stepped over to a metal case. While the beagle slowly sniffed at the seams, the solemn man in uniform waited patiently at the end of a loose leash. As Snoopy dog walked away, Glenna grew curious.

"What's he going to do?" she whispered to Gregg.

He and Mason stood watching Snoopy shove his nose under a black carry-on. His legs stiffened. His limp tail grew bushy. The bag's owner, a man in a suit and tie, glared at the officer.

Grandpa walked up, nixing their detour.

"Get a move on. Warm sandy beaches and giant waves await Mason."

"I want to see what Snoopy does." Glenna stood her ground.

"Nope. Hightail it to the elevators."

Grandpa's stern tone made Glenna turn. She walked onto the elevator, with an eye over her shoulder. The male passenger's face beamed red. As the doors closed, Gregg faced Grandpa.

"What do you think? Was the dog searching for drugs or money?"

Mason pocketed his hands. "I say explosives in outgoing luggage. That way they protect us from terrorists."

"Blaze searched for currency." Glenna folded her arms. "I wonder what happened."

"A businessman opened his suitcase, that's all." Grandpa shifted Mason's pack to his other shoulder.

The doors opened and Glenna stepped into the parking garage. The rest followed.

"Blaze didn't work this airport though," she said, wishing she could have seen the beagle make an arrest.

Gregg lifted the boogie board up over his head. Grandpa opened the car doors before adding his two cents.

"Maybe he did, Glenna. But Blaze can't tell us."

Grandpa stowed Mason's gear in the trunk and Mason texted his parents that he'd met his ride. The three teens packed into the Crown Victoria and minutes later, they split for Treasure Island. A jet roared overhead. Glenna clamped her hands over her ears.

"Watch for the puff of smoke when the tires hit the ground!" she said loudly.

The car slowed.

"You say smoke's coming from my tires?" Grandpa hollered.

"No!" She quickly corrected her mistake. "From the jet touching on the runway."

"Mind your p's and q's back there."

Grandpa sped up again and Glenna saw his eyes in the rearview mirror.

"Glenna, your sniffing Snoopy reminds me of something we saw the other day."

He flicked a hand at Gregg in the front seat.

"Tell Glenna and Mason about the attack dog we survived at John's Pass."

"You never told me about an attack." Glenna socked her brother's shoulder.

Gregg twisted in his seat.

"Oh yeah! Grandpa and I rode our bikes to the Pass."

The whole animated account of the attack Chihuahua spilled out. "They'd certified the beast as a service dog, registering mighty Cujo using the Internet."

"Did Cujo nip you? Maybe he has rabies." Mason flashed Glenna a serious look.

"Nah. I asked the guy the same thing. You should've seen that mutt. He was no bigger than Grandpa's hand. Those people proudly take Cujo anywhere, including restaurants."

They settled down for the ride. Glenna noticed a cormorant landing on a light pole. She loved Florida birds. To go with the camera Mom and Dad gave her for Christmas, Grandy bought Glenna a book to identify birds. She'd already written a paper on whooping cranes.

Grandpa flipped on the radio. As Elvis sang about blue suede shoes, Mason leaned over.

"Blaze should be certified as a service dog," he whispered to Glenna. "Could we use Grandpa Buck's computer to find that online site?"

She smiled. "I'll ask him. Maybe you can help me look up something else."

THAT NIGHT, WITH MASON'S HELP and Grandpa's credit card, a remarkable thing happened. Gregg registered Blaze as a certified service dog. He could honestly answer Blaze did not jump on people. Yes, his dog walked obediently next to his handler. Yes, Blaze sat without advancing if his leash was dropped.

Gregg logged off and Grandpa gave him a high-five.

"Well, now Blaze is a service dog just like little old Cujo."

"His service vest and 'ask before petting' patch are being sent in the mail," Gregg said.

His sister giggled and dropped to the floor to pet Blaze. Gregg had other ideas.

He pumped his fist. "Cool! Blaze can come with us to Smuggler's Cove for lunch."

"We'll see."

Grandpa stuffed his credit card in his wallet and left the den.

Gregg peered over Mason's shoulder. "Can you find another site for me?"

"What do you have in mind?"

"I found an ad in the paper about rewards," he said, keeping his voice low. "Secret Observers pays money for tips."

Mason whistled. Glenna watched over Gregg's shoulder as Mason's fingers flew across the keyboard. In minutes, Gregg stared at a screen boasting a Sherlock Holmes cameo and a magnifying glass.

You spot the Crime—We pay the Reward was blazoned at the top in big red letters.

"Look," Glenna bellowed. "You sign up to be a silent informant with your own secret ID number. If you spy a crime and phone Secret Observers, you receive a reward."

"Sshh," Gregg hissed, shutting the door.

Then eager to try out Secret Observers, he told Mason, "Okay, sign me up."

Mason went to work. Ten minutes later Gregg burst from the den, brimming with pride. Though Mason stayed at the computer to help Glenna with a project, Gregg didn't care.

He was now an official Secret Observer, with his own account, operating out of Grandpa's house on Treasure Island.

18

Gregg eased into Grandpa's backseat, letting Mason sit up front. Grandpa slipped on his shades.

"Fort De Soto, here we come," he said. "During the Second World War, pilots used the island for bombing practice. They were the ones who dropped *the* bomb on Hiroshima, Japan."

Mason buckled his seat belt. "This will be my first visit to the Fort. I guess Spanish explorers roamed there hundreds of years ago."

"I hope the waves are huge," Gregg said.

"But not too big. I'm still mastering the board."

Gregg couldn't wait to try Mason's "Mischief" board. Grandpa parked and they trudged to the water's edge. Grandpa set down the cooler and Mason gave Gregg a quick lesson. He flew to the water. In his first attempt, he fell off the board, banging his knee on the sand. After rubbing out the pain, he leapt on again.

Mason laughed, telling Gregg, "Let me show you a trick."

They traded places and the freshman zoomed across the waves. Balancing on the board, he made a perfect landing each time. Gregg ran up to Grandpa, dropping into the sand.

"If I had my own board, I'd get the hang of it."

"Your dad bought you a new fishing rod for Christmas."

"Yeah, I haven't tried it yet."

"Why not throw in a line when we get home?"

"Thanks for taking us here, Grandpa. Maybe I'll see what I find with Klondike."

Grandpa opened the cooler. "I'm ready to eat. Call Mason in."

Gregg shot down to the water where he plowed through a giant wave. When he surfaced, he chased Mason to the beach. They dried off under a big blue umbrella. Grandpa handed out turkey sandwiches and chocolate chip cookies Glenna had baked. After their picnic, Grandpa showed Mason how to use Klondike. Mason found six quarters and two dimes.

"That's more money than I've found in two weeks," Gregg grumbled.

Mason grinned. "I'll split it with you."

"Nope. You find the treasure, you keep it. That's Grandpa's rule."

"But Klondike is yours."

Gregg finally agreed, thrusting the extra change in his shorts pocket. He planned to save up for a Mischief board. They dusted off the sand, packed up the car, and headed for home.

"I'm thinking of stopping for bait," Grandpa declared. "Any takers?"

Mason smiled. "I love to fish. My gramps taught me when I was five."

Grandpa slapped the steering wheel with his palm.

"The tide's just right for fishing off the dock. It's Gregg's turn to show off his new pole."

At the bait shack, Gregg and Mason used the money he'd found plus a few dollars from Grandpa's wallet. When they reached home, Gregg ran for his pole and Grandpa loaned Mason his rod, even baiting the hook for him.

Gregg and Mason threw out their lines at the dock's end. They caught eleven fish, cleaning them on Grandpa's cleaning station. Gregg tossed the guts to brown pelicans hanging around like vultures.

Mason cast his line, chiming, "The pelican, the pelican—his beak can hold as much as his belly can."

"Did you make that up?"

"No. I learned from Gramps when we fished on Chesapeake Bay."

"Dad took me on the Chesapeake," Gregg said. "He knows a guy with a big boat."

"Was he another spy?"

Gregg didn't take the bait. Dad worked for the State Department and that was the end of the matter. A pelican soaring past got Mason reciting his lyric again.

"You've said that rhyme a zillion times," Gregg said, reeling in his line.

"Glad you invited me down. I don't miss the snow or the animals."

Gregg fastened the hook on his new pole.

"Are you happy with your Mischief board?" he asked Mason.

"What a blast. You know they're made not too far from here, over in Jacksonville."

"My stomach is empty," Gregg announced. "Fudge ice cream is calling my name."

Mason took off. "I'll race 'ya!"

Gregg ran after him, enjoying the day and the idea of having an older brother.

THE NEXT DAY, GREGG FLOATED in a red kayak on Boca Ciega Bay, near Skeleton Key. Mason paddled in the second kayak a few feet away. Gregg peered into the water, hoping to see a manatee or some kind of treasure. The Intracoastal, a wide waterway separating Treasure Island from the mainland, used to be home to pirates. Then Mom's warning flared up in his mind.

"Watch out for sharks," she'd cautioned before he and Mason left.

Gregg saw his reflection in the water. Were sharks really swimming down there? Maybe Mom had been joking. Deep rumbling behind him broke his concentration. He snapped up his head, shocked to see a large yacht bearing down on them.

"Mason, look out!" he called. "Paddle close to shore or that boat will ram us."

His friend raced for shore, but Gregg needed to turn around. He pulled hard with his right hand and spun about, finally coming alongside Mason.

"Wow. A dolphin's fin just broke the water ahead of you," Gregg said, forgetting about the boat.

"Where?"

Gregg jabbed his paddle in the air. He was so focused on where the porpoise might be that the air horn nearly gave him a heart attack.

BBBLLLAAAAAAAA. BBBLLLAAAAAAA.

The horn blasted louder than a semitruck. He and Mason tried speeding away, but their paddles crossed, locking together. Mason's eyes widened and Gregg froze. He couldn't make his kayak go. The huge boat—its massive bow pushing a wave higher than the kayaks—bore down on Gregg.

The horn blasted again. *BBBLLLAAAAAAA.*

Adrenaline pushed through Gregg. He pumped like mad, his arm muscles burning as if on fire. He strained and at last, his tiny boat surged away. So did Mason. The giant boat slowed, corralling Gregg and Mason between its hull and a boat tied to a dock.

The captain leaned over, his eyes bulging.

"You idiots! Can't you see I'm trying to dock here?"

Gregg cringed. He felt trapped. The captain pointed to the dock beyond the kayaks.

"Next time I won't stop," he yelled. "Block me again and I'll turn you into fish food."

"Squeeze closer to the docked boat," Mason commanded.

They paddled backwards. As the large boat coasted to its dock, exhaust steam rose from the water, drifting past the boat's name, *Making Mischief*. Mason shot through an opening.

Gregg struggled to catch up. When they reached Grandpa's dock, Gregg's muscles ached. Hauling the kayak out of the water, his legs were shaking. He dropped on the bench seat.

"Did you see the boat's name?"

Mason drew in a deep breath. "Yes. Isn't it crazy? I own a Mischief board and am nearly run over by a boat named *Making Mischief*."

"Maybe that captain makes Mischief boogie boards."

"We should put him in a search engine. Will Grandpa Buck let us use his computer?"

"Yeah, he's cool if he knows what we're doing. Don't mention our close call, though. My mom won't let us near these kayaks ever again."

"Wow, Gregg. What made that captain so angry?"

"I don't know, but I never want to cross swords with him again."

19

Glenna loved exploring Skeleton Key. The narrow strip of sand, a stone's throw from her grandparents' house on Treasure Island, jutted into Boca Ciega Bay after being formed by a hurricane a hundred years ago.

Warm breezes tousled her hair. She and Blaze dodged foamy waves ahead of Mason and Gregg, who carried Klondike under his arm.

Yelp!

Blaze lifted up his front paw and Glenna leaned down to investigate. The poor dog must have stepped on a cactus. His pad had a speck of blood, but no spike. She rubbed his paw, speaking gently to him.

"It's okay, Blaze. Be more careful in the bush."

He started walking with no problems. Glenna looked around. Where were Mason and Gregg? A sound on her right caught her attention. It was wind rustling dead fronds on a palm tree. She stepped backward and became tangled in Blaze's leash.

A hand grabbed her arm and pulled her down.

"Ow!" Glenna dropped the leash and fell to the ground.

"Be quiet," Gregg ordered. "Or we'll be caught."

Glenna rubbed her twisted ankle. "Why are you guys hiding in the palmettos?"

"I got winded. Gregg slowed down with me," Mason said, breathing deeply.

"Yeah, that's when he saw it."

"A buried skeleton?" Glenna asked, biting her lip.

She jostled in the sand, fearing what may be lurking beneath her. Gregg tugged her closer to the fan-like branches of the low palmetto plants.

"Drag Blaze in here too," he hissed.

She lifted her bottom up from the sand. "Did you find a skeleton?"

As Gregg rolled his eyes, Glenna lifted her chin.

"You said pirates' skeletons were found on Skeleton Key."

"You're confusing your islands. Treasure Island is named after those guys who buried fake treasure chests and dug them up. Keep your voice down. We don't want *him* seeing us."

Gregg ducked his head behind a palmetto branch. Mason nodded, pointing to a large yacht nestled by the boat dock.

"Look beyond the tiki hut," he said. "A guy just drove a mule to the metal storage building near the white yacht. It's loaded with suitcases."

"Why is a mule out here? Skeleton Key has no farms."

"I mean the motorized kind," Mason explained. "Gregg heard the noisy muffler."

"Yeah," Gregg added. "The driver had on a merchant marine uniform."

Glenna peered around the palmetto. "How do you know?"

"I'm not totally clueless about nautical stuff. Dad tells me. He also has a chin beard."

Mason's eyes grew serious. "He looks like the guy who tried smashing us in the kayaks."

Blaze shoved his nose under Mason's hand. As Mason stroked Blaze's neck, the dog settled down. Glenna gazed at the metal building tucked in among the palms. What might happen on this island named for skeletons? She shivered and narrowed her eyes at Gregg.

"Okay, describe his uniform. And who almost ran into you yesterday?"

"He's wearing a white jacket with gold buttons and a blue hat."

Gregg crossed his arms as if she shouldn't question his powers of observation.

"Silly. He must be the captain of that yacht over there," Glenna said. "Your mind is always searching for conspiracies behind every palm tree."

Her speech finished, she stood and rubbed sand off her knees.

"Come on, Blaze. Let's take our walk without these two."

Vrrooom! Vrrooom!

The mule was running straight at them. Glenna dove into the palmettos, pulling Blaze behind her. Her brother was right. She saw the uniformed man dressed like a yacht captain. The mule zoomed by, but she didn't spot any suitcases.

"What did I tell you?" Gregg demanded.

Glenna wiped her hair from her eyes. "That's not a chin beard. It's a goatee."

She was about to blister her brother for being a bad witness, when Mason pointed toward the water. Suddenly, he bent over. Blaze lunged toward him, straining at the leash.

"What's wrong?" Glenna asked, leaning over to see.

Blood squirted from Mason's nose. He plugged it and tipped his head backward. Seconds later, he wiped blood on his shirttail.

"It's nothing. It should go away like at the airport," he said. "Sorry to gross you out."

"The mule captain is getting into a Jeep," Gregg muttered.

Mason motioned with a finger and asked, "Do you see it?"

Gregg swiveled his head to look. "See what?" he asked.

Glenna had no clue what Mason meant, but she squinted toward the bay.

"He came from *Making Mischief*. He's definitely the guy who nearly clobbered us, ruining our time on the Bay."

"Oh great! Let's beat it." Gregg spun around.

Mason shook his head. "We should stay and see what he's up to."

It didn't take Glenna long to decide. One look at Mason's pale cheeks convinced her. "I know nothing about your *Mischief* boat, but we're taking you home, Mason."

She tugged on Blaze's leash, but he stayed by Mason's feet looking up at his face.

"Mason, my dog won't come unless you do."

Glenna wondered if Mason would stay here with Blaze. He blinked at Gregg and nodded.

"Okay. I could use a tall glass of lemonade."

Mason started off and Blaze did too, wagging his tail. Then he jumped up toward Mason's chest.

"What is it, boy?" Glenna asked, fighting to control him.

Blaze kept pouncing on Mason and she handed him the leash.

"I guess he wants you to walk him."

"Maybe we can come back here later."

"Dusk is a good time to see if birds are roosting here," she said, keeping her eye on Blaze, making sure he didn't step on another cactus.

"And mysterious men up to no good," Mason added. "Maybe we'll find a reason for you to call Secret Observers before I fly home."

A STORM BLEW OVER, making Saturday a perfect day to hunt on Skeleton Key for treasure. Glenna hooked Blaze on the leash. Gregg and Mason each grabbed the metal detectors. They searched every inch of sand, with Glenna working the sifter. Gregg unearthed an old bottle top, a silver earring, and a button. Mason found two quarters.

Blaze joined in the fun with his nose, but mostly he sniffed Mason's feet. Glenna felt relieved that neither the mule with the suitcases nor the surly boat captain returned to the Key. And the big yacht, the one as long as a basketball court, had disappeared.

Gregg fell to the sand as if ready to quit.

"We've got nada," he moaned. "Nothing to report to Secret Observers."

Mason emptied out the plastic strainer and held up a penny. It was from 1920.

"See," he said. "We should be vigilant. Crimes are not solved overnight."

"I want to keep searching, but I have to make lunch." Glenna tugged on Blaze's leash.

Mason stowed the valuable penny in his pocket.

"I'll show Grandpa Buck my penny. You know, my gramps and Nana Rose both died."

"Then think of our grandpa as your grandpa too. He'd like that," Glenna said.

Mason dusted sand from his clothes. "Then I'll ask him."

Glenna pulled on the leash, but Blaze wouldn't budge. She thrust the leash at Mason.

"You walk him or I'll be in trouble again."

She strode ahead, trying not to be hurt that Blaze wouldn't leave Mason's side. They made it home and after lunch, Glenna gave Blaze one of his special treats to tempt him into her room. It didn't work and she gave up trying. Mason crashed early that night, with Blaze sleeping on the porch next to his cot.

Sunday brought more disappointment for Glenna. She was eager for Mason to join them in church, but he stayed home with Blaze. When she returned home, Mason was napping on the cot with Blaze lying on the floor. That afternoon as Glenna challenged Mason to checkers, Blaze watched his every move.

Monday and Tuesday were even worse. Grandpa bought a two-day pass for Busch Gardens, but rain fell in buckets. Instead Grandpa Buck took his two grandkids and his new "grandson" to Homosassa Springs State Park, where they strolled under umbrellas. Glenna snapped photos of swimming manatees and alligators.

Wednesday brought more rain. Glenna gave Blaze a bath. She brushed his coat in the den while Mason and Gregg battled crime on their video game. Mom stuck her head in the door.

"Mason, your mother is calling. She wants to talk to you."

As he sped out of the room, Blaze trotted after him.

"What's it all about?" Glenna asked Mom.

"His folks are flying back to Washington National. The cousin watching their farm is in the hospital with appendicitis."

"So Mason has to leave?" Gregg toggled off the game.

"Not until Saturday," Mason said, walking back into the room with Blaze on his heels.

Mom wore a wide smile. "It will be great having you a few more days. Grandpa Buck will take you to the airport on Saturday."

"I hope Blaze gets his certificate before I leave."

Gregg brought out the checkers.

"Isn't there some way Mason can stay longer?"

"Mason is not homeschooled and his classes are starting again. I told your mother about the nosebleeds and how tired you seem. She wants you to see a doctor."

"Mom and Dad are overprotective. I'm their only child."

Mason ruffled Blaze's ears. Glenna's dog loved the attention. She could only sit and watch Blaze curl up by Mason's feet.

"Blaze doesn't want you to leave either," she said, grinning at their friend.

"I guess you're all staying here so Gregg won't have to testify in the counterfeiters' trial."

"For a few weeks yet," Mom agreed. "The rain should lift after lunch. Come and get it."

Mom returned to the kitchen and Glenna took a picture of Blaze leaning against Mason.

"Will you e-mail me that photo?" Mason asked.

"I'll send you one of Blaze too. You could make him your screen saver."

"I guess my father is right," Mason chimed, stifling a yawn. "You can't return to your McLean home or the farmhouse because your dad's a spy."

He wiggled his eyebrows, adding in a spooky whisper, "But we may never know because Gregg Rider is now the spy in hiding."

20

Glenna was thrilled. Blaze's certificate arrived with one day to spare. When Saturday morning rolled around, she dressed him in his blue vest. She snapped his picture.

Mason saluted Blaze. "You sure look official, boy."

Woof!

Blaze scurried to sit by Mason's feet and Mason patted his head. "I'll miss you, fella. Don't wait too long to come see me."

Woof!

"He said he won't," Glenna said, her shoulders drooping. "Thanks for helping me check out that funny money."

"I've never seen blue money before. I think it's North Korean won. The picture was of their former leader. Where did you see those?"

"Oh, around. Grandpa has one in his money collection."

She wasn't ready to admit to Mason how she'd found that money in Dad's suitcase. Such evidence might prove he was a spy.

Mason's questioning gaze prompted her to add, "Florida won't be the same without you."

Glenna enjoyed how Mason had tempered Gregg's constant teasing. Because her brother had found a new best buddy, he rarely picked on Glenna. She figured his happy ways would disappear the very moment Mason hopped on the airport's monorail.

"Glenna, your family is super. I love my parents, but as the only kid, I have no one to hang out with."

"I think I understand," she replied. "Our crew always has something happening."

Mason handed her a piece of paper. Before she could read it, Gregg bounded in.

"What did I miss?" he demanded.

"I gave Glenna my e-mail. Grandpa Buck said to use his computer to keep in touch."

Grandpa strode in. "We all will. Mason, you are family and welcome anytime."

Glenna tugged Blaze away from sniffing Mason's feet again.

"Come on, Blaze. Tampa airport awaits your first visit."

Mom walked in and she handed Mason a small container.

"Put the homemade peanut brittle in your backpack for later. And I'm praying for your safe flight home."

Glenna hadn't thought of doing that, but she did notice the worry line in Mom's forehead.

Mason shifted his boogie board and pumped her mom's hand with a smile.

"Thanks for everything, Mrs. Rider. I talked to my father this morning. Everything's okay at your house, but a little dark with Mr. Rider gone."

Where's Dad this time? Glenna wondered.

Mom darted her eyes away, so Glenna decided to ask after she came home from the airport.

Grandpa grabbed Mason's bag.

"No time for long good-byes. Hop in the car if you're coming with Blaze and me."

Glenna scooted Blaze out the front door and into Grandpa's back-seat. The ride to the airport stayed mostly quiet, with Grandpa and Mason talking up front about his strict football training for next season.

Blaze hunched between Glenna and Gregg in the back, his nose resting on Mason's arm.

"I've started doing two hundred sit-ups every day."

"Careful there, Mason," Grandpa replied. "You look tuckered out."

Gregg shot his hand out, colliding with Glenna's arm.

"Ow. What was that for?" she hissed.

"I'm walking Blaze into the airport. You act like he's your dog."

"All right, if you insist."

Glenna let out a sigh. Mason hadn't left yet and Gregg was in her face again. Maybe it was because he'd be missing Mason also. She'd go easy on Gregg until tomorrow. Then she would put her younger brother in his place.

Grandpa drove up the spiral ramp to the parking garage. Getting out of the car, Glenna handed Gregg the leash.

"Keep a better eye on him than you did at the Vault. If it wasn't for you, we could head home with Mason."

Gregg gripped the leash, shaking his head.

"You shouted my name for those creeps to hear."

"Enough, you two." Grandpa pursed his lips. "Mason deserves a happy send-off."

Glenna closed her mouth. She'd stick to positive things for the rest of the day. Blaze lumbered into the elevator and huddled against Mason's legs. She pushed the button for the ticketing level.

"Grandpa, you said you thought Blaze searched for money here at Tampa," she said.

Grandpa just shrugged and petted Blaze's head.

Mason laughed. "I think Blaze has lots of stories to tell."

THE ELEVATOR DOORS OPENED and Grandpa plunged out first. "I'm grabbing coffee while you wait in line," he said, heading upstairs.

Gregg put Mason's bag over his shoulder. Blaze walked obediently at his side. Mason followed, carrying his board and backpack. Mason stood at the end of a long line of passengers and their bags. A family came up behind. Their little boy reached to pet Blaze. Gregg put out a hand.

"Whoa!" He pointed to the circular patch. "It says to ask before petting."

Glenna hurried to intervene, telling the boy's mother, "Blaze is a service dog in training."

"Oh, I am sorry." She pulled her child close. "I did not see his service patch."

"Blaze is friendly," Glenna assured her. "It's okay to pet him, now that you've asked."

The mother touched Blaze's head and announced, "Ethan, he's a nice doggie."

Blaze sat motionless as the boy petted and pulled on his fur. The mother finally brought Ethan to the counter. With Gregg and Mason talking about the jet he'd fly on, Glenna removed the leash from Gregg's hand and let it relax.

She whispered in Blaze's ear, "Do you want to work, Blaze? Show me where it is."

Blaze walked to suitcases lined up ahead. Just like the Snoopy dog Glenna had seen at the airport a few weeks ago, Blaze's head snapped back and forth as he smelled each bag. When he reached the end of the leash, he stopped and returned to Glenna.

A man ahead of Mason asked, "Is that a service dog?"

"He's learning to be one." Gregg squared his chin as if prepared for more questions.

"You should feed your mutt. He's sniffing for food."

"Sir, we treat our dog special," Glenna replied. "Don't you like dogs?"

"Keep him away from me. I'm allergic," the man snarled.

Glenna noted his black leather jacket and darting eyes. He might be hiding something illegal in his suitcase. Had Blaze alerted? She nudged him along the line of people hugging the boundary ribbon.

When they passed a post, she asked in his ear, "Where is it?"

His leash hung loosely as Blaze patrolled passengers and suitcases. He smelled one blue suitcase, but kept going. Suddenly he turned and came back, stopping by the blue bag. Blaze sat down quickly, eying the bag. The woman passenger clutched her purse close to her body.

Gregg said to Glenna in a low voice, "Blaze is alerting. Maybe he's found money."

"Show me. Show me," she commanded.

Blaze stared at the bag, on high alert.

"That's it," Gregg whispered. "She even looks suspicious."

The woman shifted her eyes, but Glenna wasn't sure Blaze was alerting.

"Gregg, he isn't whining. Maybe he is resting."

In the noise of arrival announcements and people talking, six eyes watched Blaze.

"He's whining! He's whining!" Gregg hissed.

"No," Glenna objected. "That's the baby in the stroller behind you."

Gregg leaned forward and told Blaze, "Show me, Blaze. Where is it?"

Blaze looked more intently at the woman's bag.

Grrrrrr.

A uniformed man stepped in between the woman and Blaze.

"Why is your dog growling?" the officer asked Glenna.

She noticed the symbol on his white shirt. He worked for the Transportation Security Administration. She smiled broadly.

"Blaze is training to be a therapy dog."

The officer thrust his hands on his hips, looking unconvinced.

"Remove him from these passengers," he insisted. "We don't want him biting someone."

Gregg snatched the leash. He stalked with Blaze to the escalators.

Mason smiled at Glenna. "Blaze will get the hang of working again. Hey, they're calling me to the counter."

Glenna fought sadness while the attendant asked if he was traveling alone.

"Unfortunately, yes," he answered, flashing a grin at Glenna.

Grandpa returned in time to heft Mason's bag onto the scale.

"Any other bags?" the attendant asked.

"Oh, right. My boogie board."

The attendant handed Mason his ticket. As they neared the escalator, Gregg waved his arm.

"Glenna, you should've told the officer that woman has illegal money in her suitcase so he could search her. Instead, he thinks Blaze is dangerous."

Grandpa and Mason gathered around. Glenna defended herself.

"What if Blaze was alerting? We need a plan before acting."

"Glenna's right." Grandpa handed Mason his pack. "Your flight is boarding."

"I'm in no hurry," Mason replied, hoisting it onto his back.

Grandpa led them to the escalator and Mason stepped on, with Blaze sitting on the step next to him. After they reached the top, Gregg complained again about the woman.

"I know her suitcase is full of money. She's a courier heading to a bank in the Bahamas."

Glenna glared at her brother. "Not so."

"Enough," Grandpa said. "Head to the monorail and keep Blaze close."

Mason stuck out his hand. "Grandpa Buck, thanks for showing me a real good time. Riding my Mischief board at Fort De Soto was cool."

Grandpa swept Mason into a bear hug, clapping him on the back. "Come see your Grandpa Buck any time."

Mason hugged Glenna and Gregg, then threw his arms around Blaze's neck. The dog wagged his tail, pushing his face against Mason's.

"Missing you already, fella."

When he stood, Glenna detected Mason's eyes were glistening.

"See you soon, Mason." Glenna swallowed a lump in her throat. "Say hi to Stormy."

"I'll send her photo with my e-mail."

"I'd like that."

With a wave, Mason disappeared into a waiting monorail. Blaze watched him go and started whining.

"Time to head out," Grandpa commanded.

Gregg shoved his hands in his pockets. "Can we take Blaze to Smuggler's Cove?"

"Why not? I could eat a horse and Blaze is officially a service dog."

Blaze trotted alongside Glenna through the terminal and up to the garage. He looked like he'd spent every day working in the airport. Maybe he had.

But why had he whined when Mason left? Glenna had lots of things to figure out. The first thing she'd do when she reached home would be to find out about Dad. Where was he and why did he have North Korean won in his suitcase?

21

That night, Glenna propped her head on her pillow, flipping open a book, *The Hiding Place*. Corrie Ten Boom was a famous Dutch lady who had helped hide Jewish people from Nazis.

She heard a soft knock. Mom walked in.

"I saw your light and felt like talking. You seemed quiet at dinner."

"It's nothing." Glenna closed her book.

"Your feelings are important, but if you don't want to tell me, that's okay. Just know I'm always here."

"When Mason said Dad was gone again, your face fell. Is Dad okay?"

"He is away on business. The next time he calls, I will be sure to let you talk to him."

"Is he in North Korea?"

Mom blinked but said nothing. Maybe she didn't know.

"Here's what I wonder," Glenna said, pulling on her hair. "Does Dad think of us when he's gone? When you love someone and they are not in your life, how do you show them love?"

Her eyes gleaming, Mom rubbed Glenna's hand.

"I find it hard to believe you're already fifteen and driving. Someday, you will go to college and move away. But will you love me less because you live in a dorm?"

Glenna shook her head on her pillow.

Mom smiled. "The love you and I have will grow stronger, even when we don't see each other. Dad feels the same. He would rather be here, but it's best we stay in Florida a bit longer."

"Thanks for explaining things, Mom. Can I send him an e-mail?"

"Absolutely. We'll fire up Grandpa's computer after church tomorrow."

"How much longer before we can go home, Mom?"

"When the trial is finished. I'll phone Eva and see if there's any news."

Mom kissed Glenna on the forehead.

"Good night, sweet girl."

She slipped out, leaving Glenna to think about things. Mason had texted that he had arrived safely home. God knew where Dad was.

This thought led her to pray softly. "Dear God, it's me, Glenna. I know you hear me. Please keep my dad safe and help Mason not to miss us too much."

WEEKS FLEW BY with Glenna studying hard with Gregg in Florida. The fun vacation a distant memory, she poured over books about the Second World War and how America and her allies beat Adolph Hitler. On Friday, after Glenna finished her history test, she helped Grandy clean out closets.

"I haven't worn this heavy coat since we moved to Florida. We'll donate these clothes to the needy fund at church. These slacks hang on me."

"My jeans are too short," Glenna said, stacking clothes into shopping bags.

After grabbing an old pair from her room, she found Grandy heading to the garage with four bags. Little pools of water covered the garage floor.

"Sheryl, we just sprayed the floor," Grandpa called, winding up the hose. "Be careful."

Grandy took out her keys. "Buck, can I take the Crown Vic? We're taking clothes to church."

Gregg toweled off the front fender of Grandpa's classic 1956 Lincoln.

"The Crown Vic is clean and dry," he told Grandy.

Gregg performed a mock bow and even opened the door for their grandmother. Glenna couldn't believe her eyes. His time with Grandpa was reaping rewards. Glenna eased in the passenger seat and buckled her belt. She didn't have Grandpa's permission to drive his car. That was okay because she wasn't familiar with the roads around Treasure Island.

As Grandy pulled the car into Calvary's drop-off area, Glenna saw someone scamper away.

"Someone ran into the trees," she said. "Is it safe for us to be behind the church?"

"You lock the doors. This will take a few seconds."

Grandy climbed out and opened the back door. Gripping the bags, she closed both doors. Glenna hit the lock button. Only when Grandy returned did she unlock the door.

"Let's stop for pizza," Grandy said, snuggling in behind the wheel.

"Do you see someone watching us?"

"No."

Grandy simply pulled away and Glenna stared out the window. If only Blaze had come along, he'd protect them. Thoughts of her dog brought an idea. She and Blaze should nose around Skeleton Key. They hadn't gone there since Mason left.

Grandy and Glenna picked up two deluxe pizzas and drove home. The moment Glenna pushed open the back door, Gregg jumped in her way.

"Look what we got in the mail," he chirped, fluttering papers in her face.

"These pizzas are hot."

She slid the boxes onto the counter and faced her brother.

"What's so urgent?"

"Follow me and find out. I'm e-mailing Mason."

Glenna snatched up the white sheets. Her eyes scanned the tiny print.

"Cool," she said. "But I'm typing."

"Why should you? It's my good news."

She trailed behind Gregg saying, "I'm faster. When I'm done, I want to take Blaze to Skeleton Key and check on the mule and suitcases. Maybe Blaze will sniff out a crime."

"Go ahead and type. See if I care."

"Tell me what you want to say."

In the den, Glenna sunk into Grandpa's leather chair. The wheels rolled beneath her.

"Can't you even sit right?" Gregg complained.

She pulled forward, turned on the computer, and entered the e-mail account.

"I'm ready."

While Gregg talked, Glenna typed.

Hi, Mason. Guess what? Secret Observers sent us instructions, telephone contacts, and our pass code. We still need to uncover a crime for a reward. We're off to the Key to check on the mule. I (Gregg) want a Mischief boogie board. Let us know how you are. Miss ya, G & G

Glenna rolled back the chair. Gregg darted out of her way.

"Watch it. You almost crushed my toes."

"Sorry. I'll get the leash and meet you outside."

Glenna bolted from the den, making it to the kitchen where Mom was pulling out dishes.

"Set the table, please. Where is your brother?"

"I haven't seen Ricky since I came home. Gregg is taking Blaze out for his duty."

"Tell Gregg to take out the recycling bin. I am fixing lemonade. Then we can eat."

Glenna's plans crumbled. Maybe if they ate fast, she and Gregg could sneak out before the sun set. She checked her watch. At five o'clock, the sun would dip below the horizon soon. Reality seeped in. Their excursion to the Key would be postponed another day.

22

It was late on Saturday afternoon when a hand pulled Glenna into the den. Gregg snapped the door shut. Blaze's leash dangled from his hand.

"I have my Secret Observers' code number. Come with us to Skeleton Key."

"And if we find something wrong, then what?"

"We report the crime to Secret Observers. What else?"

"The reward, for one thing." She folded her hands behind her back. Gregg stared at her with big eyes. Then he laughed.

"Okay, we're partners. Fifty-fifty split."

Glenna liked the sound of being partners with her oldest younger brother.

"Let's go before Mom corners us into doing more jobs."

"Partner, you are so right."

He pulled open the door and Glenna listened.

"I don't hear anyone. Get outside quick."

Heading out the door, Glenna called softly, "We're taking Blaze to Skeleton Key."

She'd told where they were going, even if no one heard. The sun was dipping behind tall condo buildings lining the beach across Gulf Boulevard. Birds sang in the trees overhead, but Glenna didn't stop to identify them. Maybe she would on the way home, if it wasn't too dark.

The idea of being on Skeleton Key in the dark brought goose bumps to her arms.

"And if we run into Captain Blackbeard again?" she whispered.

"First, we do what Mason calls 'reconnaissance.'"

Glenna nodded. "That's how the Dutch resistance fought the Nazis."

The narrow sidewalk didn't hold all three of them, so Gregg walked Blaze in the street. They stepped on the sidewalk when a rare car passed by. Glenna tried to recall what other secrets the Dutch freedom fighters had used. Her mind drew a blank.

All she could think of was the reward from Secret Observers and her plans for the money.

Noisy seagulls lofted overhead as they crossed the low bridge leading onto the Key.

"Are you buying a Mischief board with your money from Secret Observers?"

Gregg stumbled on a dip in the road.

"How'd you know?"

"Mason's boogie board is all you talk about."

"So?" Gregg finally said. "Why shouldn't I have one?"

Blaze walked silently, his tail hanging limp. What was he thinking? And what about Gregg? Had she hurt his feelings?

Glenna pulled the hair off her neck, letting the breeze cool her.

"You can. I might buy Mom a new grinder for her coffee beans."

"Oh, that's my sister. Always wanting to be Mom's pet."

"I don't think Secret Observers even works," she shot back. "Grandpa says it's a scam."

"Is not. I'm gonna buy a boogie board *and* a hotrod go-cart."

"Hey, you kids!"

Glenna spun around. A man wearing a Yankees ball cap ran straight for them, a shovel raised above his head.

Woof! Blaze barked, hunkering down on his haunches.

"I knew I'd catch you eventually." The beefy man pointed the shovel at Blaze.

Glenna snatched the leash and tugged Blaze backward. Shovel-man surged forward.

"So you're the culprit. I finally caught you."

"We did nothing wrong." Glenna held her free hand in the air. "Why pick on our dog?"

The man jabbed his shovel at a green sign near the curb. On it, a dog squatted beneath the words: *Clean up after your dog.*

"Ah ..." Gregg mumbled. "Our dog hasn't made any messes around here."

Shovel-man waved his weapon too close to Gregg's chin.

"Don't lie to me. I know your big dog left a surprise on my lawn last night."

"No, he was home with us and our Grandpa Buck," Glenna insisted.

She stepped away, not trusting the wild look in that guy's eyes. Blaze didn't either. His hair bristled. The man lowered the shovel, staring at Gregg's hands.

"Where's your bag to clean up after your dog?"

Gregg shrugged.

"What about you?" he bellowed, aiming his head at Glenna like a bull about to charge.

Glenna tried to think what to do. She had no plastic baggie. Blaze always went in Grandpa's yard.

"You lazy, good-for-nothin' kids." He shook the shovel. "Git out of this neighborhood and take yer mutt before I call the police. They'll impound your dog."

Gregg took off running. Glenna's heart flipped, but she pulled Blaze closer to her.

"You are not a nice person," she flung at him, hurrying after Gregg. When she caught up to him, she let him have it.

"What a 'fraidy cat. You took off and left us there."

Gregg kept up his fast pace until they reached the driveway.

"I'm not afraid," he snapped, sounding winded. "I didn't want Blaze to be impounded."

Glenna stroked Blaze on his side. "We never made it to Skeleton Key again. Why?"

He shook his head. "Next time we'll keep away from that old crank."

"Mom says we should mind our elders."

"Yeah, I do when they're not crazy."

GLENNA DASHED TO THE MUDROOM. She'd just unsnapped the leash from Blaze's collar when the portable phone rang. She hung the leash on a peg and listened.

"Yes, Julia is right here," Grandy said.

Maybe Dad was calling. Mom started talking, her voice sounding muffled. Glenna zoomed into the living room.

Mom walked away, but not before Glenna heard, "I am *so* sorry." The door to the den swung shut and the latch clicked.

Was Dad okay? If Mason's father was right and Dad had been hurt being an American spy … She stopped her thoughts right there. She had to believe God would protect him.

The door to the den creaked opened. Mom strode into the living room, her eyes glancing at the floor as if she was deep in thought. She gripped Glenna's shoulder.

"Please find your brother. I have terrible news."

Glenna didn't move an inch.

"What happened, Mom?"

Her mother turned her around and nudged her toward the door.

"Please call Gregg. I see him in the backyard with Blaze."

A lump formed in Glenna's throat. Her eyes began to blur. What did this mean? She ran to Gregg who was at the opposite end of a heavy rope, pulling Blaze in circles.

"Gregg, hurry into the house. Something's wrong."

"Did that old guy with the shovel call Grandpa and snitch on us?"

Running back to the house, Glenna called over her shoulder, "Come on!"

Gregg whistled for Blaze to follow. Glenna found Mom and Grandy in the living room with their heads together. Things looked serious. When Gregg burst in the room, Mom stopped talking and pointed to some chairs.

"Please sit down. We just received bad news."

They sat, but Gregg wasn't waiting.

"Is it about Dad?"

Mom folded her arms together. "Remember Mason's nosebleeds?"

"He had two that I know of," Glenna replied, trying to recall for sure.

"Doctors have discovered he has cancer. That's why he kept getting tired."

"No!" She sprang from the chair. "He can't. He's too young."

"Yeah," Gregg protested. "Old people get cancer. They made a mistake."

Mom reached for Glenna's hand. "This is a serious kind of cancer called leukemia. But there is something we can do."

"Are we flying home?" Gregg asked, shuffling his feet.

"That isn't what I mean. Humanly speaking, we can do nothing, but God can. This is one of those times when even the doctor may have her limits."

"Mom, is Mason going to die?" Glenna sobbed.

Tears flowed down her cheeks and Mom squeezed her hands.

"We are going to pray that he won't."

She motioned for Gregg to sit by her on the floor. Grandy left the room, returning with Grandpa. His face looked twisted.

"Julia, what can I do to help?" he asked.

Mom reached out her hand and Grandpa knelt next to her. Everyone formed a tight circle, holding hands.

"Daddy," Mom told Grandpa, "God can cure a tough cancer even if doctors are unable. We are going to pray that he will do so for Mason."

She bowed her head. Glenna closed her eyes, concentrating with all her heart.

"Oh, Father in heaven," Mom prayed. "You created Mason and you love him. Though we do not understand, we ask you to heal him from cancer attacking his body. Give the dear boy strength to fight and help his parents during this tough time. In Jesus' name, amen."

Tears stung Glenna's eyes as she opened them. Mom's face glowed. She gazed lovingly at her children and her parents.

"Let's pray each day. God has performed miracles in our lives. He can heal Mason."

"Do you think Mason knows that?" Gregg wondered aloud.

Mom laid a hand on his shoulder. "I'm not sure if he does."

Glenna wiped her eyes. "We didn't always know about God either."

"You are right, Glenna. Your dad and I didn't understand, so we couldn't teach you of God's love for his people. We learned the truth after meeting Dr. Van Horn in Israel."

Grandpa cleared his throat.

"Your mother and I share the blame. We never took you or your brothers to church."

"But you love going now, Daddy," Mom said gently.

Gregg stood up and thrust his hands on his hips. "I don't think Mr. Lockridge knows anything about love. He's mean."

"Son, that's not nice."

"He says unkind things."

Mom folded her eyebrows together, looking stern. "Like what?"

Gregg walked backward to the doorway. "I don't remember," was all he said.

"Glenna, what's this all about? Do you feel that way too?"

"Not really. But when I met Mr. Lockridge one time, he yelled at a delivery man about being cheated on the price of hay."

Grandpa got to his feet with a grunt.

"I haven't always been the nicest character, but I am learning with Grandy's help. Gregg, want to take a ride on *Pollywog*? I could use my grandson's company."

Gregg's face lit up. "Sure."

As Mom and Grandy hugged, Glenna fled to her room. She flopped on the bed and cried. Her thoughts were jumbled and she couldn't form words to pray. All she wanted was to go home and find Dad. But she didn't even know where he was.

23

The week ground by slowly. Glenna kept busy, her heart never far from Mason. Dad texted, writing he'd try to call soon. Friday night, Glenna watched Gregg and Mason play Xbox online. After the game, she and her brother logged on Skype and visited with Mason.

"We think of you every day," Glenna said.

She turned away so Mason wouldn't see her wiping her eyes.

"My chemo has started," he announced, looking tired. "To keep me from germs, I have to stay home from school."

Gregg leaned close to the computer. "Next time you'll beat me at Xbox."

"Mason," Glenna took a deep breath. "We miss you, but Blaze misses you more."

He actually smiled. "Really? Or are you kidding me?"

"Really," Gregg replied. "For days after you left, Blaze went to the porch, smelling around where you slept on the cot. He planted his nose right where your suitcase was."

"That is amazing."

Mason briefly closed his eyes. When he opened them, he peppered them with questions.

"Have you been to Skeleton Key? What about the captain of *Making Mischief*?"

Glenna looked at Gregg. How could she tell Mason that each time they planned a trip there, something or someone had hindered them?

"Since you left, we tried several times to check out the Key," Glenna finally said.

Gregg slapped his hands. "Mom took us to visit the dolphin with the fake tail. Yesterday, Grandpa drove us to the science museum. It's boring studying the ocean. I'd rather be on it."

"Mason, we promise to sneak out there soon," Glenna said.

When he nodded, Glenna detected dark rings under his eyes. "We have a surprise." She hoped he'd try guessing.

Mason flashed a grin. "Let me guess. At the airport, did Blaze alert to fifteen million dollars?"

"We wish. We found a dog store and Grandpa bought you a stuffed dog that looks like a miniature Blaze. We shipped him to you."

Glenna tried to sound more upbeat than she felt. "Blaze's twin should arrive next week. I hope you like him."

"You guys are great. E-mail me anytime. Hey, did I tell you that I've read one of those old letters you found?"

"How ancient are they?" Glenna wondered aloud.

"My relative fought in the Civil War. During my chemo, my mother's letting me conduct genealogy research on the computer."

"That sounds like a fun project," Glenna said. "We'll Skype next Friday night."

Mason waved and then was gone. She and Gregg stared at each other.

"Wanna play checkers?" he asked, breaking the awkward silence.

Glenna dabbed her eyes. "You're like Dad. You guys ride bikes or fish to take your mind off troubles. It's not so easy for me. Guess I'm like Mom because right now I could cry a river."

"Do you want to play or not?"

Blaze ambled into the den. He plopped down by Glenna, heaving a long sigh.

"He's missing Mason too," she said. "We can play, but I'm getting up early tomorrow and heading to Skeleton Key no matter what."

Gregg set up the board, giving Glenna the red checkers.

"Maybe we'll find something cool to tell Mason. Chemo's zapping his strength."

"You noticed that too?"

"Sure," Gregg snapped. "Just because I don't show girly emotions doesn't mean I don't have eyes."

Glenna made the first move. "You never cease to amaze me, brother."

She beat him the first game and he won the second.

"We're even and I'm going to bed."

Glenna scrambled up and for the first time since they adopted Blaze, he spent the night on her rug, right by her bed.

MORNING DAWNED BRIGHT and clear. Brother and sister hiked to the Key with Blaze leading the way. He seemed to realize he was on an important mission to help Mason.

Glenna's binoculars swung around her neck. She'd also tucked a plastic baggie in her pocket. When they reached the Key, Gregg hunted for treasure using Klondike. He let fly a low whistle.

"Look here. A dangling earring made of gold."

Glenna ignored his latest find and looked past the metal building with her field glasses.

"The yacht is back. I don't see anyone. But wait!" She sharpened the focus. "The mule is leaving the building. A guy in overalls is loading suitcases onto the *Mischief.*"

"Let me see."

Glenna handed him the glasses and Gregg pressed them against his eyes.

"Two ladies and a man are stepping aboard."

"Maybe they're heading out to cruise the Gulf."

"Uh oh. A black dog is pacing on the deck. Keep hold of Blaze."

Glenna seized the leash. "What kind of dog?"

"A Doberman. He's showing his teeth at the lady. She's going down into the cabin."

"Do you think they're doing anything illegal to qualify for a reward?"

Gregg dropped the glasses. "I don't care! The dog's running off the boat. Beat it!" He snatched the metal detector and fled.

"Come on, Blaze." She sped away with Blaze close behind.

After jogging away, Glenna glanced back. The Doberman sat in the mule, which was being driven by the guy in overalls. The pair made a comical sight. Then the mule disappeared into the metal building.

"Hey, Gregg," she called. "The threat's over."

He ignored her, running full tilt over the bridge. Glenna bubbled with laughter. They caught no criminals, but at least she had a funny story to tell Mason.

24

Glenna was shocked at how pale Mason looked on the screen the next week. Chunks of his hair were missing.

"Blaze's twin arrived," he said with little energy. "I hope you don't think this is weird."

Mason paused as if waiting for permission to tell what was on his mind.

"We won't," Glenna promised, wanting to reassure him.

"I told my doctor how Blaze reacted to me and what you said about him smelling where I slept. I wondered if I could get a dog like him. The doctor said to wait until I am better."

Gregg leaned toward the screen. "We can ask Eva to find you a search dog. Say the word."

"Blaze and I really hit it off. I found out why he was always sniffing me."

"He thinks you're made of ink?" Glenna chuckled at the picture forming in her mind.

Even Mason cracked a smile. "Close. Dogs do have powerful noses. My doctor said Blaze sensed something wrong in my blood. He was trying to save me."

"Wow!"

Glenna sat back stunned. Blaze was remarkable. She wanted to fling her arms around him, but he was asleep on his fluffy pillow. Maybe she'd take a photo and send it to Mason.

"Did you check online for dogs smelling cancer?" Gregg asked.

"No, but I will. I had another treatment this week and am pretty whipped. Last night I read another letter written by my relative during the Civil War."

"Gregg even found a sword in the basement," Glenna said.

Gregg pumped his fist. "Hey, I forgot. I'll ask Dad about that sword."

"The football club is hosting a spaghetti dinner to raise money for my treatment."

Mason sounded tired. Glenna poked Gregg to move over so they both appeared on Mason's computer screen.

"Is it real expensive?" she asked.

Then she wondered if she should have asked. He didn't seem to mind.

He rubbed the back of his neck, "My parent's insurance covers some, but I may need a bone marrow transplant. That costs about two hundred thousand dollars."

"That's a fortune," Glenna said, shock rippling through her.

"I know. That's why supporters opened an account at the bank. Put Mason Lockridge in your search engine. You'll find the blog and read about my treatment."

Glenna made a mental note to check out the blog.

Then she asked, "Does everything seem okay at our house?"

"Yesterday we drove by," Mason said. "I saw your dad by his car. He came over to our car window and said he's missing you. I told him I miss you both too."

"And Blaze," Gregg added.

Mason simply grinned. Glenna shared how Gregg ran away from the Doberman on Skeleton Key.

"Mason, if you could have seen that dog sitting in the mule, just like he was driving."

"Don't forget about me," he said.

Sadness sliced through Glenna. She wanted to tell Mason how she ached for him. There was a way. She chose her words carefully.

"Mason, every day Gregg and I, and our family, are praying you'll be well."

Mason dipped his head slightly.

"Thanks for doing that," he said in a bare whisper. "My father says if there is a God, he stays in heaven and doesn't get involved in healing sick people. But I hope God hears you and heals me. See you next Friday."

He waved with both hands and disappeared off the screen.

"That's the saddest thing I ever heard," Glenna croaked, wiping her eyes.

Gregg gaped at the screen.

"I'm going to ask Mom."

Glenna walked into the living room and sat by her mom, who was gluing photos in a scrapbook. Gregg dragged in, silently staring at the muted TV.

Mom fingered a photo. "What's with the long faces?"

Glenna started crying. "Mom, we visited Mason on Skype. He might need a bone marrow transplant. I don't even know what that is."

Gregg switched his stare to his mom.

"His hair is mostly gone. Parts of his head are shiny like Grandpa's trailer hitch."

"We should have known how sick he is." Glenna wiped her tears on her sleeve. "For the second time, Gregg beat him at *Call of Duty, Black Ops*."

"Yeah." Gregg nodded. "I figured he let me win last time to be nice. But I think it's because he is sick."

Grandpa walked in from the kitchen, covering a yawn with his hand.

"I'm turning in. Lots to do tomorrow."

"Grandpa, we received more news from Mason." Glenna blinked back tears.

"What happened? That poor kid needs a break."

Glenna gathered her courage, telling him about the transplant.

"It costs over two hundred thousand dollars," she said. "His insurance won't pay it all."

Grandpa stood up and pulled out his wallet.

"People can contribute to a cancer fund. Is anyone creating a fund for his cure?"

Gregg jumped in. "They already have. There's a website to donate money."

"Well then, let's get busy raising money. We can't let this cancer beat him."

"What can we do?" Glenna asked.

She had never faced the illness of a friend before. How could she raise money? By babysitting? Families at church might need her services. Or she could bake brownies and cookies and sell them in the neighborhood.

Before she voiced her opinion, Gregg flopped on the sofa and moaned.

"It's hopeless. I found only two bucks with Klondike, which I spent on bait. I could sell my fishing pole."

"Gregg, that was your Christmas present from Dad," Glenna said, rolling her eyes.

Grandpa reached down a hand, pulling Gregg up from the couch.

"Life is like pushing a wet noodle up a hill. If you slack off, the wet noodle rolls back on you. Let's sleep on it. Tomorrow, we'll head to Smugglers Cove for lunch and talk things over."

Gregg squared his shoulders. "Okay, I'm in. What about Blaze? If Cujo the Chihuahua goes there, so can Blaze."

"Me too," Glenna said with a hint of challenge in her tone. "A working dog has only one handler. Blaze is used to working with me."

Grandpa shrugged. "She's right, Gregg. Looks like we all go."

Glenna trudged to her room, realizing Grandpa had changed the subject from Mason's illness to creating a plan to help. She was also beginning to see how her emotions often kept her frozen. Was love a feeling or was it doing for others?

She collapsed onto her bed with few answers. Her life, like Grandpa's wet noodle, was sliding downhill fast. She pulled out her Bible, searching for comfort in the pages of Jesus helping others.

25

Lunch at Smuggler's Cove provided the perfect escape from Glenna's troubles. Blaze lay quietly at her feet dressed in his bright blue service vest. Tender fried clams were tasty. Then she remembered Mason's chemo treatment and how he'd have no appetite. She pushed aside the basket, her heart heavy.

When several patrons stopped to admire Blaze, Gregg warned, "Don't touch our service dog. He's in training."

A nicely dressed couple walked away with the lady saying, "What a beautiful dog. Herb, I want a Lab."

After that, no one disturbed Blaze. Even the server accepted his presence, just like the website had predicted. From their waterside table, Glenna watched pelicans clamor around a charter boat as fishermen cleaned fish.

"Our meal is finished and our experiment is a success," Grandpa intoned. "We turn to the business at hand."

"Yeah, how to raise a billion dollars," Gregg said, collapsing his chin in both hands.

"Don't sound glum, sport. I have formed a plan."

Grandpa pulled out his keys and Blaze snapped to attention.

"Aren't you going to tell us your idea?" Glenna asked, rising from her chair.

"I like to keep a little suspense in pushing that noodle uphill. Come along."

They trailed behind Grandpa to the parking lot. Gregg complained about the hot sun and grumbled about forgetting his Tampa Bay Bucs cap. They piled into Grandpa's car and he pulled into traffic, climbing the bridge at John's Pass.

"So is this like the hill where you push up the noodle?" Glenna gazed out the side window.

"You got that right," Grandpa said, grunting.

Below, Glenna watched a V-shaped wake following a boat streaming to a dock. The bright sun shone on the coral blue water. She pressed her nose against the glass.

"*Making Mischief* is down there. I recognize her sleek, white hull."

"Who's on board and where is she going?"

"How do I know, Gregg?"

"I know who might tell us," Grandpa said, whizzing down the bridge.

Before Glenna knew it, he aimed his wide car down a narrow side street, jerking to a stop in front of a small building. A striped candy cane barber pole twirled by the door.

"I need a haircut. Blaze is welcome here too," Grandpa announced.

Gregg hopped out, but Glenna peered into the barbershop window. She didn't care to go inside. Blaze sniffed the ground by her sandaled feet.

"Home is two blocks from here," she said firmly. "Can't I walk from here?"

"If you take Blaze. But Zeke used to rope steer on the Texas range and lived in Alaska. My barber has survived interesting exploits, like your dad."

Grandpa opened the door. A tiny bell jingled. Glenna caught sight of a huge jawbone of a shark hanging above the door. Its teeth glittered in the sun. Maybe Grandpa had it right. A funny story or two would turn her mind from Mason's illness.

"Okay, Blaze," she said. "Let's check out the people-grooming store."

He followed her inside. She sat in a chair between Gregg and Grandpa along the window. Blaze took up his post at her feet. A nearly bald man sat under a gray cape in a high black chair.

Bzzz. Zeke ran an electric clipper on a customer's neck, looking over his half-glasses.

"Howdy, Buck. Who'd you bring with you?"

"Meet my grandkids, Gregg and Glenna. Blaze is their service dog."

Grandpa nodded at the tall man. "Zeke's the best barber and storyteller this side of Tampa."

Glenna had never been in a barbershop. Zeke looked sort of kooky in his loose-fitting shirt crawling with green alligators. He shut off the clippers and brushed his customer's neck. Then he pulled off a gray cape that looked like a shark.

He shook hair clippings onto the floor. The man handed Zeke cash and headed out the door, ringing the bell. Zeke swept clippings into the corner.

"Who's gettin' skinned today?" He smiled at Blaze. "Your pooch?"

He waved the clippers in the air and started lunging for Blaze. His tail wagged against Glenna's leg. Guess he wasn't scared of getting his hairs cut. But Grandpa put out his arm.

"That won't be necessary," he said.

Zeke spun around his empty chair. He seemed wound up like Grandpa's old antique clock. His hair drifted past his ears, like he never cut his hair. He tugged on a curl and Glenna tuned her ears to listen.

"I once gave a haircut to a golden. Blaze is a golden, right? Or is he a yellow Lab mix?"

Grandpa nodded and Zeke waved toward a door in the back of the shop.

"I shaved the other dog in there. He left with his tail between his legs lookin' like a greyhound. His mistress made a stink, but she did ask for a 'summer cut.' Course, you can imagine neither she nor her hound ever came back. Then another time—"

"I'm here for a haircut," Grandpa interrupted. "Gregg hinted he might like one too, but he's giving it some thought."

Grandpa sauntered over to the spinning chair and clamped a hand on its back. It stopped. Zeke held the large cape in front of Grandpa as though ready to perform a magic trick. He snapped the gray shark around his neck and began cutting.

"What does Blaze do for service?" Zeke asked, wielding the scissors like a weapon.

Gregg launched into great detail, telling how his dad had heard of Blaze and agreed to adopt him.

"We didn't discover for days that he used to be a government search dog."

Glenna stroked Blaze's soft fur.

"We love him. He even smelled out cancer in our friend Mason's blood. We're trying to raise money for his treatment."

"Is that right?" Zeke snipped Grandpa's sideburns.

Grandpa shut his eyes as the scissors came close to his eyes.

"We'll come up with something," he said. "Gregg and I met a scrawny Chihuahua at Smuggler's Cove. If a pipsqueak named Cujo can be a certified 'service dog,' so can Blaze."

"How did you manage getting him certified?"

Zeke sounded interested so Glenna told him how Mason found the site.

"He helped us answer the questions. We paid the fee, and bingo—" she snapped her fingers, "Blaze received his certificate and vest in the mail."

Zeke stopped clipping. He stalked over to Blaze, pointing his clippers at him. Blaze lifted his head. Was that a smile on his face? Glenna must be seeing things.

"I know some service dogs search and track," Zeke said. "Others help blind people or those in wheelchairs, like my mammy. She's been promoted to heaven."

He glared hard at Glenna before shifting his intense gaze to Gregg.

"You kids look healthy enough. Why bring Blaze in here posing as a service dog?"

Uh oh. Glenna squirmed, tossing a "What now?" look at Gregg. He was no help, dropping his eyes to his shoes. Grandpa sported a grin, like he was enjoying their torture. Glenna knew they were in trouble. Zeke shook his head.

"Ah, huh. You have *not* thought this through."

He went back to skimming the electric clippers along Grandpa's neck.

"So, Gregg, why do you suppose that man had Cujo in the Smuggler's Cove?"

Gregg shrugged his shoulders. "He likes him?"

Zeke set down the clippers and swiveled his head, asking Glenna, "How come you didn't leave Blaze at home when you came out today?"

Glenna swiftly calculated. Zeke didn't seem to mind having Blaze present. Maybe they weren't in hot water after all.

"Because I love him and don't want to be without him."

"So, we know the truth about Blaze." Zeke picked up his scissors and waved them in the air. "He makes you happy."

Glenna patted her friend Blaze. A smile formed at the edge of her lips.

"That's right, Mr. Zeke."

The barber snipped around Grandpa's ear.

"Without him, you get anxious. With Blaze, you're happy. Is that your position?"

Suspicion crept into Glenna's mind. She simply nodded. Zeke tilted his scissors in the air as if he had a sudden idea.

"It's like this. Blaze sniffed out bad guys when he worked for the government. For you, he's a therapy dog because he keeps you from becoming anxious."

He flashed Glenna an exaggerated wink.

"Yeah!" Gregg exclaimed. "When Grandpa and I decided to take Blaze to Smuggler's Cove for lunch, Glenna got anxious about being apart, so she made us bring her along too."

Zeke's laugh sounded like rusty gears.

"Blaze's vest patch says to ask before petting," he said, lowering the scissors. "That's true for therapy dogs. People may pet them, but folks should never pet service dogs."

Glenna was totally confused. Was Blaze their service dog or a therapy dog? She wished Grandpa would throw in his two cents.

Gregg did instead. "Blaze works. He still has searching skills."

Zeke started trimming Grandpa's eyebrows.

"But if challenged about bringing Blaze into restaurants and such, tell people he's a therapy dog. People will think young and healthy kids don't need a service dog."

Glenna smoothed Blaze's head. "Sometimes when Blaze is working, he growls."

"Yeah." Gregg nodded his head sharply. "When Blaze caught criminals in Virginia, they hit him on the nose."

Zeke stopped his clipping, swiveling Grandpa's chair so he could look in the mirror.

"Speaking of criminals, Buck, don't you live down by Sea Drive?"

In the mirror, Glenna saw Grandpa narrow his eyes.

"Why? Is there a problem?"

"Aren't you down toward Skeleton Key?"

"Spit it out, Zeke. I don't have all day for a haircut."

"As the local barber I hear things. A certain guy lives down there who has been the subject of much gossip. He's not one of my customers, 'cause I don't think he's ever had a haircut. Got those long curls, you know?"

Kinda like your hair, Glenna wanted to say, but she kept quiet.

When Zeke poised the scissors in the air again, Grandpa shook his head.

"Can't say I know any long hairs. What are people saying?"

Glenna had enough. She folded her arms.

"Mom says we're not supposed to gossip."

"Glenna, you're an old fogey before your time," Gregg hissed. "We need to hear about the guy."

"This isn't gossip," Zeke declared. "It's important scuttlebutt you should know. Some believe he's a modern-day pirate. He spreads money around."

The barber with the wild scissors laid them on a tray. He zapped Grandpa's neck with the clippers and loosened the cape. Zeke dusted off Grandpa's neck with a small brush.

"Your mystery man could have inherited family money," Grandpa offered.

"Don't think so, Buck. He's pure mean. He drives *Making Mischief* for some rich guy who owns the boat. You've probably seen that big boat cruisin' in and out of the bay."

Gregg jumped up. "That's him. He *is* mean."

"How do you know him?" Grandpa swung his head around and stared at Gregg.

"He tried to run over me and Mason when we were kayaking. Blew his horn and cursed like mad."

"Steer clear," Zeke cautioned, pointing his comb at Gregg. "That fella's up to no good. Scuttlebutt is he runs clients into international waters so they can gamble on his boat. Others think he smuggles drugs."

Grandpa set his chin. "Either way, he sounds dangerous."

Zeke whisked off the apron, waving the cape like he was a matador. Glenna stifled a giggle. The barber was funny, but she wanted to head home. Decisions needed to be made.

Grandpa hoisted himself out of the chair and reached for his wallet. Glenna rose to her feet. Before she made it out the door, Grandpa stepped over to Gregg.

"Do you want yours cut now?" he asked.

Gregg stood as if deep in thought. Glenna would hesitate too with Zeke's crazy scissors.

"Okay."

He climbed into the chair and Glenna sat down, her hand resting on Blaze's head. She tried to figure things out. Was Blaze a service dog or a therapy dog? Did it matter? And was the captain of the *Mischief* up to no good?

26

On the ride home, Glenna considered how to help Blaze adjust to crowds of people. Grandpa surprised her by abruptly turning into a parking lot.

"Stay here with Blaze," he said. "No need to ruffle any feathers until we settle on a plan. I have supplies to pick up."

He bounded out and Gregg whipped his head, facing Glenna in the backseat.

"Can you believe what Zeke said? The captain doesn't own the *Mischief*."

"We saw him loading suitcases," Glenna replied. "Maybe the people climbing aboard are gamblers."

"Is that legal?" Gregg asked.

"I have no idea, but we could find out who the owner is. Zeke forgot to tell us the captain's name."

"He was probably afraid of gossiping after you scolded him."

"Mom says if you can't say something good, say nothing at all."

Gregg sagged against the front seat. "I wish Mason was here. He knows about computers. Mom and Dad won't even buy us one."

"We'll connect with him on Skype and see how he's doing. Mason probably needs something to work on besides old letters."

Blaze shoved his nose under Glenna's hand. Had he recognized Mason's name? Believing he did, she comforted him by patting his forehead, which eased her anxiety. Grandpa handed Gregg some grocery bags and slid behind the wheel.

He pulled out of his parking spot, his seat belt warning dinging. Grandpa ignored it. He'd almost reached the street and that warning bell was making Glenna nuts.

"Grandpa."

He glanced in the mirror and finally clicked on his belt.

"Yes, I'm multitasking. I haven't entered the street yet, so driving rules don't apply." He entered traffic, saying, "I've given thought to the beagle we saw at Tampa's airport."

"The Snoopy dog that sniffed passengers when Mason arrived?" Glenna asked.

"He's the one. I've seen other dogs searching passengers in Miami who might smuggle cash to Caribbean or South American banks for drug cartels."

Glenna chewed her lip, remembering what Eva had said. "A Federal agent told us currency dogs like Blaze find hidden money that people don't pay taxes on."

"Here's the bottom line, kids. Money-movers avoid Miami currency dogs by flying from Tampa instead."

Blaze had his head in Glenna's lap. She tickled his nose, not understanding how criminals worked. Her parents taught them to live by obeying the laws.

"How does flying from another airport help criminals?" she asked.

"Simple. Your bag is full of money and you check it at Tampa. When you reach Miami, you switch planes. If Tampa has no currency dogs, the suitcase is loaded onto another plane in Miami without ever being smelled by currency dogs."

Gregg balled his fist. "Yeah, when we took Mason to the airport, I think that woman was moving money here in Tampa."

"I have an idea," Glenna said, leaning forward. "We take Blaze to the Tampa airport for socialization training."

"I'm in," Gregg quickly added.

Grandpa wheeled into the driveway. "Say, I never thought of that. What a great idea."

He stopped short of the garage door. There on the floor next to his classic 1956 black Lincoln convertible lay a kayak where Grandpa wanted to park.

"Gregg, put that kayak back where you found it. Be careful not to hit my Lincoln. I'll wait to drive in. Glenna, take Blaze out to the backyard."

After walking Blaze outside, Glenna beat her brother and Grandpa into the kitchen. Mom and Grandy were fixing dinner. Gregg walked in and Mom's hands flew to her face.

"Gregg!" she screamed. "What have you done?"

Grandy whirled around.

"Oh no!" Her eyes became huge. "What happened to you?"

Gregg beamed from ear to ear, his head completely bald.

"If Mason can't keep his hair, then I'm not keeping mine."

Mom snatched Gregg and hugged him.

"That's my Gregger. You are a true friend."

The door from the garage closed and Grandpa sauntered in.

"Did everyone see my new grandson?" He clasped his hands on Gregg's shoulders.

Gregg grinned. "It is a shock to see myself without hair."

"You're just as handsome without hair." Grandpa rubbed his hand over Gregg's bald head. "Don't forget. After dinner, we're preparing for tomorrow's canine training."

Mom picked up a tomato. "Before you make plans, there is something you should know."

Glenna's heart thudded against her chest. Had something happened to Mason?

Mom just opened her mouth when one of the twins started crying in their room. Grandy dropped a knife on the counter with a clatter and hurried down the hall.

"Grandy and I are having a bake sale at Calvary Church to raise money for Mason. It's in two weeks."

"My Classic Car Club could organize a show," Grandpa said, flexing his hand.

"Thanks, Daddy," Mom said. "Glenna and Gregg, you might think how you can help."

Gregg crossed his arms. "I can wash cars."

"I'll bake brownies." Glenna sighed. "But how much can we make, really?"

Mom looked at her with a smile. "Remember the loaves and the fishes? Jesus can multiply whatever we can do."

THAT NIGHT UNDER COVER OF DARKNESS, a sixty-one-foot Hatteras captained by Cain Denton plowed toward shore. He yanked back on the throttle and *Making Mischief* settled into the water. Cain shifted into neutral, power exuding from his fingertips.

Off to his east rose the arch formed by the John's Pass Bridge. His black eyes searched the horizon. The only boat in sight, he killed the engine. The *Mischief* rocked in total silence. Sounds of waves lapping against the hull and an occasional ping from the engine's heat made him bold. His scheme was nearly complete.

Cain had taken similar trips to the Gulf, bringing groups at night to gamble beyond the three-mile limit. He snickered. The jaunts made him the gossip of John's Pass and fit perfectly into his plans. Even the police believed his cover story as a party host. Troy Abramson, the

Mischief's owner, was an even bigger chump. Troy trusted Cain like an older brother allowing him to entertain Troy's clients at sea.

Cain plowed a hand through his carefully tended locks. On this trip, he carried no passengers, only valuable cargo. He'd keep that a secret, no matter the cost.

A voice crackled on the radio. "*Lady Luck*, how's it going?"

Lady Luck answered, "We are full and headed for Crystal River."

"*Lady Luck*, it's the *Dora Ruth*. Where you at?"

No response. The radio crackled again.

"*Dora Ruth* is calling *Lady Luck*. We'd like yer spot. We're not doin' good."

Still no answer. Cain smiled. *Lady Luck's* skipper must have a good shrimping spot and wasn't about to reveal his location. Well, neither was Cain. He rested his hand on the throttle. Then five words booming over his marine radio shook him to the core.

"He must have his lights off."

Anger shot through him. Had the voice come from a nearby boat? Cain saw nothing. Was a police boat lurking? Finally his rattled brain grasped the truth. Cops wouldn't use marine radios. What if they had grabbed the wrong microphone?

Cain started his engine and pushed the throttle forward. In total darkness, *Making Mischief* sped toward John's Pass until a sound reached his ears. He shut off the engine, but heard no other boat engine roaring like his had done.

He sat a moment before starting again. This time the bow lifted a fraction as he cruised slowly beneath the bridge, passing shops and his favorite clam place, Smugglers Cove. At three o'clock in the morning, no locals walked the boardwalk.

Cain idled along Eleanor Island before turning south into Boca Ciega Bay. Confident no one suspected the purpose of his trip, he reversed his engine. He turned aft, snuggling *Mischief* beside her dock jutting off from Skeleton Key. As he tossed the bowline over the side, something scrambled by the metal shed.

Rage shook him. He would kill that dog. As he shone the boat's spotlight on the shed, a shrouded figure started running. Was the spirit haunting him again? Then it dawned on Cain.

"It's her again," he said with a snort.

A girl carrying a bag fled into the darkness, her long coat flopping in the boat's spotlight. Why had she come back? If the imp dared to sleep in his shed, he'd put an end to her presence. The last thing he needed was a snitch poking around his business.

Cain couldn't risk Abramson discovering how Cain was using his yacht. Abramson was busy in New York brokering a baseball franchise. Cain vowed to complete his plans before his boss got wind of his scheme or returned to Florida with customers to entertain.

Too bad the urchin had gotten a head start on him. Next time there wouldn't be a next time. He'd get his hands on her, all right. Cain leaned back in his captain's chair, letting his anger subside.

After all, hadn't he just made himself a very good wage for one night's work?

27

Later that morning, Glenna sat in Grandpa's backseat as he drove toward Tampa's airport. She watched pelicans gliding in the shadows cast by the long bridge.

"I hope Blaze is ready for this," she said.

Her mind filled with doubt over what might happen. In case Blaze heard and understood her concerns, she patted his side.

"He'll be awesome. Wait and see," Gregg declared over his shoulder.

"Glenna."

Grandpa said her name quietly as if he had something earth-shaking to say. His eyes searched the rearview mirror and she caught his look.

"Zeke loaned me a documentary about drug smuggling. It featured a DEA agent in Florida. Do you know what that is?"

"Not for sure. Are they the agents who help people to quit doing drugs?"

"Partly right. Drug Enforcement Administration agents stop drug smugglers. Zeke's son is a DEA agent. Anyway, this should be a busy time in the departure lines."

Gregg rubbed his chin. "So Blaze will have tons of bags to sniff."

"You bet. Smugglers aim to leave the airports during busy times. Officials don't have time to examine luggage or ask questions."

Grandpa entered the airport. He had plenty more to tell.

"We'll see if Blaze has lost his special powers."

Glenna would not accept that he had. "Look how he tried to help Mason."

"Right, kiddo."

Grandpa spun around the corkscrew ramp rising into the parking garage.

Glenna leaned forward, asking Gregg, "Do you have everything?"

He slapped the pocket of his cargo pants.

"Spiral notebook? Check. Pencil? Check."

"That's not everything."

"Give a guy a chance." He tapped his other pocket. "Fluorescent orange tape? Check. Cell phone with Secret Observers' phone number? Check."

"Sounds like we're all set."

Glenna put her arm around Blaze and squeezed him. His soft fur tickled her nose.

"Are you ready to go to work? We need money to help buy Mason's medicine."

With her hands, she lifted Blaze's face toward hers. "You remember Mason. He's your special friend. Your doggie bones are in my pocket, but you must earn them."

Grandpa angled past a blue handicapped parking spot where a man sprinted from his car.

"Look at him go." Grandpa pointed. "He doesn't look like he needs a handicap sticker."

He shook his head and kept driving through rows looking for an open spot.

"Grandpa, you're old enough for a handicap pass," Gregg suggested.

"Wrong. Those aren't for grandparents. They're for folks who are not mobile. If I received a permit to park closer, then younger people in wheelchairs couldn't park there."

"There's a SUV pulling out. Ugh, it's a yellow Hummer," Glenna said, feeling worried.

Gregg released his seat belt. "Hey, Mom was going to call Eva. What did she find out?"

Grandpa pulled in and cut the engine. "Defense lawyers are playing their usual games. So you'll be with me and Grandy in Florida until things are resolved. For the record, stay as long as you want."

"Maybe we'll move for good," Gregg said. "Except for Mason, who cares about Virginia."

Glenna felt torn about where to live. Well, she didn't have to decide at the moment. Blaze had work to do. Grandpa waited for Blaze to hop down before locking the doors. They reached the elevator doors and when Gregg pushed the call button, Glenna blurted,

"Wait. Are we saying Blaze is a certified therapy dog?"

Grandpa didn't answer. The doors opened and he stepped in.

"Why do you think Blaze shouldn't be certified?"

Glenna wrapped the end of the leash around her hand. "Didn't you and Gregg get the idea from Cujo the attack Chihuahua?"

"Correct. Is Blaze a real working dog, trained to work around people in airports?"

The doors opened.

Gregg tugged on the leash. "Yes, and he has work to do. Come on, Glenna."

"Well?" Grandpa looked at her and smiled.

She smiled back. "Right. Let's go."

"My number is in your cell phone. I'll be enjoying my cup of joe at the BK."

Gregg was already in line, eyeing suitcases in front of him.

Glenna wandered over and whispered in Blaze's ear, "Time to help Mason. Can you show me?"

Blaze blinked as if deciding what she wanted him to do. She took his face between her hands and looked him directly in the eyes.

"Where is it?" she asked. "Where is it?"

Glenna nudged Blaze and he smelled around a suitcase by a roundish man in front of them.

He turned to Glenna, his face contorted. "Why is your dog smelling my luggage?"

"He's my therapy dog," she fired back.

Blaze walked forward in the line, keeping his head close to the floor. He smelled a lot of bags, soft ones, the hard case kind, and floppy duffle bags. When Glenna and Blaze reached a divider, they swung back toward Gregg.

"Miss, take that dog out of here."

Shockwaves rippled through her. The police officer wore a bright green vest with reflective tape.

"Dogs are not permitted in the airport," he said.

Disgust exploded in her heart. She'd failed already. The officer strode closer. Glenna lifted Blaze's laminated certification tag.

"He's a certified therapy dog," she said, trying to sound polite.

"What does that mean?"

Glenna turned her thumbs toward her chest.

"He helps me so I don't have anxiety attacks."

The officer read the tag. He lifted his eyes, looking at her skeptically.

"I don't know; you seem stable to me, not the anxious type."

"You see? He's helping me."

The officer straightened. He glared, and then he surprised Glenna. He strode away with a "humph." She looked down at Blaze to adjust her bearings.

"Where is it, Blaze?" she asked, trying to sound composed.

Her insides were still shaking. Blaze sniffed along until he reached a battered canvas case wrapped in a leather strap. He smelled that bag for a long time and then sat down. Its owner, a tan guy in his mid-twenties with gelled hair, nodded at Blaze.

"Handsome dog," he said.

Glenna urged Blaze along to check other bags, but he refused to budge. He glued his snapping brown eyes to the man's suitcase.

"Where is it?" she urged softly.

Blaze tilted his head and whined. Glenna shot Gregg a "hurry up" look. He rushed over.

Glenna told the guy with the grease mop, "My dog thinks your bag has dog food in it."

"Nope," he said with a smirk. "Just dirty clothes."

Glenna bent over to Blaze. "Do you smell dog food?"

Blaze simply stared at the canvas bag.

Then in her commanding voice, she ordered, "Show me, Blaze. Show me."

Blaze's whine changed to a loud growl. The man slung a backpack over his shoulder, nearly whacking Gregg in the nose.

"What's up with your dog?" he demanded.

Gregg stepped between Blaze and the canvas bag. He bumped the bag with his calf. It tipped over, but Gregg quickly steadied the bag.

"Sorry," Glenna chirped. "Our dog is still being socialized."

Gregg nodded. "Yeah, that's why we bring him to the airport."

Glenna glimpsed orange tape on the bag's bottom. She hid a smile. Gregg had slapped it there when he righted the bag. She brought Blaze toward the elevators, hoping the owner didn't spot the bright tape.

She snuck Blaze a doggie bone. "Good dog, Blaze. You did great."

Blaze chomped his treat. Glenna's heart pounded while Gregg talked to the guy who lifted his canvas bag on the scale by the ticket agent. Her brother was carrying out phase two of their plan: listening for the traveler's flight arrangements.

The guy hopped on the escalator, tossing a skeptical look at Blaze. Gregg's cheeks flushed and his eyes practically bugged out of his head.

"He's flying to Turks and Caicos," he told Glenna. "Just like Grandpa predicted."

Glenna held tightly to the leash. "Blaze alerted. That man must be hiding currency."

Gregg started scribbling in his notebook.

"Come on!" he hissed. "I'm making a call."

He raced to the escalator. Glenna and Blaze stayed close behind. When they reached the upper floor, they found seats with no one else nearby.

Gregg punched Secret Observers' number. He talked fast, giving his secret code and the suspect's name and flight number. Glenna grabbed his book to read his notes.

He snatched back his notebook, saying into the phone, "The bag has bright orange tape on the bottom. He's changing planes in Miami, bound for Turks and Caicos."

Gregg stopped talking and rolled his eyes as if Secret Observers was grilling him.

"He *is* hiding money in his bag," Gregg insisted. "He's smuggling to a bank there."

He fell silent before adding, "Act fast and you'll snatch his bag before the plane leaves."

Glenna stroked Blaze, whispering in his ear, "You are amazing."

She almost missed Gregg telling Secret Observer, "*Yes*, I'm sure."

As she tried for his notes again, Gregg waved her off.

"No! I don't want to tell how I know. And no, I am not related to him."

Glenna's eyes scanned his notes. He had nothing else to report.

"Uh huh," Gregg mumbled. "Good-bye."

He pushed the disconnect button with a defeated shrug.

"They're passing along my tip."

"What did they say? What should we do?"

"Stop racing your motor, will ya?"

Gregg waved a hand at the security guard hovering near the monorail entrance.

"We can't ride to the departure terminal because we're not passengers."

Glenna shook her head. "Don't give up. We could watch for the orange-taped bag to be put in the baggage hold."

"Yeah," Gregg's eyes sparkled. "Maybe they'll stop his bag before it gets that far."

"Run to the BK. Tell Grandpa we're getting back in line. I'll head down. There were more people in line for that Miami flight."

Glenna drew her partner Blaze to her side. They had much more crime fighting to do.

28

Glenna hurried Blaze to the line. She studied passengers, trying to detect which ones were criminals. Trouble was they looked like nice, normal people. Maybe Blaze wouldn't have any more success this morning. That would be too bad because Mason needed help.

Gregg stepped behind her, hissing in her ear, "Grandpa's done reading the paper."

"So?"

"So, he drank too much coffee and says we're outta here in five minutes."

Glenna swung into action. She held Blaze's chin in one hand, tapping her pocket with the doggie bone with her other hand.

In a confident tone she asked Blaze, "Where is it?"

The dog lifted his head and walked the line, smelling red suitcases of the next passenger. He surged forward as if those cases held no contraband. Glenna felt herself being pulled by Blaze.

"Gregg, save our spot," she said. "I'm giving Blaze exercise."

Glenna didn't want waiting passengers to realize Blaze was sniffing their luggage. Two young women dressed to the nines asked about Blaze. She smiled, admiring their colorful Florida outfits.

"Is he bothering you?"

The tall girl flipped sunglasses on her head. "He looks like Champ, my dog in Michigan. He rides in the bow of our boat on Lake Michigan."

Glenna walked Blaze ahead, recalling how Dad had taken them to Mackinaw Island. They had fun riding horses on an island where cars were banned.

Nothing in line nabbed Blaze's sensitive nose. They made two bends along the weaving line. Without warning Blaze plunked down by a gleaming aluminum case. It was huge. A stylish woman, her hair the color of her tan suit, stood near two other shiny suitcases.

She smiled at Glenna with white teeth. "Your dog is beautiful. Is he a therapy dog?"

"Yes, ma'am. He helps me to fly."

"I do not enjoy flying either," the woman said. "Not with reports of terrorism."

Blaze stared at her luggage, causing Glenna to nod at the burnished bags.

"Do you have food in there? He senses it."

"No," the fashionable woman snarled, heaving the large case away from Blaze.

Glenna stooped over him, whispering, "Do you smell food? Where is it?"

Blaze's stare at the aluminum case never wavered. As Glenna gave Gregg the high sign, Blaze's low whine sent excitement charging through her. Gregg ran to join them.

"I help my sister train Blaze," he told the woman.

"You silly dog," Glenna trilled. "If food is in there, show me, Blaze."

And prove she has currency in her luggage.

As if Blaze knew her thoughts, he growled. Gregg jumped in front of him, knocking over two of the big cases.

"Sorry," he quipped.

Glenna nudged Blaze away from the commotion, slipping him a treat. He happily ate his bone. Gregg's deft movements in righting the bags and sticking orange tape on them amazed Glenna. A gentleman, he helped the lady move her bags to the agent. He chattered nonstop.

"I'll push these for you. I apologize for my dog's bad manners."

Glenna stifled a laugh. Her younger brother, the hero, was on a secret mission to catch the guilty. When the lady traveler reached the ticket agent, Gregg hefted her bags on the scale. According to plan, Glenna marched up, handing Gregg the leash.

"It's your turn to watch the dog," she insisted.

This time, she would hear the flight details. The lady handed the agent her ticket and Glenna heard her say, "Bogota." Ah, drug dealers flew in and out of Colombia.

Glenna fixed a smile on her face. "Sorry my brother and dog caused such a ruckus."

The well-dressed woman lifted her chin and Glenna waited with open ears.

"Ms. Sanchez," the agent said. "Here are your passport and boarding pass."

Glenna pivoted on her heels, making straight for Gregg who petted Blaze.

"Quick, give me the notebook."

She scribbled as they rode the escalator. At the top, she showed Gregg her notes.

"Here's her name and destination. Ms. Sanchez is changing planes in Miami."

Gregg scooted to a distant seating area. Glenna saw Grandpa hustling out of the BK. She zipped over to Gregg, sweeping her hand to hurry him. He was already speaking rapid-fire to Secret Observer, giving details of the Bogota flight.

"Yes," he nodded, "that's my ID number."

Glenna held the notebook open for him to confirm the details.

"Orange tape is on the bottom of two metal cases," he said. "A third bag has no tape."

He snatched the pad from Glenna, looking over her scrawls.

"The woman has on tan slacks and jacket. Her metallic purse is over her shoulder."

Gregg winked at Glenna. Good, maybe he was being better received this time.

He added, "Her brown hair is piled on her head. Okay, good-bye."

The call ended. Glenna blew out a sigh as Grandpa strode up and ruffled Blaze's ear. "How did our secret weapon do on his first assignment?"

"Secret Observers passes along our evidence," Gregg said, shrugging.

"We wait then, Sherlock. Let's head home. I've a Car Club event to plan and Glenna has brownies to bake for the sale."

Blaze sat up on his haunches and nuzzled Glenna's arm.

"I think Blaze is ready to go, and I mean he has to *go*."

Glenna sprinted toward the elevator. In the mix of passengers hurrying from an arriving flight, she saw a man in a business suit, his hair pulled back in a ponytail. His appearance didn't add up. Waiting by the elevator, she stood by him, bringing Blaze in close.

Ping.

The doors opened. She and Blaze walked in seconds before the doors closed.

"Which floor?" Gregg asked Grandpa.

"Five."

"And I need six," the man with the ponytail answered.

Gregg punched both buttons. Glenna surveyed the traveler. He gripped the suitcase handle so tightly his knuckles had turned white.

What was he hiding in there? Blaze must have been suspicious too, because he started sniffing the man's bag.

Then her super sleuth did something startling. Blaze pushed between Gregg and the man for a better whiff. He sat, his eyes riveted on the man's bag.

Glenna couldn't help herself. She leaned over and whispered, "Where is it, Blaze?"

The elevator lurched to a stop. Blaze started whining. The doors opened and Grandpa walked out. So did Gregg. The doors were closing, but Glenna stayed by the man who was watching Blaze. Grandpa rammed the edge of the door with his hand. The doors flew open.

"Glenna, this is our floor. You and Blaze must leave," he commanded.

She didn't budge an inch, just looked defiantly at her grandpa and her brother.

"Glenna!" Grandpa barked.

Having never heard a strict tone from him, Glenna dashed out. The leash became taut. Blaze sat right by the suitcase and refused to budge. She tugged hard.

"Come, Blaze," she ordered.

At last, Blaze walked out, the doors closing behind him. Glenna spun on Grandpa.

"Didn't you see that? Blaze found another suspect."

Grandpa put a hand on her shoulder.

"Glenna, think about what just happened. That man flew *into* Tampa on an arriving flight. I don't think it's illegal to bring money to Tampa."

Grandpa unlocked the Crown Vic and eased behind the wheel. Gregg pulled open the front passenger door, rolling his eyes at her.

"He's right. Besides, Blaze needs a potty break. You said so."

Hiding irritation at her know-it-all brother, Glenna let Blaze jump in the backseat. She slid in beside him, burying her face in his fur. Had they just let a criminal go free? Their mission to help Mason was proving to be much harder than she thought.

29

All afternoon Secret Observers failed to call Gregg. He washed Grandpa's classic Lincoln and trimmed bushes, willing the phone to ring. Did they act on his tips or not?

His yard work done, he chopped walnuts for Glenna's brownies. When she turned her back to mix stuff in a bowl, he slipped into Grandpa's den and shut the door. It was easy remembering the 800 phone number.

After several rings, a woman said with an accent, "Secret Observers. We stop crime."

Gregg grew nervous. What should he say?

"Is anyone there?" the woman asked.

"I'm checking on my tip."

He gave his Secret Observer code number, scarcely breathing.

"Did you call that in earlier today?"

"Yeah."

She hummed a peculiar tune before saying, "Let me see what we have."

Gregg pulled on his bottom lip, waiting.

She finally said, "We passed your info to Miami's Department of Homeland Security."

"Miami? How come?"

"By the time we reached our connection in Tampa, the flight had left for Miami."

Disappointment shot through Gregg. What could he say?

"Ah ... then I won't receive a reward from Secret Observers?"

"We work with some law enforcement agencies that pay bigger rewards than we do."

Gregg had to find out more. He could just imagine Glenna's thousand questions.

"Have you heard anything from Miami?"

"We don't usually hear this soon. You should not get your hopes up."

Gregg dropped into Grandpa's chair. "Why not?"

"How did a tipster know about two different passengers hiding money in their luggage?"

Gregg leapt from the chair. "Why should you care? My tips are true!"

"I am not sure," was her reply.

"You're letting them get away because of doubts? Why didn't they check?"

Gregg heard clicking sounds and then she said, "When I phoned your tips to Miami, they had questions. The police may not work to find those suitcases. But you may check later."

"Okay," Gregg said dully, hanging up.

Defeat dogged his steps as he trudged out to the dock. He didn't feel like talking to anyone, let alone Glenna. How could he admit his dream of becoming a crime fighter just fizzled to nothing?

GREGG LAUNCHED HIMSELF up from the dock and shuffled back inside. He eyed the brownies in the kitchen, but remembered in time. Glenna had made the treats for the bake sale. A scratching noise in the mudroom caught his attention. He scurried around the corner.

Glenna attached the leash to Blaze's collar.

"Where are you going?" Gregg asked.

"To take Blaze for a walk. We're investigating Skeleton Key."

"Me too."

He grabbed his cap off a hook just as Mom poked her head out the door.

"Wait, I'm ordering pizzas. Your grands are at church but should be home soon."

"Glenna and I are taking Blaze on a short walk," Gregg said firmly.

Mom smiled. "Be back in forty minutes and take your cell phone along."

Glenna patted her back pocket. "Got it, Mom."

She let Blaze out on the leash. Gregg hustled up to her other side.

"I called Secret Observers. The woman I talked to said they doubted our information."

"What was her name?"

Gregg gulped. He never thought to ask.

"So you didn't get her name. Did you tell her that Blaze caught other people with money and he used to work for the government?"

"No way! Why should I?" Confusion filled his mind.

"They think you're a kid seeking reward money. I should've called. I sound older."

Gregg pushed out his jaw. "What happens if they learn Blaze is after money?"

"Nothing."

"If the government finds out Blaze can still work," he said, "they'll take him back."

"Oh." Glenna's shoulders sagged. "I never thought of that."

Gregg had silenced his older sister at last. They crossed the bridge onto Skeleton Key, each caught up in their own thoughts. Blaze nosed under a thick palmetto bush.

"Get away from me!" a girlish voice yelled from the bushes.

Gregg looked at Glenna in surprise. He thumped over to the palm fronds.

"Who is under there?" Glenna breathed in his ear.

"Some girl."

Smudges ringed her eyes, dotted her face. Her matted hair clung to her cheeks.

"Get that dumb dog outta here," the girl snapped.

She was obviously hiding from someone.

"Blaze is an attack dog," he warned. "I command him and you're dead meat."

"I ain't afraid of you or your dog."

Drool squeezed out from her cracked lips. Glenna peered down at her and then whipped out her cell phone.

"I saw you at my church," she said. "You stole cookies the night of the nativity."

The girl raised her hand. "Stop! Don't call the cops. I took 'em 'cause I were hungry."

Gregg examined her snarled hair and torn shoes. She looked a mess.

"Are you homeless?" he asked.

"I used ta' live here at Captain Cain's, but he kicked me out."

Gregg dropped to his knees. "Why? What did you do?"

"None a yer business." She curled her lips and shot a spitball on Gregg's shoes.

"That's it." He grabbed the leash from his sister. "Why should we care?"

Glenna scrambled to her feet. Blaze sniffed around the bush and Gregg tugged his leash. They walked roughly a hundred feet, when Glenna spun around.

"Keep walking," she said. "I'll be right back."

Glenna ran back to the bush and stooped down. A minute later she sprinted back to Gregg.

"Who is she?" he asked.

"I'm not sure. Nothing's happening by the shed or tiki hut. The yacht is gone."

They reached the turn when Gregg checked over his shoulder. "That girl's following us."

Glenna poked him with her elbow. "Don't scare her."

"I don't want that wild kid knowing where we live."

"She's a young girl who is homeless and afraid."

"You're kidding!" Gregg protested. "Are you brave enough to sleep outside at night?"

"That doesn't mean she's not scared, Gregg."

Gregg ran home with Blaze. He entered the garage. Glenna turned up the driveway but kept looking back. Gregg didn't see the girl. Where had she gone?

30

Glenna shot into the house, washed her hands, and set the table before Mom noticed she was late.

The doorbell rang and while Grandpa paid the delivery guy, she hurried to her room to pick up something for after dinner. Back in the kitchen, she set a tray of raw veggies on the table.

Grandy put Ricky in a blue high chair while Mom nestled Annie in her yellow high chair.

"I'm starving," Gregg said, tearing open a pizza box.

Grandpa shook his head. "Let's join hands for the blessing."

Glenna ignored the tempting aroma of spices and grabbed her brother's hand. After Grandpa thanked God for the food, Mom served the pizza.

"Save room for strawberry shortcake," she said.

Grandpa held his pizza in midair. "Did I miss a special occasion, Julia?"

A light beamed from Mom's eyes. "We are splurging because—"

"Grandpa found an old coin worth thousands of dollars," Gregg mused.

Mom fed Annie food from a jar. "I'll save the surprise until we eat our shortcake."

"Sorry I interrupted. Please tell us," Gregg urged.

Mom spooned more food into the open mouths of the twins.

Grandpa shoved his plate away. "In that case, I'm ready for dessert."

Mom laughed and Ricky gurgled.

"I never could put anything over on you, Daddy," Mom said, tilting her chin.

Gregg tapped his fingers on the table. "Drumroll."

"Dad is flying in for a *long* weekend."

"Yahoo!" Glenna cried, happiness flooding her heart.

At her shouting, Annie burst into tears. Mom fussed over her and tried coaxing her with mashed up food. Glenna did a double take. Did she ever eat such gross stuff as a baby? She took a big bite of her veggie pizza, relishing the peppery taste. She snuck a second piece on her plate along with celery sticks. Gregg helped himself to another slice.

"I hope Dad and I can go fishing," he said.

Glenna ate in silence, planning how she'd tell Dad that Blaze sniffed out criminals at the airport. Then her heart squeezed. If he learned of Blaze's success he'd tell Eva and she might take Blaze away. Her appetite gone, Glenna dropped a napkin over her plate.

"May I be excused?" she asked. "Blaze needs to go out."

Mom nodded, still smiling. Glenna took her plate to the sink. The shortcake looked delicious, even without strawberries being piled on yet. She snatched a piece. Hands full, she stepped into the garage and at the side door, she gazed over her shoulder.

Gregg hadn't followed. She breathed easier and went outside, stopping by a trash caddie. A small hand reached from between the caddies and snatched the napkin.

Glenna crouched down, saying gently, "My name is Glenna. What do I call you?"

The girl tore off the napkin, ripping her teeth into the pizza.

"Krystal," she mumbled between bites.

"Where are your parents?"

Krystal ate the pizza, crunched the celery, and then consumed the shortcake.

"Sleep here tonight," Glenna finally said. "I'll unlock the side door to the garage."

A cloud passed over Krystal's dirty face. She looked worried.

"What do ya want from me?"

Glenna wadded up the napkin. "To help, of course."

"Why? Ya don't know nothin' about me."

"You need food and a place to sleep."

"What's it to you? Ya callin' the cops?"

"No." Glenna started thinking fast. "Do you know the Micky D's on the boulevard?"

"I guess."

"Meet me in the morning after the sun's been up a few hours. Say, at ten o'clock."

"Why should I trust ya?"

"I'll bring money for food. Leave by daylight, so no one finds you here. Understand?"

Krystal dipped her head and Glenna led her into the garage, wondering if this girl with no home was even ten years old.

"Sshh," Glenna cautioned. "If my dog smells you, he will bark."

"Does he bite?"

"He's friendly to most people, unless you're a criminal."

Krystal's eyes rounded and she whispered, "I ain't."

"See you in the morning. There's a blanket by the car for you to sleep on."

Krystal's head disappeared and Glenna debated if she was doing right. After all, why was she living under a bush on Skeleton Key? Where were her parents? Glenna closed the door, vowing to find out. She let Blaze out the slider doors, keeping him away from the garage. She saw Grandpa casting a line on the dock and stepped forward. Glenna was anxious to tell him Krystal was sleeping in his garage.

Gregg shot past, calling, "I found the frozen bait."

She shrunk back, waiting for Blaze to finish his tour of the backyard. If Gregg discovered Krystal, he'd insist she leave. Glenna didn't exactly trust Krystal either, but if Grandpa kicked her out, the poor girl would have no home.

THAT NIGHT GREGG called Secrets Observers, afraid they'd already be closed. Grandpa's clock chimed seven o'clock. Mason's mother had just phoned with updates on his treatment. He was pretty weak and tired, she had said.

Gregg listened to the phone ring. He sure hoped to give Mason some good news. But why didn't the ringing stop? He was about to hang up when a voice answered, "Secret Observers. Do you have a tip?"

Gregg blurted his secret code, then said, "I already gave one. The lady told me to call back."

"Sorry, as the dispatcher, I only receive tips. The staff is gone until Monday."

Glenna's words from the other day haunted Gregg: *You sound too young.*

He lowered his voice. "I called in my first tips. Did someone get caught?"

"I can't access all the files, but your tips must have been right."

Gregg sat up straight in Grandpa's chair. "How do you know?"

"The asterisk by your code number means your tip had value."

"Really?"

Gregg jumped up, remembering he was supposed to sound older. "Can you tell me anything else?" he asked in a husky voice.

"Here is something. Did your tip involve money on a flight from Tampa?"

"Yes," Gregg answered, pride swelling in his chest.

"Three hundred thousand dollars were found by DHS in Miami."

"Did you say three thousand or three *hundred* thousand?"

"Sir, I said the Department of Homeland Security found …"

The dispatcher stopped talking and Gregg's heart started racing.

"Yes?" he prompted.

"Three hundred thousand dollars! That's the most money I've ever seen."

The dispatcher sounded awed.

"Do I receive a reward?" Gregg felt comfortable asking the friendly guy.

"I don't know, but I think they should give you a reward, don't you?"

Fear seized Gregg. "Not if it's counterfeit."

"Call on Monday, young man. It doesn't say the money is counterfeit."

Gregg ended the call, stunned. How much would he get if the government found three hundred thousand dollars? Before he figured that out, he heard the garage door go up.

"Your mom and I are going to pick up your dad," Grandpa called.

"Wait for me!"

Gregg shot out of the den anxious to tell Dad about his tips. A few nights ago, Dad had been gone on company business. Because Gregg couldn't phone, he'd sent him an e-mail about how an Air Force bomber flew beneath the Mackinaw Bridge years ago. Dad had e-mailed back.

Thanks for sending me the cool plane picture, pardner. Maybe we should take a family trip back to Mackinaw Island this summer. Glad to know you haven't forgotten me.

Gregg piled into the backseat of Grandpa's car. He wanted to spend time with Dad, but once the counterfeiter's case ended they'd have to leave Florida. Then he and Blaze might not catch enough money couriers to pay for Mason's treatment.

31

By late morning a nip still hung in the air. Glenna walked down to Mickey D's with her jacket on and money in her pockets. She sat inside with Blaze at her feet. Minutes ticked by. Glenna stared out the window, catching the sun shining on the Gulf between high-rise condos across the street. Too worried to enjoy the beauty, she wondered if Krystal would come.

Then she noticed a sign on the wall, *Thirty-Minute Maximum While Eating.*

She'd need to buy something soon or leave. But she'd already eaten with Dad.

Over pancakes he had told her, "The counterfeiters' trial is set. Eva thinks they may take a plea deal. Then you can come home."

"We're okay in Florida, for now," she had said, wanting to ask him about North Korea.

The communist nation had fired off a missile toward Japan. But Glenna hadn't the nerve to ask if he'd been over there risking his life.

A motion out the window grabbed her attention and she saw Krystal sit on a bench across the street. She seemed to have on a new coat, just as massive. Her hair fell in her eyes.

Glenna waved, but Krystal didn't react. So Glenna snatched Blaze's leash and dashed outside. Again she beckoned with her hand. Still Krystal did nothing. Was she ill?

"Krystal!"

This time the girl shook her head.

"Krystal! Come over here."

Finally she stood and walked to the curb waiting for the light to change. She trudged over to Glenna, her head down and shoulders slouched. She stooped to pet Blaze.

Glenna smiled. "I thought you were meeting me inside."

"They don't let me in. I never buy nothin.'"

Glenna reached for Krystal's dirty hand. "I am buying you break-fast."

They had barely taken a table when a woman hustled from behind the counter and rushed at the girls. She glared at Krystal, pointing to the trash can by the door.

"I caught you eating food thrown out by customers. I told you never to come back."

"Ma'am." Glenna waved dollar bills in the woman's face. "We are here to eat."

The woman thrust her hands on her skinny hips. Glenna glanced at her tag. Olga, the manager, gaped at Glenna before fixing her eyes on Blaze.

"Oh no, dogs aren't allowed. You both must leave."

"But he's a service dog." Glenna lifted the laminated tag on Blaze's vest.

Olga leaned over and read Blaze's certification. She straightened, her gaze sweeping from Blaze to Glenna to Krystal. She shrugged her bony shoulders.

"Okay, this once. Be quick and order. Don't plan on staying all day."

Glenna let Krystal hold the leash. At the counter she ordered two of everything: egg biscuits, milks, and cinnamon melts. The piping hot food was put on a tray under Olga's watchful eye. Glenna slid behind the table. Krystal dove into the biscuit like she was starving.

"Was that yer brother you were with?"

Glenna watched Krystal gobble her food. *Was I ever so hungry? I don't think so.*

"Yes, Gregg's my brother. You slept in my grandparents' garage last night."

Krystal opened her milk, drinking it in one huge gulp straight from the bottle.

"I crashed in the black car. I cleaned up before I left."

Uh oh. Krystal had slept in Grandpa's untouchable classic car. He wouldn't like that, *if* he ever found out. Krystal sunk her teeth into the biscuit. In her eyes, Glenna saw fear and hunger mixed. She glimpsed something else. Was it a longing for a friend, someone to care for her?

Glenna's mind pulsed with questions, but she didn't want to scare Krystal. How had she sunk so low? Who abandoned her? Maybe she ran away to save herself from a terrible situation.

Glenna wet her lips before asking, "Do you have brothers or sisters?"

"Maybe. But I never met any of 'em."

Glenna weighed the risks. If she probed too deeply, she'd end their budding friendship. She looked at Krystal's streaked face and decided. She must take a chance.

"Where do you live?"

Krystal stopped chewing. "In the backseat of yer grandpa's convertible."

"What about your family?"

"I've got two of 'em."

Krystal wadded the paper wrapper and tore open the cinnamon melts.

"I told ya. I been livin' on Cain's boat. He kicked me off."

"Who is Cain?" Glenna demanded.

"Cain Denton. He runs *Makin' Mischuf*, the big boat near where I was hidin' in the bushes."

"Where's your mother?"

Krystal stuffed gooey bits into her mouth, lifting her skimpy shoulders.

"She cleaned the boat. Me and her lived on it. Cain gave her clothes."

"How about your dad?"

"Misty said Pa died when I was a baby," Krystal said, gazing at Glenna's second milk.

Glenna slid the container forward and Krystal twisted off the cap.

"What about school?" Glenna pried.

"I went to one once." A tear slid down Krystal's nose, which she flung off with her hand.

"Know what crack is?"

Glenna did some thinking. Mom had taught her people did drugs and lost their jobs.

She nodded. "It's an illegal drug, right?"

"Ma's addicted. She's hooked on crack. Steals stuff to buy it. I was a crack baby."

"What's a crack baby?" Glenna really had no idea.

"Ma was takin' drugs. I was addicted when I was born."

Glenna was startled by Olga stalking up to their table.

"You two girls have stayed long enough."

Glenna pointed to her unwrapped sandwich. "I haven't eaten mine yet."

Olga turned, snapping over her shoulder, "Get eating or start paying rent for that seat."

"Yes, we are eating," Glenna replied, leaning forward. "Krystal, if you were a crack baby, what happened to you?"

"Once I had me a nice house, like your grandpa's. They took me away from Ma and the Fosters let me live with 'em."

"Where do the Fosters live?"

"Michigan. Same place I was born."

"Did they bring you to Florida?"

"I had me two older sisters. We sang in church school. I were happy, I think."

"Why did you leave?"

"Ma came." As Krystal said this, her voice sounded flat.

Glenna's mind whirled. "Where? To Florida?"

"She made me call her Misty." Krystal eyed Glenna's sandwich. "You gonna eat that?"

"No. It's for you."

Krystal tore off the wrapper and bit in. She chewed quickly before returning to her story. "Her boyfriend got Misty hooked on crack again. She stole money and he kicked us out."

Glenna tried following the broken threads of Krystal's story. "So is he Cain?"

"Whad'ya mean?" Krystal frowned.

"Is Cain her boyfriend?"

"Nah." Krystal shoved the biscuit in her mouth. "Cain runs the boat for a rich dude who makes bugle boards."

"Let me see." Glenna tried deciphering Krystal's words. "Cain's the captain of *Making Mischief*. My brother and I have seen that boat. But the owner is actually a man who builds boogie boards. My friend Mason owns a Mischief board."

Krystal shrugged. "I guess so. Misty's gone."

"Where is she?"

"Don't know. She stole Cain's food and drinks for his gamblin' people. To buy crack, Cain said. He warned if she robbed him again, we'd be gone."

"She left without you?" Glenna sat in disbelief.

Krystal chewed her lip. "Cain says she fell in a sinkhole. He brung her to the hospital."

"Did you check at the hospital?"

"I hung around. Misty never came out."

"I'll help you find her."

"You can't," Krystal said, shaking her head. "I heard Cain tell some Colombians he sold Misty to 'em. He's a rat."

It made little sense, but Glenna was starting to figure a few things out.

"So you hide in the bushes by Cain's boat in case Misty returns."

A tiny smile erupted on Krystal's thin face. "Cain lives in a small house by *Mischuf's* dock. At dark, I sleep in the shed so Misty can find me."

If Misty fell in a sinkhole, she might never return. Glenna had seen horror stories on the news about the gaping holes swallowing houses and people. She didn't tell Krystal. Glenna dashed to the counter to order a third sandwich. Olga shook her head.

"If you put the fresh sandwich in a bag," Glenna said smiling, "we are leaving."

Olga dropped a brown bag on the counter. "You'd better be."

Glenna sped to the table, dropping the extra cinnamon melts in the bag. She picked up the leash, telling Krystal to follow her. But the girl plunged away from Glenna. Had she hurt her feelings? Glenna headed after her.

Krystal swung into the restroom and Glenna waited, petting Blaze's head.

"We must help her, boy."

He pushed his head against her hand and shut his eyes as if deciding what to do. Krystal walked up, her face clean and her long hair pushed behind her ears. Glenna pictured her own soft pillow and nice clothes. She was glad she could buy her breakfast. Outside, she handed Krystal the bag.

"Eat these later. Where do you go from here?"

Krystal snuggled the bag under her arm. "I got places to go."

"Can we be friends?" Glenna asked, flashing a tender smile.

Blaze sniffed at Krystal's torn tennis shoes and she giggled.

"You wanna be friends?"

"Yes. I prayed for you last night."

Krystal started walking away.

"Wait!" Glenna said. "I'll talk to Grandpa. You can sleep in the garage, but not in his convertible. I'll leave the door unlocked."

"Okay." Krystal clutched her bag and turned the corner.

Along the water's edge, Glenna shared her heart with Blaze. "She can't live in a garage, but Grandpa's house is full. Before the twins, Mom might have said yes."

Glenna's mind whirled and Blaze's tail hung limp.

"I know, boy. Jesus said we should care for the poor. I'm trying. If I talk to Dad, maybe he can find the Fosters. Are they in Florida or Michigan? What do you think?"

The twinkle in Blaze's eye confirmed she was on the right path. A squirrel ran across the neighbor's yard but Blaze didn't even try chasing the furry creature. He marched by Glenna's side, her silent partner in solving this riddle.

32

Later that morning, Glenna trotted up the driveway with Blaze staying alongside. Gregg flew out of the side garage door holding a fishing pole.

"Mom and Dad are heading to the outlet stores. I'm going fishing with Grandpa on the *Pollywog*. Want to come?"

"Are you really going fishing or are you up to some mischief?" Glenna asked, fingering the leash.

"Along with catching supper, we might do a little spying."

Glenna jumped at the chance to check out the *Mischief* and see if she could spot Misty.

"Grab me a pole. I need to talk with Mom and Dad first. Will you take Blaze out back?"

Gregg rolled his eyes. "You're up to something, I can tell."

"If Secret Observers gives us a reward, I have a project to spend it on."

"Oh, no. You're soft for that homeless kid. We've pledged money for Mason, or did you forget his bone marrow transplant?"

"I pray for Mason every day. I want him healed."

"Me too," he replied.

Glenna lifted her chin. "All I mean is, let's save a few dollars to buy Krystal decent clothes. I just bought her breakfast from my allowance. She has no home or family."

"She's that bad off?" Gregg scowled. "I figured she'd run away."

"Her life stinks. Her mom's an addict. Krystal is alone and I'm asking Mom and Dad what to do."

"We can help her some, but most of our money is for Mason."

Glenna wanted to say they should earn a reward first, but Gregg disappeared with Blaze around the garage. She ran into the kitchen.

"Will you help Grandy make lunch?" Mom asked. "Dad is taking me shopping."

Glenna lifted up her arms. "Mom, Dad, there's a girl—"

"Stop," Dad said, shaking his head. "Remember rule number ten? Don't make excuses."

Mom's pale cheeks caused Glenna to change gears. She'd say nothing yet about Krystal. Her parents were too tired to think right. Instead, she hauled out the cutting board.

"You're right. I guess I can make lunch."

"Don't plan on us," Dad said, "I'm taking my beautiful wife to Smuggler's Cove."

Glenna shuffled to the fridge. She would miss Grandpa's excursion.

Mom and Dad headed for the back door.

"Wait." Glenna hurried over. "Grandpa took us to Smuggler's Cove. The clams are tasty. I hope you like them. If the twins nap, when you get home, Mom can rest too."

Glenna couldn't make her tongue stop talking. She always prattled on when she was nervous. Mom must have caught on. She came over to rub Glenna's upper back.

"That's my daughter, always wanting to please."

Dad jangled the keys in his hands. "You said something about a girl. What happened?"

Tears hovered on her lashes, and in seconds, some of the story spilled out. How Krystal's mother had gone missing and she had become homeless.

"My heart breaks for her and Mason."

Mom hugged her tightly. Glenna choked back tears as Mom stroked her hair.

She pulled back, asking softly, "Have you prayed for them?"

"Yes! My heart tells me to do something to help."

Dad touched Glenna's shoulder.

"What we are doing for Mason will help, with bake sales, Car Club, and washing cars. Our church back home is also involved."

Glenna wiped her eyes. "They are?"

"Your youth group is hosting a basketball game. Proceeds go to Mason's fund."

"Wow. I've lost touch. Who is organizing the tournament?"

Mom smiled. "All your friends back home. Sarah is captain of the girls' team and Steven is captain for the guys. Annelise, Leah, Kira are playing too."

"Wish I could, but I'm so focused on helping down here …"

Glenna broke down in sobs.

At Dad's warm hug, she dried her eyes and said, "I have a confession."

Mom gazed intently. "We are listening."

"Better tell all," Dad urged. "We'll deal with any sharp edges before you get hurt."

Glenna bit her lip, telling how she'd asked Krystal to stay in the garage. Somehow she omitted that Krystal had slept in Grandpa's classic car. Dad shook his head, looking stern.

"Your motives are pure but misguided. You should've talked to one of your grands. This is their house and they have a say in what goes on here."

"I planned to when I went fishing with Grandpa and Gregg." Her lower lip trembled. "But I'll make lunch instead."

Mom took her by the shoulders and turned her toward the door. "Hurry and fix peanut butter sandwiches. Then run out and have a good time."

"I'll get you some water and bring down the cooler," Dad offered.

Glenna whirled, kissing her mom's warm cheek.

Dad brought out three water bottles. "If she comes, Krystal should join us for supper. We need to learn more."

Dread seized Glenna.

"Please don't cross-examine her and scare her off."

Mom tapped Glenna's nose with a finger. "We won't let her roam the streets."

Feeling relieved after telling her parents, a thought pierced Glenna's mind. "Dad, have you ever been to Colombia, like in South America?"

He pulled down the soft-sided cooler with a thump.

"That came out of nowhere. Why?"

Glenna lobbed a glance at Mom. Her eyes were narrowed to slits, warning her not to ask Dad about his job. Glenna took Mom's non-verbal hint and headed for the door.

"Oh, never mind."

GLENNA HUNKERED DOWN BENEATH her baseball cap as Grandpa motored by the dock in Skeleton Key. They'd been fishing for hours and were heading home. A man with a goatee stepped quickly off *Making Mischief* and onto the dock. His hair curled under his Greek fishing cap just as Zeke had said.

"That's him!" Gregg hissed. "The captain Mason and I saw."

"He sure has long hair," Glenna pointed out.

Grandpa slowed the motor. "He must be Cain Denton."

"Grandpa, I mentioned Krystal needs a place to live," Glenna said, pulling down her cap.

"Yes, and I said I would talk to your grandy."

"Right, but that's not all. Cain let Krystal and her ma, Misty, live on the *Mischief.*"

Grandpa snapped his head around, facing her.

"What did you say?"

"Misty takes cocaine," Glenna said, shaking her head. "Krystal thinks Cain sold her to Colombians that he owes money to. It's a tangle. Dad said I should talk to you about it."

A funny look erupted on Grandpa's face.

"He did, huh. What can I do?"

"Let her sleep on the porch until we find her a home," Gregg said, handing Grandpa a cold soda. "Sip this orange crush and think on it."

Glenna could have hugged her brother. Grandpa twisted off the top and took a long swig. Glenna gazed around at Cain's dock, hoping to see a woman. Then she realized Krystal had never described Misty.

Glenna sighed. She had much to learn before becoming a Federal agent like Eva. Grandpa nodded at their big fish coolers. When he smiled, his peculiar look disappeared.

"We didn't do too badly. Three sheepshead and six snappers should be enough to invite your little lassie for supper. I'll ask your grandy, but I think a few nights on the couch won't hurt. Is your mom up to homeschooling another student?"

Glenna put her hand on the wheel, her fingers touching her grandfather's.

"Do you have any ideas how to find Misty?" she asked.

Grandpa turned, circling back to his dock. The wind was picking up. Glenna scanned the sky for tornadoes. Thankfully, no dark clouds swirled overhead. Only fluffy white clouds jetted past. Still, bad weather could blow in without warning. She'd learned that much about Florida.

A great blue heron soared off, tucking in its long neck. Dad had taught her and Gregg how to fish and feed the big birds. A sudden thought sizzled through her brain.

"Dad should contact Eva. She's a Federal agent, Grandpa. Eva might shed light on Krystal's suspicions."

He hopped off the *Pollywog* and secured her lines.

"Don't get your hopes up. I sense your dad's pretty involved with his recruiting job."

"He's never too busy to help us. Told me so last night," Gregg shot back.

He handed the fishing rods to Grandpa. Meanwhile, Glenna hurried into the house to find Dad. If he called Eva before Krystal arrived, she might answer Glenna's troubling questions.

33

Glenna had no chance to talk with her dad during the meal. Afterwards, he washed dishes with Gregg. Glenna gave up trying and let Blaze run in the backyard. Cold air blew down her neck and she wondered how Krystal survived on such nights. Blaze barked up a storm near a bush.

Thinking Krystal might be hiding in the yard, Glenna rushed over. Blaze had cornered a squirrel. She coaxed him away.

"Come on, boy. I don't have all night."

He nosed around the side yard while Glenna searched for Krystal. The young girl was not to be found. Glenna whistled for Blaze to come. She sauntered into the living room where he shuddered and sprawled out by her feet. Seconds later, he was snoring.

Glenna took up a post by the front window, concerned Krystal would never return. She roamed over to her grandmother who was knitting with her mom. Glenna toyed with a ball of yarn.

"I shouldn't have let her leave Mickey D's."

"You invited her to come back," Grandy reminded her.

Mom clicked her needles rapid-fire. "Where else does she have to go?"

"Nowhere."

Glenna watched her grandmother knit several rows with pink yarn.

"What are you making?" she asked.

"Would you like to make caps for girls and ladies who lose their hair from cancer?"

"Yes, if you'll teach me. I have never held a needle."

Grandy patted Glenna's hand. "My friendship group at Calvary is knitting caps after I told them about Mason. We'll sell a selection at next week's bake sale."

Glenna fingered her long hair. "I wonder …"

Before she finished, Gregg burst into the living room. He shoved a piece of paper in Grandy's hands so fast she dropped her knitting needles.

"Gregg, what in the world are you up to?" Mom asked.

"Quick, I need Grandy to write down the address here. Include the zip code."

He handed her a pen and she scribbled the address.

She handed it back. "You're not ordering pizza, are you?"

Gregg darted out. Mom pinned her eyes on Glenna. "What is he doing?"

"I'm not my brother's keeper."

Her mother peered at her closely. "Please go into the den and check."

"Why do I always have to corral him?"

Gregg swaggered back into the living room, grinning.

Mom's eyes shifted. "Okay, buster. What scheme are you cooking up?"

"I spoke with Secret Observers. They needed my address to send me a check."

Glenna jumped to her feet. "What do you mean *me*? You and I are partners."

"Checks? Partners?" Mom's eyes bounced from Gregg to Glenna and back again as if she was watching a tennis match.

At their silence, she folded her arms. "One of you better tell me what it's about."

"Not me!"

Gregg pointed at Glenna and plopped down by Grandy. Glenna gathered her thoughts before facing Mom.

"You might as well bring Dad in here so I don't have to repeat everything."

Mom set down her knitting needles by her chair and hurried away. Gregg rolled his eyes at Glenna.

"Thanks a lot, Gregg, for bursting in here talking about the reward."

Grandy jabbed a needle toward them both. "I told Buck he should inform your parents, but he wanted you to break the news in your own time. This is the time."

Mom and Dad walked in holding hands and sat down. While they looked more rested than this morning, their eyes betrayed worry. Glenna's hands started sweating. She and Gregg would be grounded for years. She exhaled slowly.

"Okay. Grandpa had the idea at first."

"Forget the blame game," Dad snapped.

"It's the simple truth. Grandpa can explain when he's back from his Car Club."

Dad crossed his legs. "A given. What happened next?"

"Mason helped us certify Blaze," Glenna said, perching on a chair. "We took him to the airport to snoop out illegal currency."

"How did you get to the Tampa airport with a dog? Take the bus?"

From the intense look on Dad's face, Glenna knew he'd dig for answers until he received them.

"Grandpa drove us," she said, suppressing a giggle.

Gregg interrupted excitedly, "Last week, we gave tips for two passengers who hid money in their suitcases. Secret Observers just told me they seized one hundred and twenty thousand dollars from the man's suitcase. Last Friday they got three hundred grand from a lady's bag."

Dad zeroed in on Gregg. "What is Secret Observers?"

"I report suspected crimes using a secret code number."

"Dad, your son and my brother has become a super snitch."

Glenna poked Gregg's arm, hoping the gesture and her comments would make her dad laugh. He did, but not Mom. She swung into action big-time.

"We have been separated from home and your father so you wouldn't be drawn into a criminal case. Here you are in Florida, going behind my back with my daddy's consent and putting yourselves in harm's way. I can't believe this!"

Mom's cheeks turned beet red. Dad put his arm around her.

"Honey," he soothed. "We don't know they are in danger. Gregg has a secret code, so the tips are anonymous. Right, son?"

Gregg nodded furiously. Mom looked anything but convinced. Glenna snuggled her face into Blaze's neck. He snorted and jerked up his head. Even Mom chuckled.

But then she pushed out her bottom lip. "Gregg, who did you give the address to?"

"Secret Observers gives rewards for good tips. They're sending us two checks, each for one thousand dollars."

"Yes!" Glenna jumped up. "That will help Mason get his treatments."

At the sound of Mason's name, Blaze lifted his head as if wanting in on their plans. Glenna dropped to her knees and patted his soft nose.

"You're trying to help Mason?" Mom asked.

Looking confused, she turned to Dad. He raised his eyebrows.

"So you're not doing this for kicks?"

"No way," Gregg replied. "Glenna and I agreed. If Blaze sniffs out illegal cash, we're sending all rewards to Mason's fund."

Dad rested a hand on Gregg's shoulder. "How do you know your identities are safe with Secret Observers?"

"They gave me a code number. I never even told them my name." Grandy cleared her throat.

"Oh, yeah," Gregg admitted. "Not until they agreed to send me a check."

"So they do have your name," Dad pressed.

"What was I supposed to do, Dad? Mason needs the money. Besides, Secret Observers demanded to know how we discovered money hidden in those suitcases." Gregg shifted his gaze to Glenna.

"You didn't tell them about Blaze, did you?" she asked, bending down and petting Blaze.

"No, but this woman was really wondering."

Grandy's needles stopped clicking. "I think you've been robbed."

"What?" Mom cried. "Did something else happen that I don't know about?"

Grandy shook her head. "I mean the government keeps four hundred thousand dollars and give my grandkids two thousand bucks. It's not fair."

"Two thousand is peanuts." Glenna's shoulders sagged. "With that and what we earn at the bake sale, it will take forever to save enough for Mason."

"Rule number five, no gloomy thoughts."

As Dad smiled, Blaze went over and pressed his nose against the window. He barked softly once. Glenna zoomed over to the window. She spotted Krystal sneaking across the street. Glenna sprang to the front door and opened it.

"Krystal!" she called, motioning for her to come.

The girl in the heavy coat disappeared behind the garage.

GLENNA GRIPPED HER CUP OF COCOA wondering if Grandy would let Krystal stay.

"It's good," Krystal piped, smacking her lips.

Grandy smiled, pouring out more cocoa for everyone. Glenna relaxed.

"We love drinking hot cocoa in the evenings," she said. "Dad tells us stories."

Krystal drank with gusto, acting more refreshed after having showered and eaten a meal. She looked cute in Glenna's capri pants and striped sweater. Grandy produced a carrot cake, slicing off a big piece for Krystal.

"Since Grandpa's still at his car meeting and your mom is busy with the twins, would you all like to play a game?" Dad asked.

"I vote for one of my video games," Gregg replied before biting into his cake.

"I was thinking of 'My Grandfather owns a grocery store.' I'll start."

"How do ya play a game?" Krystal flexed her eyebrows.

"It's simple," Dad said. "My grandfather owns a grocery store. In it he sells something starting with the letter 'B.' You all guess what I'm thinking of."

"Cool, mind games. Is it bagels?" Glenna asked.

Gregg guessed bananas. Dad shook his head to both and fired a warning glance at Glenna. Sensing he was up to something, she ate her cake. Krystal scrunched up her tilted nose.

"Bread?" she croaked.

Dad clapped his hands. "You win. We can play this game or try another."

"I ain't been goin' to school," Krystal admitted.

Glenna decided to take a chance. "Dad, can you help us find Misty?"

As if on cue, he picked up his pen.

"Krystal, you told Glenna how you were born addicted to crack and lived with Mr. and Mrs. Foster in Michigan. To find your mother, I have to ask some questions."

She set her cup down with a thud. "That were private—"

"So now that your birth mother abandoned you," Grandy interrupted.

"She didn't abandon me!" Krystal cried.

Grandy lightly touched her arm. "I am sorry. Your mother would be here if she could."

Gregg shot out of his chair and rummaged in the cupboard, returning with a tin of cookies. He took one out for himself, then pushed the tin toward Krystal.

"Have one. Glenna made 'em and they're good."

Glenna grinned at her brother's rare compliment. Having eaten the last crumb of her cake, Krystal snatched a cookie. Dad set down his pen.

"What do you think happened to your mother?"

"Cain sold her to crooks in Colombia."

Dad nodded. "I see, as in South America. Where do the Fosters live? In Michigan? How old were you when you left them?"

Krystal gazed out the kitchen window. "Ma took me outta the second grade."

"Were the Fosters nice?"

Krystal briefly shut her eyes. "They gave me a big, white bed. My mind sees me walking up a hill from the old house to my school. They took me to church. On Christmas, I sang."

"Wow, you remember a lot. Want to come to church with us?" Glenna asked.

"I already been to yer church."

"Come inside with us next time. We can sing together."

Krystal looked so tiny. Glenna pictured her stealing cookies and her heart ached. Glenna had two bedrooms, one in Virginia and one here. Dad was asking more questions so she listened.

"Do you know the town's name?"

Krystal lips fell open. "A river falls over a dam. Toy ducks race on the river. Lights are in the trees at Christmas. The snow is real pretty."

Because Krystal kept mentioning Christmas, Glenna thought maybe the Fosters celebrated Jesus' birth too.

"Did you like snow?" she asked.

"Yeah, but it's cold." Krystal forced a giggle. "There's a place called Panda's. You slide down a hill on a tube. Popa held me on his lap. The Fosters all piled on one tube."

Dad wrote some notes on his pad. "So you had brothers and sisters?"

"Two sisters older than me. Nicki and Bree."

"You must miss them," Dad said.

Tears rolled down Krystal's cheeks. She dropped her head on her arms.

"Sweetie, you're tired. We can talk after a good night's sleep." Grandy patted her hands.

Krystal lifted her head. "No. I wanna tell. Misty put my clothes and church books in a bag. I were screaming. They forced me in the car. My family were all cryin.'"

Grandy gave Krystal a tissue from a box. As she wiped her face, Glenna nibbled a cookie, not knowing what else to do. She glanced at Gregg and he shook his head.

"A cop car came," Krystal said, tears hovering on her lashes. "He put Misty in the backseat. My worker let her out."

Dad began writing again. "Did you move to Florida after that?"

"Yup, with her rich boyfriend. He kicked us out for her drugs. So Misty worked for Cain."

"Did you try contacting the Fosters in Michigan?"

"Wouldn't do no good. They moved."

"Where to?"

Krystal sagged. "Misty took me 'cause they left and couldn't keep me no more."

"They probably didn't really ..."

Dad lightly squeezed Glenna's arms so she didn't finish. She really believed Misty just wanted to get Krystal away from the Fosters.

"We should try to find your family. Do you know the Fosters' first names?" Dad asked.

"No!" Krystal wailed. "I can't leave. Misty always comes back."

Glenna had to clear up something. "How long has she been gone?"

"She left before and came back."

"But didn't Cain tell you she's not coming back?" Glenna watched Krystal's face.

Grandy stood up. "Meanwhile, you will stay here. Buck and Bo can check by the boat in the morning. They'll see if Misty returned. I'll put sheets on the pullout couch."

"That sounds like a plan." Dad folded up his pad.

"No, Dad!" Glenna cried. "Don't go near Cain. He's mean."

Gregg bobbed his head. "Yeah, ask Grandpa."

"I intend to, as soon as he comes home. How about another game?"

Krystal yawned. Grandy put her to bed and Glenna took Blaze outside. Because Misty had abandoned Krystal, would she become part of their family?

34

A week passed with Krystal sleeping on the pullout couch. Mom worked with her on sounding out common words like "was" instead of "were" and writing sentences. A smart girl, Krystal made surprising progress. On Friday afternoon, Grandy took her shopping for new clothes.

Glenna wandered to the den watching Gregg and Mason play *Call of Duty, Black Ops*. Mason quit after only a few short minutes. She and Gregg squeezed together by Grandpa's computer with Glenna sitting on a folding chair. When they connected on Skype, she did a double take. Mason's hair was gone. He looked frail, but his grin never wavered.

"Sorry I'm zapped. Couldn't eat much today."

Silence, and then Gregg nudged his sister with his elbow.

"How's Stormy?" she blurted.

"She's being a watchful good guard donkey, but Stormy isn't as friendly as Blaze."

Gregg laughed and leaned into the webcam. "Kaley Montanna sent Glenna an e-mail. She said your football team raised three thousand dollars at the spaghetti dinner."

"Mrs. Montanna came with Kaley. Even though she carries a gun, she's nice."

"Gregg and I wish we could have been there," Glenna said, feeling left out.

Mason's grin widened. Glenna was glad to see that Mason still had a sense of humor.

"Firefighters stretched their ladder all the way to the top. My teammates tossed footballs and dunked our coach in a tank. He said he'd stay all day because it was helping the team's passing game."

He stopped talking to guzzle from a big glass.

"Sweet! Glenna and I are sending money to your fund. Grandpa is raising money from his Car Club."

Glenna's heart surged for her friend. "Besides a bake sale at church, Mom and Grandy are knitting like crazy. They're teaching me how to knit."

"Mother said two thousand dollars came in anonymously from Florida," Mason said, his voice getting weaker. "Did you find old coins on Skeleton Key?"

Gregg nodded. "No, it's amazing. You helped Blaze become certified and he's working again."

Mason scratched his chin. "So did Secret Observers send a reward?"

"Right!" Glenna jumped in. "It's because of you that we're even doing this."

"You guys are my best friends. Any idea when you're coming back?"

Glenna traded looks with Gregg. "The trial is a month away. But it keeps being delayed."

"That long?"

Mason sounded winded and discouraged. Glenna decided to test the waters. "How are your treatments coming?"

He looked away.

"Are there more than two left?" she wanted to know.

Mason's eyes widened. "My treatments aren't working as the doctors hoped, so they are quitting."

"Quitting?" Gregg wailed. "No! You can't quit."

Mason nodded. "The doctor is referring me to a special hospital for a possible bone marrow transplant. They say it's my only hope."

"Oh, so you are not quitting," Glenna said with a tortured sigh.

"I have to be accepted for the program first. I might be because I am young."

Gregg poked Glenna with his elbow. She struggled to tell Mason how they felt.

"We are going to keep praying for you to receive the transplant and to be made completely healthy. We want you to play football again. Don't we, Gregg?"

"Yeah! You have to beat me at *Black Ops* again."

"But your prayers have not worked so far," Mason said, looking wounded.

"We won't quit praying. God knows exactly what you need and when. We never stop bringing you to his attention."

"The transplant costs two hundred, maybe three hundred thousand dollars. My family can't afford what the insurance won't cover, even if the whole town buys spaghetti."

"Don't give up!" Gregg urged.

Mason blinked and he seemed to sag in the chair. "I'd better lie down."

Glenna thought of something to perk up his spirits. "Mason, don't go yet. I'll be right back."

She sped away, catching snippets of Gregg telling about the fish he and Grandpa caught.

"Blaze, come here, boy," she called in the hallway.

He didn't come so she called him again. She was careful not to wake the twins. In seconds, she heard Blaze's nails screech on the kitchen tile. She rushed to pet him.

"Mason needs you."

At his name, Blaze started whining and followed her into the den.

"Look who wants to say hi."

Glenna propped Blaze's front paws on the desk so he could see Mason on the computer.

Woof!

Mason rallied. He smiled and his eyes grew bright.

"Blaze, old buddy. I hear you've been busy busting criminals."

Woof! was Blaze's curt reply. His tail started wagging.

"Don't forget me, you guys," Mason said in a firm a voice.

"We won't!"

The screen flickered to black and Mason was gone. Blaze jumped down and pushed his nose under Glenna's hand. She stroked his fur.

"I'm scared," Gregg said, his eyes glistening.

Glenna felt numb. "He needs so much money. What are we going to do?"

Her brother gawked at the blank screen, biting his lower lip.

"If we'd stolen those suitcases, we could have paid for Mason's bone marrow."

"Gregg, don't say such things. Dad will have your hide if you even hint about stealing."

He puffed out a breath. "I'm not serious, but think about it. Criminals have money when Mason is sick and needs help."

"You can fuss, but I'm going to do something," Glenna cried, leaping up from the chair.

"Like what?"

"Like asking God for help. This is way too big for you and me."

SUNDAY MORNING ROLLED IN WITH RAIN. Glenna walked with Krystal to church. The girls talked and laughed, huddling under umbrellas. A kid passed riding a bike in his bare feet. He was drenched. Garbage bags hung off his handle bars.

"He looks homeless," Glenna observed.

Krystal wiped water off her new yellow coat. "He is."

"You know him?"

"Yup. For two days after I lost Misty, I stayed at a camp. It's where homeless people live." Krystal's eyes narrowed. "That kid stole my blanket."

Glenna stopped beneath the awning and shook her umbrella.

"You've been through so much. Look, here comes Grandpa's car."

The family rushed into the church. Once inside, Glenna snuggled in a packed row between Krystal and Mom. Her heart soared. Her entire family was here. Well, except Grandy and the twins stayed in the nursery.

She grinned at Dad as he slid next to Grandpa and Gregg. Lights dimmed.

Mrs. Hernandez sang about Jesus calming a mighty storm with his words. Gooseflesh covered Glenna's arms. She remembered the tornado and how they'd survived. Krystal's eyes and mouth opened wide. Glenna wondered where she hid when the tornado had thundered by.

Pastor Brighton stepped up front to welcome new visitors. Everyone clapped. Krystal smiled, looking happy. The pastor lifted his Bible. He read some verses about Jesus and a man called the Good Samaritan.

"You may wonder who the Good Samaritan is in our church family," he said. "Some had homes damaged by the tornado. Many of you pitched in, buzzing trees and fixing roofs. Let me tell you about an amazing event."

Glenna watched Krystal lean forward, her eyes on the pastor.

"A tree fell on Ralph's house, leaving a gaping hole in his roof. He paid two men who came door-to-door to fix his roof. They left with Ralph's money to buy supplies, but never returned. Ralph was robbed. Some of you may have been struck down by others. Perhaps life has you beaten."

Krystal nodded like she knew people like that. Glenna wondered if those thieves lived in the homeless camp.

"Jesus knows our every hurt," Pastor Brighton assured. "So what happened to Ralph? His neighbor on the north fixed a hole in his own roof, ignoring Ralph when he told him he'd lost his money. Ralph's neighbor to the south heard the sad story but insisted Ralph remove the tree that fell on their fence."

"I believe it," Glenna heard Krystal mutter.

Who was Ralph? Glenna hadn't heard of his troubles.

Pastor reached out with his hands. "If you're like me, you are ashamed to think you might have seen Ralph and ignored his horrible situation. Listen, another man from a distant neighborhood stopped at Ralph's house. You may wonder if he also robbed poor Ralph."

Glenna glanced at Dad. Maybe he and Grandpa had already helped Ralph.

"No, this stranger did something wonderful. He climbed on Ralph's roof and fixed the hole, covering it with a tarp. He *gave* Ralph money to buy supplies. When he returned to his own neighborhood, he left Ralph enough money to pay a roofer for a new roof.

"Jesus wants to know, who was a neighbor to Ralph? Friends, the stranger who lived far away but who helped Ralph, who showed him mercy, is truly his neighbor."

Just when Glenna was going to pen a note asking Dad about Ralph, Pastor opened his Bible and said, "Isn't my story similar to the one Jesus told about the Good Samaritan helping a beaten man?"

Glenna had read Jesus' parable before, but the way pastor told it made her think of Krystal's woes. She peeked at Krystal. Her eyes were wet with tears. Pastor Brighton walked down a step.

"Jesus wants us to be like the stranger who helped Ralph. Let's ask ourselves. Do we love God so much that we will help others, even when doing so is inconvenient or even dangerous?"

Gregg leaned around Dad, shooting Glenna a look. What was he trying to tell her with his eyes? She couldn't ask him in church. Krystal twisted her coat sleeve. Glenna felt overwhelmed at her needs and Mason's too. Was she doing enough? After church, she'd ask her parents.

Pastor held up Mason's photo. Where had that come from?

"Our church family is raising money for Mason's bone marrow transplant. We are holding a bake sale and car event. This young friend of Buck and Sheryl's lives in Virginia next to their grandkids, Gregg and Glenna Rider. We are praying for him to be healed of leukemia."

Krystal started fidgeting as if she found church boring.

"Ask Jesus to calm your storms of life. He never fails." Pastor lifted his hands. "He might send a neighbor to help. Mrs. Hernandez and I are down front if you need help. We are here to listen, to pray."

Krystal shot past Glenna, plunging down the aisle. She started talking to Pastor Brighton. Mom nudged Glenna and they both scurried after her.

When Glenna reached Krystal's side, she heard her ask Mrs. Hernandez, "Will you pray for Misty?"

She did pray with Krystal and gave her a small pink Bible.

"I love pink," Krystal said in awe.

Mrs. Hernandez smiled. "Me too. I hope you discover Jesus' love for you."

"I want to."

"Would you like to ask him to help you every day?"

"Yup." Krystal fidgeted with her coat sleeve. "Um … you prob'ly know I stoled cookies from this church. I need all the help I can get."

Mrs. Hernandez kneeled down. "Jesus forgives our wrongs and mistakes if we ask him to. He never leaves when we ask him into our lives."

Krystal nodded, her cheeks turning pink. "Then I'm askin'."

She bowed her head. Glenna grabbed Mom's hand. After Krystal prayed, Mom hugged her and went to find Grandy and the twins in the nursery. Glenna walked with Krystal outside. Though the rain had stopped, tiny drops glistened from the palm trees. A single drop fell on Glenna's head from the side of the awning. She brushed it away.

Krystal opened her Bible, stopping at a picture in the back. "Look, he's in a boat in a storm like she sung."

"That's Jesus calming the storm," Glenna said, peering over her shoulder.

Krystal touched her finger to Jesus' face.

"I told the lady about the homeless kid on the bike needing help."

"Wow, Krystal. I forgot about him. But he took your blanket."

"Yup, and I swiped cookies. Jesus saved me by bringin' you to Skeleton Key."

Tears burned in Glenna's eyes. She remembered that day when she'd almost called the cops on Krystal.

"And Jesus can help us find Misty," she replied. "I know he can."

35

When Glenna returned home from church, she let Blaze out the back door. He rocketed straight for a palmetto bush, barking up a storm. Was he harassing another squirrel? She zoomed over to see and nearly collapsed in fear.

"Dad! Come quick!"

She tried tugging Blaze away from the creature, but he barked sharply. Dad ran up, breathing hard.

"Look!" Glenna pointed with a trembling finger.

Dad's eyes locked onto what made Glenna so scared: the biggest snake she'd ever seen.

"Ooh, a python is dangerous. Run and get my cell phone off the dresser."

"Don't let him eat Blaze!" she cried before dashing off.

Tearing inside, she screamed, "Blaze caught a python. Dad needs his cell."

"Protect the twins," Grandpa yelled at Grandy. "I'll help Bo wrestle that monster."

Mom grabbed the portable and crossed the yard with Grandpa. Glenna swiped Dad's phone. Just as she reached the sliding doors, his cell rang. The screen said, "Restricted." She handed him the phone. Then she tried getting Blaze away from the invader. He just kept growling.

"This is Bo," Dad answered.

Glenna didn't listen in, turning her ears instead to Grandpa who called the wildlife office.

"A twelve-foot python is in my yard," he said. "You'd better hurry. The snake is starting to unwind, like it wants to slither into the water."

He hung up. Glenna heard Dad say into his cell, "Frank, make my flight for first thing in the morning."

He folded his phone, holding out his arm like he was saving her from the snake. Gregg ran up with Krystal.

"We were e-mailing Mason that Krystal's cutting her hair and donating the proceeds. What's the fuss?"

"A big snake." Mom herded them to the house. "Grandpa called the experts. Stay clear."

"We'll watch from the back door," Gregg said, puffing out his chest.

Dad took Mom aside. When her shoulders drooped, Glenna figured he must have told Mom he was leaving. Why did his job have to take him away with so much happening?

She turned to Krystal. "I want to cut my hair too. Grandpa can drive us to Zeke's."

"Your friend Mason is worse off than me," Krystal said, fingering her hair.

She really did have pretty hair now that it was washed. Before Glenna could tell her so, the snake experts barged around the corner carrying hooks and nets.

"Stay back, kids," Dad warned, joining them by the garage.

One snake catcher put his staff on the snake's head and grabbed him. The snake opened its mouth wide and began wrapping around the man's body. His assistant struggled to unwind the snake. Soon they stretched the beast out in the yard, but the snake twisted and turned.

Dad and Grandpa held open the cage door. The two men fought to stuff the snake inside. Once the door was closed and latched, they carried the caged reptile to their truck. When they drove away, Dad assembled them around the kitchen table.

"The excitement is over and I fly home in the morning. I'll ask Eva about the trial."

"Yeah, Dad. We are so ready to get home," Gregg said.

Krystal's lips sagged.

"Yer leavin' me?" She groaned.

Glenna touched her arm. "Pay no attention to my brother. We aren't going anywhere."

"Krystal, I'll check with our friend who is a Federal agent. She can help us search for Misty or the Fosters," Dad said, holding his cell phone.

The young girl burst into tears and ran from the room. Glenna started after her, but Grandy beat her to it. Glenna sat down, thrusting her elbows on the table.

"She'll be all right," Dad said. "Listen, Eva's agency seized the money on your cases."

"Does that help us?" Glenna turned to Gregg who rubbed his chin.

Dad smiled. "With her help, you might earn serious moiety for Mason's transplant."

Gregg pumped his fist. Tears burned in Glenna's eyes. Wouldn't that be incredible?

GLENNA WOKE EARLY the next morning. The first thing on her mind was that awful snake. She dashed to the window and checked, but didn't see anything. Still, she shivered just thinking of creepy, crawling reptiles. After their family meeting yesterday, Dad took them online to research pythons and boa constrictors.

She and Gregg were supposed to write about those snakes invading the Everglades and eating native birds. Last night, Mom had started working on Krystal's reading, which was pretty weak.

Glenna dressed and hurried into the kitchen to fix breakfast. She poured scrambled eggs into sizzling butter, toasted waffles, and cut up strawberries. Then she set the dining room table to accommodate the burgeoning family. Arranging Dad's plate, she realized life would be so different with him gone again.

Grandy squeezed oranges for juice.

"You and I make a great team in the kitchen," she said. "I'll miss you, sweetie."

"Please come visit us. You and Grandpa will want to see Mason after his transplant."

"What a wonderful idea. I'll speak to Buck about flying up soon."

The Rider clan sat around the dining room. Glenna focused her mind on taking Dad to the airport. Plus, she and Gregg had work planned for Blaze, their crime fighter. Mom shocked her back to the present.

"Glenna, will you say grace, please?"

She gulped. Praying in front of people was out of her comfort zone. Mom smiled so convincingly that Glenna closed her eyes. She talked to God as if he was right there with them, ending with a plea for Mason.

Dad opened his eyes, giving her a wink. Grandpa dug into his eggs.

"Guys are bringing their classic Chevys and Mustangs to the car show. Bert's driving over in his '36 Ford coupe. Sorry you won't be here, Bo, with your Austin-Healey."

"I have an important conference. Business types are coming from Asia."

Glenna peeked at Mom, but she shook her head. No problem.

When Glenna had Dad to herself, she'd ask about that North Korean money. All too quickly, breakfast was over.

"I'll get the car," Grandpa announced, pushing back his chair.

Dad wiped a napkin over his mouth. "Buck, I'll get my bag."

"Better keep your hidden cash away from Blaze," Gregg said, laughing. "He'll find it."

Glenna's eyes darted to her brother. Did he know about the foreign currency? Dad was going to meet someone from Asia.

She jumped up, ready for their mission. Two thousand dollars down and one hundred and ninety-eight thousand to go. She felt like she'd pushed Grandpa's noodle a few inches up the hill. Would she ever reach the top?

36

In the airport terminal, Glenna hugged Dad close. He kissed the top of her head, promising to call after he talked with Eva. Before she knew it, the doors to the monorail opened and he hustled inside. She and Gregg waved good-bye. Blaze wagged his tail.

"That's my cue for a tall cup of hot coffee," Grandpa said, heading to the BK.

Gregg pulled a carry-on suitcase behind him. Glenna and Blaze joined him in the ticket line.

She whispered to Blaze, "Let's go to work. Where is it?"

Blaze put his nose close to suitcases. Glenna chatted with waiting travelers about their destinations and even the Tampa Bay Buccaneers until her throat felt dry like cotton. For all her talking, Blaze never alerted. Gregg flopped into a chair.

"My feet hurt," he grumbled.

Glenna didn't want to admit their outing was a bust.

All she said was, "Blaze is tired too."

They joined Granddad in the BK where he bought them burgers and shakes for lunch.

"Is Blaze getting old?" Gregg asked. "He's forgetting how to search."

Glenna set down her shake. "Wrong. Not everyone hides money in foreign countries."

"What do you think, Buck?"

Glenna rolled her eyes. Her brother shouldn't use Grandpa's nickname behind Mom's back. But Grandpa didn't seem to mind. He folded his newspaper.

"I think after Blaze rests, you should try again. I'm happy to sit here and people watch."

Glenna tossed out her wrapper and cup. She took Blaze outside to do his business, using a plastic bag to clean up. After returning to the departure area, she found Gregg back in line with his carry-on, his orange tape, and notebook. Glenna gave Blaze his go-to-work command.

He walked to the front of the line, never stopping. Glenna grew tired of talking to people. A terrible thought plagued her. Had Blaze lost his touch? Gregg changed to the back of the line and Glenna shuffled there also. Blaze's tail hung limp.

Gregg kicked at his carry-on. "We'll never help Mason if we don't find something."

"Let's try one more time for his sake."

"Come on, Blaze," she whispered. "Help Mason. Where is it?"

Blaze sniffed a bag of a man talking on a cell phone.

Nothing was found. The dog smelled onward while Gregg remained in his spot. Glenna neared the front when Blaze stopped by a black suitcase, its owner clad in blue jeans and a leather jacket.

"Is he your service dog?" the middle-aged man asked Glenna.

"Blaze is a therapy dog."

To Glenna's delight, Blaze sat and stared at the man's bag.

"What's he smelling for?"

"Perhaps he is hungry," she replied with a smile.

In a low voice, she commanded, "Do you smell food, Blaze? Show me."

Blaze sat still but started whining.

The traveler chuckled wickedly. "He's smart. He knows I packed doggie bones in there."

"Oh really," she said.

The man was a smart currency smuggler pretending to have doggie bones.

"I'm visiting my niece in Seattle. I always bring her Labradoodle doggie bones."

"Does he have food, Blaze? Show me."

At Blaze's low growl, Glenna's spirits soared. Her dog hadn't forgotten. Gregg hurried toward them, orange tape hidden in his hand. Quickly stepping by Blaze, he knocked over and then righted the black suitcase, slapping orange tape on the side.

The man folded his arms. "I thought your dog was nice until he growled."

Gregg took the leash, nudging Blaze to the rear of the line.

"Wait," the traveler said, unzipping the bag. "Maybe he is hungry."

The man pulled out a plastic baggie and handed Glenna two doggie bones. "Your dog worked hard to find these."

Glenna slipped the bones into her jeans pocket. She wouldn't reward Blaze for failure. "Thanks, but if I give him these, he won't eat his dinner."

Gregg extended both hands palms up as if asking, "What now?"

Glenna couldn't decipher the facts. Did this guy have money in his bag? He probably stuffed doggie treats in there to confuse search dogs. He might be flying to a bank in the Bahamas or South America.

To learn more, she stayed with him asking about Labradoodles. They reached the agent and he handed over his ticket.

"Good morning, Mr. Earp. Just one bag going with you to Seattle?"

"Righto."

The man was weird but for real. Flying to see his niece, he wasn't leaving with cash.

"Mister, thanks for the doggie bones," Glenna said. "Have a nice trip."

That snake had messed up Blaze's power to smell. Confused, Glenna stomped over to Gregg and Blaze.

"What's going on? Does he have money in his suitcase?"

Her brother's twenty questions didn't help her to think.

"Mr. Earp is flying to Seattle. Blaze probably alerted to food."

She showed Gregg the doggie bones and then hurried to a trash can. She tossed in both bones with a vengeance. She looked back at Blaze and shook her head.

"No treats for false alerts." Glenna thrust her hands on her hips. "Let's find Grandpa. We're done."

TWO WEEKS PASSED SINCE the failed airport trip. In Gregg's opinion, Grandpa's house was too crowded. Between their homeschool classes and Grandy helping Krystal learn about living in the house, everyone was getting in everyone else's way. He hatched an escape plan.

Shoving on Grandpa's earphones, he trooped to Skeleton Key, trusty Klondike at the ready. Glenna was knitting caps for cancer victims. She and Krystal had cut their hair short, donating the rest for women with cancer to make wigs, or so Glenna had told him. The bake sale and Car Club event had netted nine hundred dollars.

Big deal.

Gregg kicked a stone on the dirt drive leading to the dock. He had to raise more money for Mason. Gregg stopped in his tracks. There was *Making Mischief,* tied up. His senses pulsed on high alert. Things seemed quiet, like no one was around. Still, he'd never forget Cain's dire warnings to keep out of his way.

Gregg thought of Krystal's tale of Cain selling Misty to drug runners. He shrugged. The young girl probably had mixed it up. He waved Klondike across the ground and listened for a tone. Gregg meandered toward the water, ready to find a treasure.

The alarm blasted his ears.

"Wow!" he cried. Maybe he'd find gold coins or a pirate's saber. He thrust his scoop in the ground and shook it, dirt falling through the strainer. He found a dirty coin. Excited, he wet his finger and rubbed the surface. Before his eyes the words *fifty cents* appeared.

Gregg squinted at the date. *1953.* This must be an antique, left by early settlers. Possibly someone had carried a chest full of fifty cent pieces from the water to a waiting horse cart. When he got home, he'd ask Grandpa. After securing the coin in his pocket, he adjusted the earphones, continuing to search. But he heard no more tones.

Gregg trod near the water's edge. He swung his halo stick back and forth, desperate to find more coins. Close to *Making Mischief,* he spotted something unusual. Suitcases were stacked at the top of the gangplank leading to the boat's deck. He whistled.

"There must be fifty of them," he said under his breath.

All those suitcases should mean people, but he saw no one. Gregg swept with his detector along by the dock and turned right. A loud tone blared in his ears. He passed Klondike over a leather boot with metal lace eyelets.

Gregg was shocked to see a foot in the boot and then a leg above the foot. He looked up in horror. A man with a goatee glared down at him. Gregg ripped off the earphones.

"You're the kid from that stupid kayak. I *never* forget a face."

Gregg stumbled backwards. He recognized *Mischief's* captain. He was the angry man who'd yelled at him and Mason in the kayaks. This must be Cain.

"Now you're trespassing on my land." Cain strode closer.

Greg opened his mouth to speak, but he couldn't even talk.

"The last time I saw you, I warned you. I'll make you into fish food yet."

Fear stabbed Gregg. His legs wouldn't go. He gripped Klondike, terrible thoughts running through his addled brain. *Will he sell me to Colombians? I should've brought Blaze.*

Cain reached to grab Gregg, but Gregg ducked. He spun around, fleeing to the road. Heavy boots gained on him. He ran full speed, his heart pumping mega rams of blood. Would he make it to Grandpa's house in time? He looked back. Cain was gone. Had Gregg only imagined the footsteps?

He slowed, checking back in case Cain sneaked out from between some houses. In minutes, he flew up Grandpa's drive. Glenna and Krystal were parking bicycles after their ride.

"Where have you been?" Glenna demanded.

"That Skeleton Key guy chased me, but I beat him here. He's mean as a gator."

Krystal's eyes bulged. "You met Cain?"

Still huffing, Gregg nodded.

"Yer lucky to be alive. Cain hit Misty and chases me off his land."

"He's piled up dozens of suitcases," Gregg said, leaning over to catch his breath.

Glenna put down the kickstand to her bike. "Does he run a business there?" she asked Krystal.

"Misty said he's a crook. He takes people into the Gulf to party."

Gregg wiped his face. "From all those suitcases, he must keep partiers out for weeks."

"Nope." Krystal shook her head. "They head back before morning. Misty served food and drinks on the *Mischuf*."

Gregg could finally breathe normally. "There's fifty suitcases on deck, but no partiers."

"Oh no!" Krystal cried.

Gregg whirled around to see if Cain lurked behind him.

"What's wrong with you?" Glenna demanded.

Gregg pointed at Krystal. "She cried 'Oh no!' I thought he was sneaking up on me."

"Nah." Krystal shook her head. "When he hauls suitcases, he don't want no one around. Not me or Misty. He made us leave."

Glenna pulled on Gregg's sleeve. "With Mason, we saw the mule hauling suitcases."

Krystal's arm started shaking and her bike fell over. She picked it up.

"First they come in vans," she said, looking scared. "Then the mule hauls them cases on the dirt path to the boat."

Gregg's mind turned. "When he loads the suitcases, does he leave for days or overnight?"

"Overnight. If he's got cases, he's leavin' tonight."

Gregg stared at his sister, detecting a glimmer of adventure in her eyes.

"Are you thinking what I am?" she asked Gregg.

Gregg marched to the front door, calling over his shoulder, "Yeah. We have work to do."

37

The setting sun painted the sky orange, but Gregg paid no attention. He crept under the palmetto cluster, upset he was so late. Before he could walk Blaze to the Key, Mom had made him wash Grandpa's car. Glenna had to read Krystal a chapter about Misty, a wild horse. When the girl started sobbing, Gregg knew it was time to launch out.

Glenna joined him and Blaze beneath the palmetto.

"Stay here, boy," she whispered.

Blaze did sit, but not before sighing. Gregg focused his eyes on Cain's compound.

"I see a white van," he said. "No one's in sight."

Glenna patted Blaze's head. "If Mom knew of our surveillance, she'd go crazy. What did Grandpa say when you told him we were heading to Skeleton Key?"

"To call if we needed him. He's standing by."

Gregg thumped the pocket where he'd stowed the cell phone. A scurrying noise got Blaze whimpering. Glenna poked her head around the palmetto.

"I don't see anything."

"Me neither."

Gregg hunkered down, listening to noisy seagulls calling overhead. Then he heard an engine sputtering.

"The mule's coming," he hissed. "Make sure Blaze doesn't give us away."

Glenna spoke quietly in Blaze's ear. Two men whizzed by on the mule. Neither of them was Cain. Gregg prodded Glenna's arm.

"Look! They're stopping at the van."

"What should we do?"

"Wait. They're turning off the mule's engine." Gregg rose to his knees. "One guy's in a Red Sox jacket. A beefy guy's in a crummy t-shirt. They're lifting suitcases from the van onto the road."

Glenna scooted to better see. "I don't like how fast the sun's going down."

"The dock's lights just turned on. The guys are loading suitcases … about twelve onto the mule. Red Sox is starting the engine. He's driving the mule toward the yacht."

"Is the t-shirt guy staying by the van? Where's Cain?"

"I think Cain's loading the yacht. The beefy guy is guarding suit-cases by the van."

"Let's go see if we can spot Misty," Glenna said, her voice hushed.

Brother and sister snuck from the bushes and walked Blaze to the van. The beefy man watching the cases lit a cigarette. He blew smoke in the air and turned as Blaze's nose reached the suitcases.

Gregg waved. "Hi. How are you tonight?"

The guard grunted and smoked his cigarette.

"My sister and I love walking our dog down this road. He looks for snakes."

"La vibora!" Mr. T-shirt tossed down his cigarette.

Glenna stooped over Blaze, whispering, "Tell me, where is it?"

Blaze sniffed the suitcases on the ground. To distract the guard so he didn't realize Blaze's true purpose, Gregg pointed to *Making Mischief.*

"That's a nice boat. Do you live on it?" he asked.

"No, I make delivery."

In spite of his Spanish accent, Gregg understood his English okay. He kept an eye on Blaze, who stared at the bags.

Glenna said to Blaze more forcefully, "Show me. Where is it?"

Blaze dipped his head and growled. The guard waved his arms.

"No dog around de bags."

Vrroom. Vrroom.

At the sound of the returning mule, the guard shook his head wildly.

"You escape, quick."

Gregg didn't have to be told twice.

"Forget Blaze looking for snakes," he told Glenna with a wink.

She pulled the leash. Blaze gave another deep growl before turning to leave with her.

Gregg tossed a friendly wave. "Nice talking to you."

"Hasta la vista," Mr. T-shirt called back.

Glenna jogged alongside Blaze, who swiveled his head like he wanted to go back to his find.

"We'd better hurry and tell Grandpa. I've never seen Blaze so anxious," Glenna said.

"Okay, but I'm calling Secret Observers first."

They rushed home. Blaze strained at the leash. Gregg's feet pounded the dirt, excitement building in his chest. He hurried in the side door and darted to the den. With Glenna tiptoeing behind, he punched in Secret Observers' number. Tail wagging, Blaze lifted his nose.

"Good boy, Blaze." Glenna held a doggie bone in her hand.

A voice answered, but Gregg's heart pounded so loud in his ears, he couldn't hear. He pressed the phone against his ear, crushed to realize he'd reached a recording.

"Secret Observers cannot take your call. Leave a message at the tone."

"It's a recording," he hissed and then cleared his throat to leave a message.

"This is … I mean, my code number—"

Beeep.

He hung up and tried again, saying, "The yacht, *Making Mischief*, is docked at Skeleton Key. It's loaded with suitcases full of money. It's lea—"

Beeep chimed again in his ear.

"What's happening?" Glenna insisted.

Blaze started whining.

Grandy called out, "Is that you, Gregg and Glenna? Dinner's ready."

Gregg redialed as fast as his fingers could punch. The phone rang once. Then the recording clicked on for him to leave a message. He was ready to talk when something terrible happened. A voice announced: "Mailbox full."

Beeep.

His heart contracted.

"We're toast," was all he said.

Glenna took off the leash. "We tried."

She left with Blaze sniffing behind her. A burning desire not to give up drove Gregg to the dining room. He'd been so sure he could give Secret Observers a hot tip about the suitcases being loaded with cash. But reaching voicemail after voicemail and being shut down by a full mailbox made him feel like his brain could explode.

He plunged to the table like a boxer about to fight in the ring. Every seat was occupied but his. Every eye trained on his face.

"Get over here and sit down."

Grandpa sounded so much like Dad that Gregg instantly sat. Grandy uncovered a large dish of chicken pieces asking Glenna to pray the blessing. Gregg bowed his head, but his eyes didn't want to close.

"Dear God," his sister said, "We thank you for the food and ask you to bless it. Amen."

"What's going on?" Mom asked. "You're not praying for Mason anymore."

Glenna's lips parted, showing her teeth. "Oh, I forgot."

Gregg's heart pounded. Glenna bowed her head and this time Gregg closed his eyes.

"Dear God, I forgot about Mason's sickness. Our friend needs healing. You know what else he needs too. Please help him. You love him more than we ever could. Amen."

Glenna wiped her eyes and Gregg passed around a platter of potatoes. He didn't feel like eating.

Instead, he gazed out the window for any sign of the white van speeding off Skeleton Key. No traffic went by. He switched to the picture window overlooking the Intracoastal Waterway. Sweat rimmed his forehead.

What should he do? *Making Mischief* could be passing Grandpa's dock right now, steaming for the Gulf. Adrenaline pushed him to tell. He pushed away his uneaten plate.

"Listen. Blaze alerted to currency in suitcases being loaded on the *Mischief*," he said. "I think Cain is hauling cash out of the country."

"You should've called me," Buck snapped, his fork swaying in midair. "How many?"

Gregg's eyes caught Glenna's, but she toyed with her chicken leg, saying zip. Gregg did some quick math.

"Between the ones I saw on the boat deck and the ones being hauled from a van to the boat, about a hundred."

Grandpa dropped his fork. "How much money was hidden in the luggage Blaze found at the airport? The ones seized in Miami?"

"Three hundred thousand, and in another, one hundred and twenty thousand," Glenna answered, her eyes shifting.

"Okay." Grandpa tapped a finger on the table as if adding. "Say there's three hundred thousand dollars in each of *Mischief's* cases and Cain has one hundred of 'em."

He gazed upward. Using his finger like multiplying on an imaginary calculator, Grandpa whistled sharply. "That's thirty million dollars!" he bellowed.

"Buck, I just phoned Secret Observers. Their mailbox is full. I can't leave a message!"

Mom frowned at Gregg. "Do not call your grandfather Buck."

"We have bigger problems." Grandpa wagged his finger. "Course those bags could belong to the folks Cain takes out to gamble."

"Nope." Krystal shook her head.

Everyone turned toward her.

"Cain don't let nobody on the boat with that many bags. The men helpin' him have guns. They sneak the cases out into the Gulf at night."

Grandpa plugged his nose. "There's something rotten in Denmark."

"They're taking the *Mischief* to Denmark?" Glenna asked, sounding confused.

"That's an old saying," Mom said. "Your grandpa means something is wrong."

Grandpa folded his arms across his chest. "Who else can we call?"

"I'll try their number again." Gregg didn't know what else to do.

"Dad might know," Glenna said.

Gregg started up to phone him, when Glenna lifted her chin. "If they seize thirty million dollars, we should get more than a thousand for reporting it."

Grandpa pushed his chair back and stood up. "More importantly, I don't want criminals making hay down the street on Skeleton Key."

"What can we do?" Grandy's eyes clouded with worry.

Grandpa headed for the door. "I'm lowering *Pollywog* in the water. I'll track Mister Cain if he heads to sea before Gregg finds help."

He stopped walking. "Glenna, you and Krystal walk Blaze down to the Key. Check if the *Mischief* is still there."

"I'm not sure this is a good idea. I'm coming along." Mom launched out of her chair.

"Too many people will raise unwanted attention," Grandpa replied.

Mom cupped a hand under her chin as if debating. "You kids didn't tell me you were going down there," she finally said.

Gregg shook his head. "We told Grandpa."

Mom shot Grandpa a hurt glance. He simply shrugged.

"Dad and I taught you kids to act right," she said. "I don't know."

Glenna touched her shoulder. "Mom, we should help Krystal find Misty."

Krystal's eyes teared up. "Cain knows where she is."

"Okay, but take Blaze and your cell phone."

"Don't go near Cain or the *Mischief*," Grandpa ordered. "Just see if she's there and hurry back."

With Glenna and Krystal heading to eyeball *Making Mischief*, Gregg darted off to call Secret Observers. If they didn't pick up this time, he was calling Dad like Glenna suggested.

38

Glenna hiked with Krystal to Skeleton Key in the dark. Armed with a flashlight and cell phone, the whole episode seemed right out of a spy movie. Blaze trotted with his head held high as if aware he should protect them. Glenna's arm swished against a plastic bag popping out of her jean pocket.

She was prepared in case Blaze left evidence in someone's yard. City lights ended and trees shrouded the road. Glenna understood the dangers Krystal must have faced when she'd slept outside. At least she had a home for the time being.

Krystal slowed. "Watch out. We're crossin' the bridge."

"In the moonlight, I see tree trunks, but not much else. I won't turn on the flashlight unless we have to."

They crept over the short bridge in silence, reaching Cain's place. Glenna heard voices in the distance. A car door slammed.

Krystal jerked Glenna's arm and they ducked inside a palmetto bush. Its giant fan-shaped fronds surrounded them. Krystal dug into Glenna's arm.

"I hid here at night."

"Were you scared? I would've been."

Glenna peered between the branches. Seeing shadows moving around, she was growing afraid of the unknown.

"I got used to it," Krystal whispered. "Being hungry is worse."

An engine fired up in the distance. Two headlights roared toward their palmetto bush. Glenna pulled Blaze deeper into the bush.

"Sit," she directed and held her breath.

The white van crawled by at a turtle's pace. Just as Glenna dared to exhale, the van came to a stop. White back-up lights flashed on and the van backed up. Glenna clapped a hand over her mouth so she wouldn't scream. Had the driver spotted them or Blaze moving in the bushes?

Krystal crouched as if used to living in secret. Seconds passed. What should they do? Glenna felt Blaze's back tremble beneath her hand. He was getting ready to attack.

With no warning, the van's white back-up lights went out. The men drove off. Glenna breathed. As she stood up, Krystal yanked her down.

"It's not safe yet."

Loud voices echoed from Cain's house. Krystal knew how to hide.

"We have to creep closer and see if *Mischief* is still there," Glenna whispered.

"Not me. I hear Cain talkin'."

"Then the boat must be at the dock. Let's make sure."

Krystal needled Glenna's arm with her fingers. "Stay off the road."

The girls sneaked through the palmettos. Blaze kept his nose to the ground. Krystal stopped and held up her finger. From the direction of the bay, Glenna heard *blub-blub-blub-blub*.

"A boat engine," she said in a hushed voice.

They crept toward the sound with Blaze on guard, his nose leading. Glenna spotted a man walking on the gangplank, stepping aboard the *Mischief*, its lights on and engine running.

"They're about to leave. Hurry!"

She pivoted away from the dock, tugging on Blaze's leash. Once she and Krystal reached the bridge, they started running. They were halfway home when Blaze hit the brakes. *Woof!*

Glenna whirled. Was Cain running after them?

No one was there. Blaze smelled around until he found a suitable place and made a mess for Glenna's plastic bag. She cleaned up before they took off running again.

Finding Grandpa and Gregg sitting on the dock, her arms started flailing before she could form any words.

Krystal gasped for air but managed to say, "His engine's on."

"What?" Grandpa stood, knocking over his collapsible chair.

Glenna found her voice. "*Mischief's* engine is running. The van just left Cain's."

Her brother leapt up, his voice reaching a fever pitch.

"I can't reach Secret Observers! Dad won't answer!"

Grandpa shrugged, seeming quite calm.

"Too bad. I'd like to follow in the *Pollywog* and report on the *Mischief's* location."

Glenna's mind whirled like a giant computer.

"Let's phone Mrs. Montanna," she said.

Grandpa turned his head, peering off in the darkness of Boca Ciega Bay.

Krystal edged closer. "Who's Mrs. Mountain?"

"Mrs. *Montanna* will know what to do," Gregg said, pronouncing her name carefully.

"Who is Mrs. Montanna?" Grandpa insisted on knowing.

Blaze shoved his nose under Glenna's hand as if he agreed with her plan.

"Eva's with Homeland Security. She's the agent who asked Dad to adopt Blaze."

Gregg nodded. "When Blaze found counterfeit money, Eva knew who to call."

"Sshh!" Glenna said. "Listen!"

Blub-blub-blub-blub.

Glenna stared out into the dark bay. One red light shone behind the *Pollywog*, coming closer and bearing for John's Pass and the Gulf.

"That's gotta be Cain's boat," Gregg snarled.

Krystal nodded at the large boat passing. "When he has cases, he's meetin' other boats."

Grandpa took charge.

"Gregg, be quick. Tell Grandy and your mom we're taking *Pollywog* for a ride." He clicked the cell phone onto his belt, adding, "Bring your cell phone."

"I have ours!" Glenna called to her brother.

Gregg raced to the house taking an unwilling Blaze with him. Glenna and Krystal climbed aboard *Pollywog*. While Grandpa started the engine, Glenna strode to the stern. She listened to the bubbling of the engine exhaust. Gregg back ran toward the boat.

"Get those lines and throw 'em aboard," Grandpa yelled.

Gregg loosened the bowline, throwing it to Krystal. He ran to the aft end of the boat and grabbed the stern line. Holding one end, he jumped. Glenna was relieved when he landed safely aboard. She didn't even want to ask what Mom had said about their night flight.

Grandpa steered away from his dock. A hush fell over their boat.

"We risk being stopped by the marine patrol or Coast Guard," he said. "But I won't turn on the running lights. It could be bad if Cain notices us back here."

Then Glenna sneezed.

"Be quiet!" Grandpa commanded. "Sounds amplify over the water."

She put both hands over her mouth. Had she blown their cover? *Pollywog* eased along Eleanor Island in total silence. Grandpa turned left, headed toward John's Pass Bridge.

"See the light on the stern of that boat? That's Cain passing under the bridge, heading west into the Gulf. He's about to make some mischief, all right."

Gregg laughed. "I like your joke, Grandpa."

As Grandpa passed under John's Pass Bridge, entering the vast darkness of the Gulf, Glenna shuddered. They'd left the safety of land behind.

Grandpa tapped Glenna. "Call your mother and get Mrs. Montanna's phone number."

Glenna made the call, but Mom's voice mail answered.

"Mom! I need Eva's phone number. Grandpa says it's important."

Crushed at leaving a message, Glenna slumped in her seat. Then she remembered—she had entered Kaley Montanna's number in her contact list. She punched in Kaley's cell. Her voice mail came on too.

"Kaley, it's an emergency. We're following a boatload of currency. Blaze found more like at the Vault. We need your mom's help. Call ASAP."

Glenna hung up and sent Kaley a text, just in case. Her body sizzled with the danger that lurked in the darkness. Grandpa increased *Pollywog's* power, the boat shuddering as the bow rose. He pointed at *Mischief's* dim white light.

"Cain is traveling faster than we are."

Glenna peered across the water in the moonlight.

"His light's gone!" she shrieked.

Grandpa groaned. "You're right. He doesn't want other boats seeing him."

Pollywog charged forth in the darkness. Grandpa stood tall by the wheel, craning his neck and staring through the windshield.

"I see him, hazy like, in the moonlight," he hollered.

Glenna held up her cell phone. "Mom never checks her messages. I just remembered."

"Call the house!" Gregg cried. "They're getting away!"

Before she could call, her phone vibrated in her hand.

"Hello," she shouted.

"Glenna? This is Eva."

"Did you get my message to Kaley?"

"She showed me your text. What's this about a boat loaded with money?"

"Wait, I can hardly hear you."

Glenna ran to the rear, but the engine noise grew louder. She lunged for the bow. Knowing Cain was speeding away with the money, Glenna talked fast.

"Eva, Grandpa took us to the Tampa airport. Blaze alerted to cash in suitcases."

"How do you know money was found?"

"Gregg has a Secret Observers code and phones in tips. The cops found four hundred and twenty thousand dollars. We need rewards for Mason's cancer fund."

"Quickly, give me all the evidence about the boat with cash."

Glenna told Eva everything she knew about Cain Denton and *Making Mischief*. She added, "Blaze smelled currency on dozens of suitcases being loaded onto the boat."

"Your message said there's an emergency. Is that still true?"

"Yes. The suitcases are on the boat. *Mischief's* already in the Gulf. We're chasing her."

"You're chasing the boat? How can that be?" Eva yelled into the phone.

"Grandpa is skippering *Pollywog*. We're behind Cain in the Gulf. We're both running without lights."

"Let me talk to your grandfather."

"He's at the helm," Glenna said, dashing to Grandpa. "It's noisy, but here he is."

She handed him the phone. "Eva wants you."

"This is Buck. Cain Denton is the captain of the boat we're after. He's shut off his lights, but we're on his tail."

Silent for a moment, Grandpa steered the *Pollywog*.

"*Making Mischief*," he said loudly, "is a sixty-foot Hatteras. Cain motors her out to international waters for private gambling junkets. The kids' hunch is correct, or I wouldn't be flying along with my lights off. We could use help, if you have any influence."

Grandpa gave their exact location and his speed all the while nodding and steering.

"Eva, a young girl worked on the *Mischief*. She says Cain and crew have guns on board."

Krystal put her tiny hand into Glenna's.

"Misty ain't with Cain," she squeaked. "He takes no people when he's runnin'."

"I know. You told me." Glenna rubbed Krystal's hand.

She tried listening to Grandpa, but that proved difficult with Krystal chattering in her ear.

"Where'd she go then?"

Krystal's hand trembled in hers. Glenna realized this chase meant more than catching Cain. Both Mason and Krystal's futures depended on the outcome.

Please, God, help us succeed. Help us find Misty.

"Reach me at this number," Grandpa growled into the phone.

He handed Glenna the phone. "Eva is doing her agent thing and then is calling back."

39

Thirty minutes passed with Glenna pacing the boat, waiting for Eva's call. Grandpa kept up the chase, aiming *Pollywog* at a dark spot ahead. Finally, Glenna's phone whirled. She answered.

"Glenna," Eva shouted. "My people doubt the whole gambling boat loaded with suitcases scenario. Tell me about Blaze alerting at Tampa's airport."

"What do you need to know?" She rushed back to the bow.

"I'm at my computer," Eva said. "When did this happen?"

Glenna gave the date. "One man flew to Turks and Caicos and a woman traveled with three aluminum suitcases. Both were caught changing planes in Miami."

"Miami!" Eva said. "I've been looking in Tampa."

"Sorry. We spotted them here and told Secret Observers. No one acted in time."

Eva clicked on a keyboard. "Okay, three hundred thousand dollars seized on a tip from Secret Observers. Does that sound right?"

"Sure does." Glenna's cheeks flushed warm. "You should find one more."

More clicking and Eva said, "Here's one hundred twenty thousand dollars called in by Tampa's Secret Observers. Did Blaze find those bags?"

"You should see him work, Eva. He's tremendous."

"So, Blaze detected money in *Making Mischief's* suitcases the same way?"

"Of course! I told you!" Glenna yelled, sarcasm lacing her voice.

"I'm trying to convince people I don't know to take action and it's difficult. Give me to Buck."

Glenna rushed to the cabin, pleading, "Make her do something, Grandpa."

"Nothing much has changed," he told Eva. "We're further out in the Gulf, both running without lights."

He listened before telling Eva their exact location and speed. Grandpa flipped the phone to Glenna and in seconds pulled back on the throttle. Her neck snapped with the decline in speed. The engine quieted, *Pollywog's* bow dropping against the dark horizon.

"He's stopped."

"What?" Glenna squinted into the darkness.

"The *Mischief* is dead in the water. Cain's sitting out there with his lights off."

Gregg sauntered up with Krystal in tow.

"Why did we stop?" he asked.

"Eva is sending the Coast Guard and what she calls Homeland Security 'assets.' We sit here and float. See what happens next."

Grandpa folded his arms and then jumped up.

"You kids sit down, now!" he boomed.

"What's happening?" Glenna's heart fluttered like a leaf in a storm.

"*Mischief's* racing right at us!"

Fear rocketed through her body. Her scalp felt like it was on fire.

"Has he spotted us?" Gregg sounded scared too.

Krystal started blubbering, "Oh no. Get me outta here. He'll sell me to Colombians."

"Hunker down in the cuddy cabin. Kids, stay out of sight."

Grandpa rushed to the rear and plunged a fishing rod in a pole holder. He sat calmly.

"If he confronts me, you kids stay in the cuddy."

Seconds passed. Glenna ducked, chewing her lip. She put an arm around Krystal. "Act like you're in the palmetto and don't want Cain to find you. Jesus sees us out here."

"I forgot," Krystal whimpered. "He's watching me."

"Right, so we're safe."

Glenna lifted her head. The boat loomed larger, which meant Cain was coming. Panic nearly erupted, but Glenna tried believing what she'd just told Krystal. A searchlight pierced the darkness from *Mischief's* deck, the bright beam sweeping across the water.

"Stay down," Grandpa hissed.

Krystal and Gregg crawled on all fours. Glenna scrambled away from the door, blood pounding in her ears. The spotlight flooded the *Pollywog*. Glenna stifled a scream. Gregg peered up, but Glenna grabbed his arm.

"*Stay down.* Cain's a breath away. Grandpa knows what he's doing."

Glenna started praying that he would.

Grandpa called to them, "No matter what, keep outta sight."

He sounded worried. Vivid light reflected through the cabin's port-holes, making it seem like daytime and not the dead of night. Krystal panted and her arms shook. Glenna vowed Cain wouldn't take her. She'd kick and scream. Besides, Eva was sending someone. Soon, she hoped.

The *Mischief's* engine roared. When Cain drew close enough to hit *Pollywog*, his engine stilled.

A voice bellowed, "Ahoy there."

Glenna raised her head barely an inch. Grandpa stood, a hand resting on his fishing pole.

"Howdy," he said.

"What are you doing here with no lights?" the voice demanded.

"That's Cain," Gregg hissed.

Shaking her head, Glenna pressed a finger against her lips.

"Fishing," Grandpa replied. "Need something?"

Cain shouted, "Yeah. To find out why you're following me."

"I told you, I'm fishing. Why should I follow you when I can be catching some nice eatin' fish? Times are tough, you know. I eat what I catch."

That should convince Cain. But what if it doesn't? Where's Eva's team?

Glenna squirmed, willing Cain to take Grandpa's word and leave.

"You followed me from John's Pass."

"True enough," Grandpa admitted. "I came out of the Pass, but only to my favorite fishing spot. There was nobody ahead of me. At least I saw no other lights."

The *Mischief* circled around *Pollywog*, shining its beacon into the cuddy cabin. The tiny cubicle filled with light. Glenna cringed. Would the light give them away? She nudged Gregg.

"Pull in your feet."

The phone vibrated in her pocket. She didn't dare answer.

Will gunshots ring out, leaving three orphaned kids? Grandpa, be careful.

Her heart pounded with each terrible thought.

"Keep away," Cain growled like a junkyard dog. "Or the fish will be catching you."

Gregg poked Glenna. "He warned me that I'd be fish food."

The cuddy turned dark. *Making Mischief* pulled away, its wake rocking *Pollywog*. Glenna's stomach reeled and for the first time ever on a boat, she felt sick. She tried breathing in deep and did feel steadier. Grandpa strode into the cuddy.

"That was close. The Coast Guard better arrive soon or Cain will get off scot-free."

"Someone called, but I was too afraid to answer."

"Check and see who called. Quick!"

Glenna whipped out the phone, looked at the number, and hit redial.

"Is that you, Glenna?" Eva asked. "I need Buck."

Glenna thrust him the phone. He wasted no time filling Eva in.

"That Cain fella nearly rammed my boat and threatened me." Grandpa waited and said, "I think he saw us following on his radar. I tried convincing him I was fishing. He just left."

"Oh that's good," he said with a nod. "When?"

His far-off look out the windshield made Glenna wonder. Was Eva sending anyone?

"Cain's headed northwest," he told Eva. "He's flying along at about twenty knots."

Grandpa bent down and peered into the darkness. "Hold on, Eva."

He ran out of the cuddy cabin to the port side. Glenna folded her sweating hands, wishing she was anywhere but in Cain's sights.

Soon Grandpa hurried back in telling Eva, "I see the shape of a big ship, much larger than the *Mischief*, sitting about six miles away in total darkness. Cain is bearing straight for her."

"Eva, my radio's on," Grandpa said, reaching for the marine radio.

Then he turned his head, checking off *Pollywog's* stern. "I see nothing on the water or in the air. We'll keep our eyes open."

Grandpa hung up, motioning for Gregg, Krystal, and Glenna to draw around his chair.

"Are you all okay?"

"Wow, Grandpa," Gregg said, his voice rising. "I thought Cain was going to get us."

"Me too." Glenna finally dared to breath.

Krystal leaned against Grandpa's arm. "You and Jesus saved me."

Grandpa adjusted his marine radio, which so far had been very quiet. "Eva says to stay here like we're fishing."

40

"What's happening?" Glenna gazed past Grandpa's shoulder straining to see.

Sounds of a flying airplane erupted in the dark sky. *Thump-thump-thump* of a helicopter vibrated, its blades shaking the air over *Pollywog*. The low-flying chopper screamed right above their heads. Grandpa started the engine.

"We'll be ready to leave if things become rough."

Glenna pointed at a beacon beaming down on *Making Mischief* along the horizon.

"It's like the bright light from our nativity scene," she said in awe. "Only this light descends from the sky like it's lowered from the heavens."

"Cool!" Gregg shot to the bow. "The chopper's circling over *Mischief* and the big ship."

Grandpa put power to the *Pollywog*. She jumped forward in the water. He grinned. "With the police on the scene, we'll creep a bit closer."

As they sped forward, Gregg pulled back from the edge. Krystal stayed near Grandpa. Glenna clutched the railing. The marine radio crackled with voices.

"*Making Mischief, Making Mischief*! This is the U.S. Coast Guard. Get all hands on deck. I repeat. Get all hands on deck."

Grandpa pulled back the throttle and they coasted to a stop. He pointed northeast. Flashing blue lights raced from Clearwater toward the *Mischief* and the bigger ship Glenna knew was out there but hadn't really seen.

Gregg bounced on his toes. "Wow! I wish Dad could be here."

Glenna's eyes flickered like busy bees. She watched the airplane buzz over, the helicopter circle, and the lights blazing. It was the most amazing adventure she'd ever been on.

"It's pretty scary, though," she said.

Her brother playfully slugged her arm. "Remember the fighter jet exploding above our heads in Israel? You screamed bloody murder."

Well maybe she had.

"That was then and this is now," she snapped.

Cain breathing down their necks after taking Misty was more frightening. Could this race to catch Cain have some deeper meaning? Maybe she would become a Federal agent like Eva, striving for justice and nabbing the guilty. But did she have Eva's courage?

With God's help, I can. I will.

Krystal slipped her tiny hand into Glenna's, staring at the action.

"She's out there maybe."

Krystal's voice sounded so fragile against all the noise. Before Glenna could remind her how Cain didn't take people on these trips, the helicopter descended, stopping over the *Mischief*.

"Look! Men are sliding down ropes onto the deck from the chopper."

Glenna's eyes followed Grandpa's finger. Flashing blue lights burst from behind the *Pollywog*. Glenna spun around. Sirens blared. Police and Coast Guard boats thundered past, their waves tossing *Pollywog* from side to side. Glenna's spirits soared. She didn't feel sick at all.

Another chopper arrived from Clearwater, hovering close to the bigger ship, flooding its deck with intense light. More men slid down ropes onto the ship. Grandpa's gallery of spectators watched along the bow, *Pollywog* rocking in the waves.

Gregg elbowed Glenna's side. "Move. You're blocking my view."

"Ouch. I have every right to watch from here."

Grandpa tapped the back of Glenna's head.

"Don't complain. These are free seats. A few hours ago we never imagined such fun."

Glenna smoothed her hair, asking, "How much money is on the *Mischief*, do you think?"

"I'd say, conservatively, thirty million dollars."

"I don't think so," Gregg said.

"Oh no?" Glenna challenged. "How much do you guess, Mr. Smarty-pants?"

Gregg jerked his head up at the helicopter.

"All those agents are about to find one hundred suitcases full of doggie bones."

"What?" Grandpa fired.

Gregg thrust out his chest. "Yeah, like last time. Blaze alerted to doggie bones."

Grandpa shot Glenna a searing glance.

"Is it true?"

"Yes, but that bag probably had currency too. We didn't report it because the flight was going to Seattle and not leaving the country."

"Does Eva know Blaze's smeller locked onto doggie bones?"

Glenna licked her lips. Was she in trouble?

"No, I forgot. But those bones could have disguised money."

Grandpa held his stomach, laughing. "By now they've found millions of Blaze's treats."

He split for the cuddy cabin. The kids followed.

"Let's head home *before* the feds come searching for their Secret Observer."

He skillfully turned the boat. Glenna walked aft, her heart in her throat. As they raced for John's Pass, she blinked at the flashing blue lights and pictured a terrible headline in Grandpa's paper: *Police seize tons of doggie bones.*

Her ears burned. If Blaze had alerted in error and agents risked their lives, Blaze would be retired for good. Dad might force him to leave their house. Hot tears rolled down Glenna's cheeks and her knees wobbled. She had really messed up this time.

THE HOUSE WAS MOSTLY dark when Grandpa docked *Pollywog.* Glenna hopped down and helped Krystal, who was a nervous wreck.

"I could'a been on *Mischuf* with Misty," she kept repeating.

While Grandpa secured his boat, Glenna brought her to the bench seat and sat by her.

"But Misty couldn't be on Cain's boat with the cases. You said so many times."

Grandpa walked over. "I'll check on Misty in the morning. Will that help?"

Krystal nodded weakly.

"Once the sun comes up, I'm bringing Blaze to Skeleton Key," Gregg said, squaring his shoulders. "I'll take Klondike too. With Cain gone, we can hunt for valuable treasure."

"Let's go in," Glenna said. "I'm beat."

She and Krystal headed through the garage entrance. But she couldn't put the girl to bed on the couch. Mom had fallen asleep on the cushions, a calico quilt on her lap. Grandy shuffled into the kitchen in her robe and switched on the light.

Mom called out, "What kept you? Is everyone all right?"

"The Feds stormed onto Cain's boat," Glenna said, hoping Mom hadn't worried much.

She'd forgotten about leaving her a message.

"They probably seized tons of doggie bones."

Gregg's criticism further crushed Glenna's spirits. The morning news would be the end of everything good in her life.

"I'll make eggs and toast," Grandy declared, setting a pan on the stove.

Mom hurried in, rubbing her eyes. "Glenna, your message said you needed Eva's number. What's the emergency? Why didn't you call back?"

"You never answered." Grandpa wiped his forehead. "We were busy helping out."

He winked at Glenna. Krystal scampered to the gold bathroom, closing the door.

"Is something wrong with Krystal?" Mom asked.

"The Coast Guard boarded Cain's boat," Glenn said. "She's afraid it could have happened to her."

Grandpa toyed with his keys. "I'd like to find out if Cain's been arrested."

"I'm in," Gregg said, pulling on a ball cap. "But may I eat first?"

"Daddy, what are you planning?" Mom asked, setting bread in the toaster.

"An excursion to John's Pass with my grandkids. Want to join us?"

Glenna looked toward the bathroom. "Maybe you should stay with Krystal."

Mom poured milk into glasses, her lips pressed together as if deep in thought.

"Eat first, and Daddy," she fixed a keen eye on Grandpa, "call once you know *anything*."

She walked down the hall and knocked softly on the bathroom door, coaxing Krystal out. The girl dragged her feet into the kitchen.

"Grandy's cooking eggs. Are you hungry?" Glenna asked.

Krystal wiped her cheeks and took a seat. Mom sat beside her, talking low. Glenna buttered toast. Being a parent and knowing the right thing to do seemed hard. After eating, she found Blaze sleeping. Had his nose been right or was Glenna about to be grounded for life?

41

At three o'clock in the morning, Glenna piled in Grandpa's backseat. Gregg hopped up front. After crossing the bridge, Glenna spotted *Making Mischief* tied to the dock by Smugglers Cove. Police and Coast Guard boats surrounded the area, their blue lights no longer flashing.

Grandpa parked on the street. Glenna slid out, her heart racing.

"We stroll along the boardwalk and watch below. Don't get too close," he warned.

Looking down on the dock, Glenna felt a surge of adrenaline. Agents wearing bulletproof vests bustled around, carrying automatic weapons. Others loaded suitcases onto a large truck backed up to the dock. Glenna tapped her grandpa's shoulder.

"I don't think they'd guard doggie bones with guns, do you?"

Grandpa gripped her shoulder. "Excellent point. Me thinketh it's real money. And you?"

"Me thinketh it's really money too."

She giggled, feeling so relieved. Blaze was her mighty hero.

Several armed agents hauled suitcases off the boat. An agent wearing a jacket with ICE letters stood by the cases. Glenna watched him type into a small computer, which spit out a label. Another ICE agent stuck labels on the suitcases before they were put in the truck.

"Maybe that ICE agent knows Eva," Gregg said.

Glenna smiled. "But he has no orange tape like you bring to the airport."

Gregg whacked her upper arm with a wide grin. Grandpa sauntered over to a middle-aged man leaning on the dock's railing. Glenna scooted behind, curious what this man might know about the raid. In the eerie light he resembled a lion, his hair bushy and eyebrows thick.

"What's the hubbub?" Grandpa asked as if he had no clue.

The onlooker raised a shaggy eyebrow at the Secret Observers' crew.

"A big arrest. I wonder why?" the lion rumbled as if on the prowl.

"I heard the choppers. My grandkids want to see police catch criminals."

"My scanner alerted me," the man said. "Cops were talking about chasing that boat."

Grandpa aimed a finger at the sleek yacht. "Who owns the *Mischief*?"

"I've seen her around and did some snooping." Mr. Lion shook his mane. "The owner lives in Jacksonville. His captain, Cain Denton, uses the boat for private poker parties, taking his victims out into international waters."

"Victims?" Dread pulsed through Glenna at what may have happened to Misty.

"Don't think the worst, young lady. I mean, card players often fall prey to sharks."

Gregg's eyes rounded. "Cain dumps the losers overboard?"

"Hmmph," Mr. Lion grunted. "Your grandkids have lively imaginations."

Grandpa narrowed his eyes at the man. "Why do you suppose the Coast Guard is after the *Mischief*? I don't imagine they're enforcing card playing."

"I heard the officers say the suitcases are full of money."

"You taking notes, kids? That could be tons of money."

"They caught a trawler stuffed with cocaine and took her to Clearwater." Mr. Lion raised a finger. "Look! There's Captain Cain."

Glenna gulped. Cain's hands were cuffed behind his back. Two agents in ICE vests hauled him off the *Mischief*.

"He doesn't look very tough," Gregg said.

Cain jerked up his head. He glared at the boardwalk railing. His eyes searched the people standing there. Like a laser, he shot venom at Gregg, mouthing something. Gregg darted behind Grandpa's back.

"What's he saying? Is he threatening my brother?" Glenna asked Grandpa.

Grandpa turned to Mr. Lion. "I think Cain's looking at you. Do you know him?"

Mr. Lion grunted and moved down the railing. Behind Cain, an ICE agent walked with another man wearing a Boston Red Sox jacket and handcuffs. Glenna nudged Gregg, who still played safe behind Grandpa.

She whispered, "We saw him on Skeleton Key. He loaded suitcases onto the mule."

"I'm glad we snuck out to the Key. Did you see Cain shoot me that 'I'll get you' stare?"

"Cain looked right at you, brother. We'd better call Dad."

"Yeah, first the counterfeiters and now Cain is after us."

"After *you*," Glenna corrected.

Grandpa cleared his throat. "I think Cain was checking out that other man."

"You mean Mr. Lion?"

Agents leading a third man to a black SUV caught Glenna's attention below. "Who is that guy in the funny hat?" she asked.

Grandpa leaned forward. "Beats me."

The guy was decked out in black pants, black jacket, and a military-style hat. He turned his face up to the railing and stared with steely eyes at the gawkers. Gregg jumped behind Grandpa again. An ICE agent shoved his hand on the military hat, stuffing that guy into the rear seat with Cain.

Grandpa drew Glenna and Gregg close.

"I don't like the way your Mr. Lion stepped away from us. Something's fishy."

The prisoners were driven away. A million questions seared Glenna's tired mind. Should she warn Dad about the scary look Cain flashed their way? Did the third man know Mr. Lion?

She saw Grandpa start talking to him again so she elbowed Gregg. They walked down to join them. Grandpa folded his arms across the railing.

"This started as a chase?" he asked.

"So I heard on my scanner."

Mr. Lion spiked fingers through his mane, making his hair stand on end. Glenna forced herself not to laugh.

"But one of them ICE agents," he pointed to the agent checking bags into the truck. "He told another agent they learned from a tip about the mischief Cain was making."

"He told your joke, Grandpa," Glenna quipped.

Her grandfather fired a "be quiet" look. Too late she realized she'd let it slip. Grandpa knew all about Cain and his boat. Mr. Lion must've heard her because he narrowed his eyes.

Glenna edged away. Down on the dock, the agents were busy locking the rear door of the truck with a padlock. A female ICE agent slapped a sticker on *Making Mischief*'s window.

"I think they're seizing the boat," Glenna said.

"Hmm." Mr. Lion nodded. "The Feds are taking the poor guy's boat to sell at auction."

Two Coast Guard officers boarded *Mischief*. A third officer loosened the mooring lines and threw them aboard. Engine running, the sleek yacht turned and headed under John's Pass Bridge.

"Where are they taking her?" Gregg asked.

"To Tampa where the Feds keep seized boats until they're sold. Too bad. Cain's probably lost everything."

Gregg yawned, but Glenna was curious about something.

"You know a lot about government seizures and how they work."

"Oh? You think so?" His bushy eyebrows shot up. "I learn by watching."

Glenna stared at Mr. Lion, wondering who he really was. She stepped close to him, extending her hand.

"I'm Glenna and my brother—"

Grandpa pulled her shirt, tugging her away.

"I hate to break up our party, but we need sleep. What say we head for home?"

He hustled them toward the car where Glenna stopped and folded her arms.

"Grandpa, we didn't get the lion man's name."

He unlocked the car door. "We don't want him knowing our names. I don't trust him."

"He seemed nice," Gregg grumbled.

"Get in before he sees our license number."

They all hopped in and Grandpa drove toward the bridge.

"Didn't you catch Cain looking up at him? The third man did too. Why haven't we seen him around these parts? I'd never forget that mane of hair."

Glenna ducked her head, steeped in worry. "What should we tell Krystal?"

"The truth. Our search for Misty has just begun."

Grandpa turned into their neighborhood, but Glenna stared out the back window. She had a weird feeling they were being followed.

THE NEXT MORNING, Gregg's feet hit the floor. He dressed quickly, finding Grandpa poring over the newspaper. Gregg rushed to Glenna's room.

"Rise and shine," he chirped. "Grandpa already ran down and bought the late morning edition of the paper."

Glenna tossed on her robe and dashed with Gregg to the kitchen. Krystal stumbled in too.

"Our entire Secret Observers crew is here," Grandpa said. "Let's find out the skinny."

"Who's Skinny?" Krystal fingered her shorter hair.

Grandpa ruffled the pages of the newspaper. "Skinny means 'what's happening.'"

Fuming at Krystal for distracting Grandpa, Gregg urged, "What about Cain?"

Grandpa took a swig of coffee before looking up.

"That trawler we spotted out in the Gulf is the *Grey Shark*. She's the mother ship for carrying cocaine. The *Shark* distributes drugs to smaller boats like Cain's all along the Gulf coast. Recognize anyone?"

He lowered the newspaper. Glenna and Krystal peered over Gregg's shoulder.

"That there is Cain," Krystal said. "Why's he in the paper?"

"It's him!" Gregg shrieked.

Glenna pulled the paper to her eyes. "Mr. Lion was arrested?"

"Correct. Sinbad Brown is Cain's accomplice." Grandpa lifted his chin. "Gregg, you thought he was nice."

"I did, but Grandpa Buck, who's this third man? I can't even pronounce his name."

Grandpa took back the paper. "The reporter says he's thought to be an agent from Iran."

"Whatever that means?" Gregg said.

"He's with Iran's CIA, silly." Glenna pumped her fist. "We caught a spy!"

"I am proud of you both." Grandpa said. "It must be the government of Iran is sending their spies to Colombia to be smuggled here along with drug shipments."

Grandpa pointed to his newspaper. "Okay, seven Colombian citizens, the Iranian agent, and one U.S. citizen were arrested aboard the *Grey Shark*. ICE agents seized eleven tons of cocaine."

Krystal hung her head. "Misty got herself strung out on crack."

"I'm sorry for you and your mother."

Grandpa lowered the paper and said gently, "Krystal, Misty Harper is the American who was arrested."

"No!"

Her hands flew to cover her ears. Breaking into sobs, Krystal ran from the room. Glenna tore after her.

"Cain lied to that young girl," Grandpa said. "Misty never disappeared in a sinkhole."

"Yeah, poor kid." Gregg slumped on the chair, thrusting his chin into his hands.

Mom scurried into the kitchen. "Why is Glenna chasing Krystal?"

"You might want to sit down."

Grandpa motioned to a chair, but Mom remained standing.

"What happened?"

"Krystal's mother was arrested on a Colombian ship. Blaze alerted to suitcases out on Skeleton Key. We followed Cain's boat and Eva called in the Feds. Your kids, my grandkids, are heroes."

Mom dropped to a chair. "So Misty truly abandoned Krystal. She's on a foreign ship while her nine-year-old daughter lives in palmetto bushes."

"You are my daughter and I'm asking you, what are we going to do about it?"

Grandpa folded his newspaper. Tears flowed down Mom's cheeks.

"Bo planned to ask Eva about Krystal's family in Michigan," she replied, drying her eyes with her hand. "But he's just returned from the overseas conference. I may call Eva myself."

Gregg drummed his fingers on the table.

"Good thinking," he said. "Dad would want us to find the Fosters in Michigan."

Mom pulled a tissue from her pocket.

"That is easier said than done," she said, dabbing her eyes. "Krystal said they moved."

Glenna hurried up to the table with the cell phone. "Mom, don't wait any longer to find Krystal's family. You need to call Dad."

Mom took the phone and Gregg felt a twinge of pride in his sister. Guess he couldn't accuse her of being a crybaby anymore. Still he wondered. He cared what happened to Krystal, but did he share Glenna's deep interest in helping her find her family?

He turned his ear to Mom, but it sounded like she had to leave a message for Dad.

Gregg reached for Grandpa's paper, opening to the page with the Iranian's picture. Had they really caught a foreign spy? He rubbed his chin. Maybe it was something he could ask Dad about. He knew plenty of agents and what was going on around the world.

Then he came up with a better idea.

"Mom, can we call Mason? I want to tell him the good news."

42

Late the following afternoon, Gregg tugged on a chew toy while Blaze pulled on the other end. He thought of his phone conversation with Mason last night. He'd sounded weak but very interested in the Iranian spy being caught.

The phone rang on Grandpa's desk.

Gregg dropped the toy and rushed to answer. Dad was finally calling.

"Dad! We have so much to tell you."

"I heard, Gregger. Can you put Buck on the phone? I'll wait."

Gregg hustled to the living room where Grandpa had his nose stuck in the newspaper.

"Dad needs to talk with you."

Grandpa shoved aside his paper and headed for the den. Mom and Glenna bustled in the front door with packages. Gregg tilted his head toward Grandpa's back.

"Dad's on the phone."

"Where is Krystal?" Glenna asked. "Maybe he has some news about Misty."

Gregg shot for the den, calling over his shoulder, "Peeling potatoes in the kitchen."

As Grandpa picked up the phone, Gregg crowded around with Mom and Glenna.

"Bo, your family's here in the den. I'll put you on speaker."

Dad chuckled. "Sounds like a great plan. Hi, everyone."

"Hi, Dad!" Gregg and Glenna chimed.

"Bo, did you get my voice mail?" Mom asked.

"Sure did, and I spoke with Eva just briefly."

"Where are you calling from?" Grandpa asked.

"Sorry, I can't say."

Glenna lifted an eyebrow at Gregg. "He's going after Iran's spy."

Gregg shook his head. He'd rather listen to Dad than Glenna's ideas.

"I'm calling to learn what mischief my kids and their Grandpa Buck have been into."

Grandpa winked. "We haven't been into *mischief*, but we were after the *Mischief*."

"Say again. You confused me."

"Bo, I couldn't help the play on words. What have you heard?"

"Eva called. She said you and the kids led to the arrest of an entire drug smuggling operation. She said Blaze discovered it."

"Yahoo!" Gregg high-fived his sister.

"Great job, you two," Dad said, his voice ringing as if really proud. "I have good news to share."

Grandpa leaned toward the phone. "We're all ears."

"Eva is amazed. ICE is still counting the seized money. They have counted … drumroll, as Gregg says … they have one hundred *million* and they're still not done."

A cheer went up in the den.

"Wow!" Gregg whooped, jumping off the ground. "Mischief boogie board, here I come."

His brain clouded with doubt. Did he really want one after Cain's illegal deeds on the *Mischief*?

"Our kids are wonderful," Mom said, her eyes beaming. "Blaze too."

At the sound of his name, Blaze careened from around the corner, joining the festivities with a loud *woof*. They all laughed, including Dad over the speakerphone. Glenna darted off, bringing back a doggie bone.

"Good boy, Blaze. This is for being so smart."

She gave him the bone, which he ate in one bite.

"Here's the best part," Dad said. "Buck, do you know what moiety is?"

Buck shook his head. "Can't say I do."

"We do." Glenna looked at her brother.

Gregg pushed his way to the phone. "Dad, are we getting a reward?"

"Eva says to apply for moiety. Homeland Security could give you as much as a ten percent reward."

Grandpa turned pale. "Are you kidding?"

"How much money is that?" Gregg couldn't multiply such big numbers in his head.

"Buddy, that's over ten million dollars!" Dad hollered.

"Yeah!"

Glenna did a Snoopy dance around the den. Blaze barked and Mom shushed him. Gregg didn't understand how much ten million was, but it must be huge. Grandpa looked like he was in shock.

Glenna voiced what rolled around in Gregg's mind.

"Dad, if Eva pays us moiety, we could afford Mason's bone marrow transplant."

"Good thinking, Pumpkin. Eva will help us apply for the reward right away."

Mom reached for Gregg, giving him a hug. Then she asked, "Bo, how long does the process take? May I tell Mason's parents so they are able to plan?"

"I'll ask Eva. To know God has provided a way will lessen their anxiety."

Mom's face looked tense. "It will help Mason too. When I spoke to his mother last night, she said he's worried about them taking out another loan on the farm."

Glenna folded her arms. "Dad, you know Krystal has been staying here, right?"

"Is she in the room with you?"

"No, she's helping Grandy make dinner. Her mother was arrested on the *Grey Shark*."

Dad sighed. "That's tough. But it's good news she didn't die in a sinkhole."

"I agree," Mom broke in. "What if Misty is released? She might come take her away."

That silenced everyone. Gregg's celebration ended. They should do something before that happened. He scratched his head and listened to Dad.

"Julia, wasn't she once in the care of a Michigan family?"

"Yes, but the Fosters moved. And theirs is such a common last name."

"Listen, in Homeland Security's custody, Misty will head straight to jail."

Grandpa made a timeout sign with his hands. "Grandy and I want Krystal to stay here."

"Let's not be hasty," Dad cautioned. "Eva might learn more from Krystal's mom."

Gregg hadn't thought of that angle. Dad was smart. Mom turned to the others.

"How about letting me talk to Dad alone," she said.

"Honey, you and I do have a few things to sort out," Dad replied. "Buck, thank you and Sheryl for watching after my family. I hope your being on duty will be over soon."

Gregg hurried behind Grandpa out of the den. Glenna hung by the door, but Grandpa pointed to the kitchen. As she trudged off, Gregg pulled on his grandfather's arm.

"Misty is toast, but do you really want to raise Krystal as your own?" he whispered.

"Your Grandy and I heard what Pastor Brighton said about loving our neighbor. Krystal will miss you kids, but I'll teach her to fish. Grandy can help with her schooling."

Gregg swallowed. "Yeah, maybe she'd like riding to school in your classic car."

"Good thinking." Grandpa clapped him on the shoulder.

"I was wondering something else. Do you think I can call Mason and tell him about the ten million? Or should I wait for Dad to ask Eva?"

"We wait. After we eat, how about if you and I take *Pollywog* for a ride?"

"Yeah. Let's bring Blaze and Glenna. We should nose around Skeleton Key."

"But we can't go without Krystal," Grandpa said with a wink.

43

In her ICE office near the Washington Monument, Eva pressed the phone against her ear.

"Bo, you sound like you're in a tunnel," she complained. "Say again."

He shouted, "I'm at Dulles Airport about to park my Austin-Healey. I said, when you told us to adopt Blaze, I had no idea my kids would discover his searching abilities."

"Me either." She chuckled.

"Glenna wants to be like you, a Federal agent."

"When she finds out who you work for, she'll want to be just like her daddy."

"My daughter is gutsy. I avoid telling her that I'm with the Agency."

The phone to her ear, Eva said loudly, "Your dog and your teens served to me on a silver platter one of the largest seizures in ICE history. Co-workers are singing my praises from all around the country."

"Kudos to you, Eva. How long before ICE processes the reward? We'd like to tell Mason's parents right away."

"I'll submit the application using the info you just gave me," she promised. "We are all praying for Mason. Marty, my youngest, sent him a paper airplane."

Bo sighed. "His doctors are eager to schedule the bone marrow transplant ASAP."

"As far as Misty Harper, she refused to give our Florida agents any leads on the Fosters. They moved, end of story. So I'm turning on my computer to start digging."

"You have Michigan sources, right?"

"Absolutely. As a trained investigator, I never give up. Stay tuned."

She said good-bye to Bo and made another call. Forced to leave a message, Eva finished the application, e-mailing it to the moiety officer. She drank her lukewarm coffee, thinking about what Bo had just said about Glenna.

Eva's kids, Kaley and Andy, knew what she did for a living. Yet they had little idea of the dangers she faced as a special agent. When her case made the news, she simply mentioned criminals being caught and brought to justice.

But Bo worked for the CIA, America's secret spy network. He couldn't tell Glenna and Gregg that he risked his life to keep the country safe. That would violate national security. It was unusual for Eva to even know his true identity. She touched a photo of her kids flying a kite on a Michigan beach. They didn't know that she helped Bo, the CIA agent, work on secret cases.

She checked her watch. It was time to head for Andy's basketball game or she'd be late. Before she made it out the door, the phone rang, startling her. She answered it quickly.

"You called?" Jim Webber asked.

Eva closed the door. "How are things for ICE in Grand Rapids?"

"We're up to our eyebrows in an illegal smuggling case."

Eva cleared her throat. How much to tell Jim about Bo? She'd keep things vague.

"A good friend works for one of those D.C. agencies no one can talk about."

Jim laughed and waited. Eva popped a mint in her mouth.

"I work with him. He and his family took in a homeless girl named Krystal Harper. She once lived with a Michigan family."

"Too many kids are homeless these days. What happened to her mother?"

"Krystal's mother is irresponsible. Did you hear of ICE's big cocaine and money seizure near Tampa a few days ago?"

"Wow, Eva!" he hollered. "That huge case is yours?"

She pulled the phone away an inch and rubbed her ear.

"I received a very good tip. When the ship from Colombia was seized, her mother was arrested on board."

"But had the mother already abandoned her daughter?"

"Yes. That's why I'm calling. Krystal was born a crack cocaine baby. Michigan protective services took her from Misty Harper, placing her with a family named Foster. I hope I can find them. Maybe they'd welcome her back."

"I'll help if I can," Jim said. "Where do they live?"

"Krystal lived with the Fosters in a small town until she was six. Then Misty took her away. She's almost ten and had two sisters, Nicole and Bree. She recalls a river with a dam and lights at Christmas. Krystal's birthday is this month, but she doesn't know the date. That's it."

"We have Grand Rapids and Lowell on rivers, but Ada has a dam and covered bridge."

Jim grew silent as if thinking hard. Eva chewed her mint, her eyes dropping to her notes. She spotted a fresh clue.

"Here's something. The Fosters took Krystal tubing in the snow at a place called Panda's."

"Bingo! I know the place, but she's not recalling the name right."

"Is it enough to figure out the town?"

Eva held her breath.

"I know Rogue Rapids well. My wife and I walked on the dam at Christmas. The whole town is decorated. There's a boardwalk and shops on the river. Fun stuff people come to see."

"They have tubing in the snow?"

"Nearby there's a place with a name similar to Panda's."

"Great. Now what?" she asked.

"Todd Kaminga is the police chief in Rogue Rapids. I'll ask him to call you."

"Thanks, Jim. Watch your six."

"Look me up when you come to Michigan. My kids would like to catch up with yours."

Eva hung up. Should she give Bo an update? No, she'd wait until she heard from Todd Kaminga. In case the chief never called, Eva quickly put together Plan B.

Ten minutes later, she picked up her car keys and heavy purse, which served as the holster for her gun. Plan B had also fizzled. Her friend, the police chief in Zeeland, was out on a burglary call.

She shut her computer when her phone rang. If she answered, she'd miss Andy's basketball game. But what if Chief Kaminga was calling?

She grabbed the receiver and the caller fired off, "This is Chief Kaminga. Is it true you've found Krystal Harper?"

She blinked, dumbfounded. "You know Krystal?"

"Possibly. Webber told me you know a little girl who lived in Rogue Rapids."

"Perhaps, but Krystal is not so little. She thinks she turns ten this month."

"Ten, huh?" the chief said. "Let me see. It happened four years ago. She was about six years old then. Yup, I think she could be our little girl."

"Yours?" Eva exclaimed. "But your name isn't Foster."

"No. No. It's not like that. But there's a good chance the girl you described might be Krystal Harper. She was taken in as a crack baby by Justin and Becca Simms. Justin owns the Rogue Rapids Insurance Agency and is a member of our village board."

"Krystal was a crack baby," Eva said, excitement filling her heart.

"If you have time I'll share the sad story."

She set down her purse.

"Go ahead."

"Becca and Justin Simms cared for a crack baby as foster parents. Maybe that's why Krystal thinks their name is Foster. The Simms raised and loved her along with their two daughters, Nicole and Bree. They even started adoption proceedings."

"Krystal was traumatized the day her mother came for her."

The chief sighed. "We took the call for a problem at the Simms' house. My officer found Misty trying to grab Krystal. Because we respect the Simms, I rushed over. Misty sat in handcuffs in the back of the squad car. Then a caseworker showed up waving a piece of paper under my nose."

"Let me guess. She had a court order giving custody to the mother."

"The court ordered Krystal removed from the Simms and returned to Misty."

Eva imagined the heart-wrenching scene.

"And there was nothing you could do," she said, shaking her head.

"With lumps in our throats, we watched Becca and Justin pack her clothes in a small bag. Misty drove away with Krystal, who was crying buckets. The whole town hurt."

"Krystal was that well known in town?"

"The Simms are."

"Krystal said they moved from Rogue Rapids. Do you know where?"

"No, they still live here."

Eva smiled. "Chief Kaminga, you've made my day. My friend wants to locate Krystal's foster family. I'd like to put Bo Rider in touch with the Simms."

The chief gave her the phone number. "I will tell Justin to expect Bo's call."

"Bo and his family wonder if Krystal and the Simms might be reunited."

"People here will hold bake sales and plastic ducky races on the river to raise funds, if it's a matter of money. That's how we are. We would love to see Krystal return here."

"Thanks," Eva said. "Now we have to hope she'll want to live with the Simms again."

She signed off and immediately called Bo. His voice mail clicked on so she left a detailed message. Eva snatched her purse, and felt grateful for how Jim Webber knew Todd Kaminga, who knew the Simms and Krystal. Such a result could only be an answer to prayer.

Eva hurried to the elevator, anxious to reach home and tell Kaley and Andy how Krystal's foster family had been found. When Eva slid behind the wheel of her car, she thanked God for using her to help Glenna and Gregg earn a huge reward.

"Thank you, Father, for putting it on their hearts to use the money to help Mason receive his transplant. His life is in your hands."

Eva's cell phone rang. It was her husband Scott.

"I'm leaving the office," she said, starting the car.

"Eva, we're in the gym. Andy's game is starting."

"I'm on my way. Honey, you won't believe who I've just discovered."

44

At Tampa's bustling airport, Glenna adjusted Blaze's service vest and stroked his shiny fur. Over the past few weeks, she'd started telling the handsome dog her deepest hurts and fears. He always listened.

"I'm sad leaving Grandpa and Grandy," she said softly his ear.

Blaze looked at her, searching her face. He understood. The twinkle in his bright eyes gave her courage to fly back to Virginia and start life anew. He'd be at her side after all. Still the thought of leaving her grandparents brought tears to her eyes.

She stole to the ladies' room, bringing Blaze. After splashing cool water on her face, she walked with him to the departure area. She dropped in a leather chair and reached in her pocket, pulling something out.

Grandpa took a seat next to her. "Why are you sitting here by yourself?"

"I'm rewarding our secret weapon," she said, giving Blaze a doggie bone.

"Perfect. This is where he started his new career, putting us on track to help Mason."

Glenna patted Blaze's head. "Because of him, we captured Cain. I had no idea we'd earn such a large reward. Mason receives his transplant in three days. I hope it works."

"I do too. Grandy and I want to see him soon."

"He'll have to keep away from germs for a month or so. Mom told me the fund we created will pay for his college."

"And college for y'all too," Grandpa said, smacking his lips.

"Don't forget Krystal."

"Right now she is scared of flying. Make sure she sits by you. You show her the ropes."

Glenna nodded. "I'll be missing you. You've become a good buddy to me and to Gregg."

He treated her to a wide smile. "Oh, I saved a newspaper clipping for you. Mr. Abramson, the owner of the *Mischief*, has sold his yacht. He donated the proceeds and more for leukemia research. It says here he's giving the Secret Observers' tipsters a reward."

She frowned. "But Grandpa, we don't need more money."

"I know, but don't deny him the blessing. He is honoring you for exposing Cain as a crook. The papers said Troy Abramson knew zilch about Cain's shenanigans; that's why the government didn't keep his yacht. Besides, you and Gregg will find someone else to help in the future. That seems to be how God is working this out, showing us how to love our neighbors."

"What if our neighbor is a bad person, like Cain?"

He grabbed her hand in his. "He will get his just desserts. Grandy and I are proud of you and Gregg. You've changed our lives being here."

Blaze tickled Glenna's free hand with his nose. He must smell the second treat hidden in her pocket. She let him chomp another doggie bone. Then he turned his brown eyes to hers as if asking, "What should I do?"

"You did well, boy. Are you ready to fly home?"

Blaze started wagging his tail. Glenna reached for him, but the dog evaded her grasp. As he bounded for the family, the leash slipped from her hands. She hurried to grab it. Blaze seemed as excited as she to be going home.

Mom cuddled Annie. Grandpa held up his arms to Grandy for Ricky. Krystal looked frightened, her eyes round and arms shaking. Glenna laid Krystal's hand on Blaze's head.

"Pet him a few times," she said. "Wait and see how safe he makes you feel."

Krystal dropped to her knees in her new jeans and nuzzled her cheek against his side. Blaze sat on his haunches, looking happy to be helping. No longer jealous when Blaze befriended others, Glenna walked over and gave Grandy a hug.

"I love you," she said, a lump sticking in her throat. "Fly up and visit us soon."

Blaze stood up, wagging his tail.

"Look!" Gregg laughed. "Our dog wants you to come too."

"Our dog is so smart. Blaze doesn't want us leaving him behind." Glenna made sure she had a firm grip on his leash.

Annie looked ready to cry so Mom walked her in her arms. She settled right down, looking happy. Glenna could relate. That's how she felt when Dad was around.

"Mrs. Lockridge called this morning," Mom said. "Mason is thrilled to know you and Gregg became crime busters with Blaze's help."

"He must be anxious about the transplant," Glenna said, nudging Blake to her side.

"Mason asked us to pray for him."

Glenna's lower lip trembled. "Can we talk with him on Skype when we get home?"

"He's receiving his final chemo at the hospital, but I think that might be arranged."

Mom blinked rapidly as if holding back tears. Glenna wiped her eyes while Grandpa moved his foot away from Blaze's front paw.

"As soon as that young man is allowed visitors," he said in a husky voice, "your grandy and I are flying up to Virginia. We're already missing y'all."

"Me too."

As Glenna wrapped her arms around Grandpa's neck, she sensed a stream of people exiting the monorail.

"Dad!" Gregg cried.

Glenna jerked up her head. Dad came bustling toward them, a giant grin on his face. Glenna rushed into his arms.

"You surprised us," was all she could say, happiness flooding her heart.

Dad kissed the top of her head and pulled Mom into a hug. Glenna introduced him to Krystal. The shy girl left her hand on Blaze's head and stared. Dad stepped back. He gestured to some nicely-dressed people behind him.

"I'd like you to meet Becca and Justin Simms."

Krystal looked shocked. Then she leapt at them.

"Mama, Papa," she said, sobbing.

They engulfed her in a bear hug. Glenna could only stare.

"Her mother is Misty," she insisted. "Who are these people?"

"Krystal lived with them in Michigan."

"Oh. Are they the Fosters?"

Dad smiled at Glenna. "Krystal was too young to realize the Simms were her *foster* parents."

"Why are they here, Dad?"

With a gentle hand, he prodded Glenna away from the group gathered around the Simms.

"I'm flying home with you and our family. Becca and Justin didn't know until the last minute if they could find someone to watch their baby daughter, who Krystal hasn't met. We didn't mention them coming for fear of disappointing her."

"She loves them, I can tell. But is she still flying home with us?"

"If she's willing to go with the Simms to Michigan, they'll change our ticket for her from Virginia to Michigan. I think Krystal will travel with her foster family, don't you?"

Glenna had such mixed feelings. "Mom said the counterfeiters plead guilty. Is it over, Dad?"

Thoughts of the crazy guy with the baseball bat made her shiver.

"Yes, the judge sentenced them to twenty years in Federal prison."

She drew in a deep breath, knowing this might be her only chance. Glenna stood on tiptoe to whisper in her dad's ear.

"With our gigantic reward, can you stop being a spy?"

Dad acted cool. His face didn't flinch. But his left eyelid closed over his eye. Did he wink? Before she could ask him a single question, Krystal grabbed her arm.

"Mama and Papa want to know if you'll visit me this summer."

Blaze looked up at Glenna. Did she imagine it or was he nodding his head yes?

45

Glenna wrapped her scarf around her neck. She was freezing on the cold bleacher seat, but there were only three minutes left. She sat wedged in between Kaley Montanna and Gregg. The stands of Wheatland's football field were filled with cheering fans from both teams. Eva Montanna and the rest of her clan filled the row. Wheatland and Middleville were battling to win their conference. The score was 14–7, with Wheatland leading. Gregg turned his back to her and she poked him.

"Don't you care? Kaley earned her driver's license."

"Go Chargers!" he yelled, rooting for Mason's team.

Glenna turned her cold face to Kaley.

"I still need more hours," she admitted.

Her friend wrinkled her nose. "You've been back in Virginia, what, six months?"

"Nine," Glenna corrected, her eyes on the scoreboard. "Too bad Grandpa and Grandy left yesterday. They're missing the game."

"Kaley, move your legs and let Mr. Rider pass," Eva scolded.

Dad stepped over Kaley and her parents' feet, sitting next to Glenna.

"Dad, where did you go?" She pulled her jacket up to her neck.

"I had a phone call and it's too noisy up here."

"Was it a spy call?" she asked in a quiet voice.

Dad said softly, "Some things are heating up and I may have to fly out tomorrow." Then he winked his left eye, asking loudly, "What did I miss?"

Before Glenna could fill him in, everyone in the bleachers stood, raising their arms forming a passing wave. As they sat back down, Glenna noticed Dad's smirk. He was starting to trust her about his job in tiny ways.

Maybe later, she'd ask him more about what he just said and what it was like working for the CIA. But she'd make sure Gregg was nowhere around when she did.

She watched the action, yelling, "Oh no! Middleville scored."

"Guess we're all tied up," Dad said. "Has Mason played?"

Eva leaned over. "Not yet. He's down on the bench with a minute left."

"We're still at midfield," Dad complained.

Glenna clapped her hands. "We want Mason to play."

"Yeah! He could kick a field goal," Gregg hollered.

Dad let out a ragged sigh. "Their regular kicker missed two already, but it's Mason's first game back after his recovery. I don't think the coach will rely on a sophomore to win the championship."

The crowd jumped to their feet. So did Glenna, not knowing why. Then she saw Wheatland's quarterback throw a pass to Middleville's twenty-three-yard line.

"We have a chance to win," Dad shouted, raising his hands.

"Look!" Gregg elbowed Glenna pointing at Wheatland's bench. "Mason's warming up."

Mason's uniform was spotless. His teammates were grass-stained and muddy. He kicked a practice football into a net as if he'd never been sick.

"Dad," Glenna pulled on his jacket sleeve, "look. The coach has Mason practicing."

"Uh oh." Dad shook his head.

Glenna locked her eyes forward. Wheatland's quarterback lay sprawled on the turf.

"He's sacked," Dad said. "Fourth down and eighteen yards to go."

Gregg jumped up. "There's seven seconds left."

"Time out, Wheatland," Eva roared.

Their quarterback ran to the sidelines. The coach draped an arm over Mason's shoulder.

Dad nudged Glenna. "Hold on. Mason's going to make the last play."

"Will he be able to make a field goal?" Glenna chewed her lip.

The coach swatted Mason on his back. He raced on the field, snapping on his helmet.

The announcer yelled above the screaming crowd, "Returning for his first time after a long illness, sophomore Mason Lockridge will attempt the field goal for Wheatland."

"Go, Mason!" Glenna called, jumping up.

Dad and everyone else rose to their feet. They hollered like crazy for Mason.

Wheatland's center snapped the ball.

The holder placed it perfectly.

Mason took four steps and kicked.

The football soared too far to the left. Glenna's spirits plunged to her toes.

Then the ball wobbled, passing just inside the upright.

"He scored! He scored!"

Glenna danced on the narrow bleacher, hugging Kaley. Cheers rang throughout the stadium.

"That's my boy. My boy made the winning score!"

Mr. Lockridge turned to Dad, giving him a high-five.

Dad yelled, "He sure did. Your son won the game."

Gregg thumped Glenna's back. She looked at Mason riding on the shoulders of his teammates. They cheered wildly, carrying him toward the sidelines. In one hand he held his helmet. With his other hand, he pointed up with one finger.

"He's pointing to heaven," Glenna shouted.

A thrill coursed through her. She couldn't wait to talk with Mason and plan a trip to spend time with Grandpa and Grandy over Christmas. Just then, Dad whisked out his cell phone. He put it to his ear, but she saw him shake his head.

He dashed past her feet, exclaiming, "Oh no!"

Glenna pulled on his sleeve. "Dad, are Mom and the twins okay?"

He nodded and winked with his left eye.

That could only mean one thing. Dad's spy thing was heating up again.

She watched him hurry away and she wondered, would they have to move again? Glenna's cell phone vibrated in her pocket. She plucked it out. Mason had sent a text message hours ago, maybe just before the game. Why hadn't the phone alerted her before? That was odd, but Mason's message was even stranger.

Tell Gregg that sword in the basement is from the Civil War. I just learned my family's secret legend. Call me after the game!

Glenna's heart raced. What could it all mean? More importantly, what exciting adventure waited for her and Gregg?

A Note to Readers from Glenna:

In *Night Flight* you learned that Gregg and I lived in Israel during my dad's last assignment. Some exciting things happened to us there, so we had to leave our home in the Washington, D.C. suburbs to live in the farmhouse owned by Mason's family. We had fun and exciting experiences in Israel, but I didn't realize until just recently who my father worked for while we were there. Gregg still doesn't know. If you feel you are a sophisticated reader and want to tackle an adult novel, you can read about our adventures in Israel in *The Joshua Covenant*, also written by Diane and David Munson.

I hope you love Blaze as much as I do. What an amazing nose. I was interested to discover there are lots of working dogs like Blaze in the Department of Homeland Security and in police departments. One such dog is Kahlua, a golden retriever assigned to Immigration Customs Enforcement (ICE). For many years, Kahlua held the record for seizing more U.S. currency than any dog in the nation. Blaze, the currency dog in *Night Flight*, was inspired by Kahlua. In the Munsons' second adult, family-friendly novel *Confirming Justice*, Kahlua had a minor but critical role in securing justice.

Stay tuned for the next installment of the "Truth Seeker Series."

The Munsons have authored six, family-friendly adult thrillers.

The Munsons' Thrillers May Be Read In Any Order.

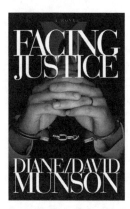

ISBN-13: 978-0982535509
352 pages, trade paper
Fiction / Mystery and Suspense
14.99

Facing Justice

First in the Justice series, Diane and David Munson draw on their true-life experiences in this suspense novel about Special Agent Eva Montanna, whose twin sister died at the Pentagon on 9/11. Eva dedicates her career to avenge her death while investigating Emile Jubayl, a member of Eva's church and CEO of Helpers International, who is accused of using his aid organization to funnel money to El Samoud, head of the Armed Revolutionary Cause, and successor to Al Qaeda. Family relationships are tested in this fast-paced, true-to-life legal thriller about the men and women who are racing to defuse the ticking time bomb of international terrorism.

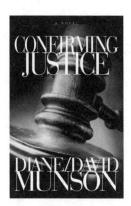

ISBN-13: 978-0982535516
352 pages, trade paper
Fiction / Mystery and Suspense
14.99

Confirming Justice

In *Confirming Justice*, all eyes are on Federal Judge Dwight Pendergast, secretly in line for nomination to the Supreme Court, who is presiding over a bribery case involving a cabinet secretary's son. When the key prosecution witness disappears, FBI agent Griff Topping risks everything to save the case while Pendergast's enemies seek to embroil the judge in a web of corruption and deceit. The whole world watches as events threaten the powerful position and those who covet it. Diane and David Munson masterfully create plot twists, legal intrigue and fast-paced suspense, in their realistic portrayal of what transpires behind the scenes at the center of power.

The Camelot Conspiracy

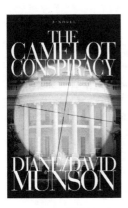

ISBN-13: 978-0982535523
352 pages, trade paper
Fiction / Mystery and Suspense
14.99

The Camelot Conspiracy rocks with a sinister plot even more menacing than the headlines. Former D.C. insiders Diane and David Munson feature a brash TV reporter, Kat Kowicki, who receives an ominous email that throws her into the high stakes conspiracy of John F. Kennedy's assassination. When Kat uncovers evidence Lee Harvey Oswald did not act alone, she turns for help to Federal Special Agents Eva Montanna and Griff Topping who uncover the chilling truth: A shadow government threatens to tear down the very foundations of the American justice system.

Hero's Ransom

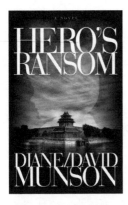

ISBN-13: 978-0982535530
320 pages, trade paper
Fiction / Mystery and Suspense
14.99

CIA Agent Bo Rider (*The Camelot Conspiracy*) and Federal Agents Eva Montanna and Griff Topping (*Facing Justice, Confirming Justice, The Camelot Conspiracy*) return in *Hero's Ransom*, the Munsons' fourth family-friendly adventure. When archeologist Amber Worthing uncovers a two-thousand-year-old mummy and witnesses a secret rocket launch at a Chinese missile base, she is arrested for espionage. Her imprisonment sparks a custody battle between grandparents over her young son, Lucas. Caught between sinister world powers, Amber's faith is tested in ways she never dreamed possible. Danger escalates as Bo races to stop China's killer satellite from destroying America and, with Eva and Griff's help, to rescue Amber using an unexpected ransom.

ISBN-13:978-0982535547
320 Pages, trade paper
Fiction/Mystery and Suspense
14.99

Redeeming Liberty

In this timely thriller by ExFeds Diane and David Munson (former Federal Prosecutor and Federal Agent), parole officer Dawn Ahern is shocked to witness her friend Liberty, the chosen bride of Wally (former "lost boy" from Sudan) being kidnapped by modern-day African slave traders. Dawn tackles overwhelming danger head-on in her quest to redeem Liberty. When she reaches out to FBI agent Griff Topping and CIA agent Bo Rider, her life is changed forever. Suspense soars as Bo launches a clandestine rescue effort for Liberty only to discover a deadly Iranian secret threatening the lives of millions of Americans and Israelis. Glimpse tomorrow's startling headlines in this captivating story of faith and freedom under fire.

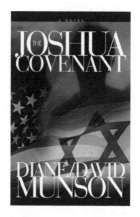

ISBN-13:978-0-983559009
336 Pages, trade paper
Fiction/Mystery and Suspense
14.99

The Joshua Covenant

CIA agent Bo Rider moves to Israel after years of clandestine spying around the world. He takes his family—wife Julia, and teens, Glenna and Gregg—and serves in America's Embassy using his real name. Glenna and Gregg face danger while exploring Israel's treasures, and their father is shocked to uncover a menacing plot jeopardizing them all. A Bible scholar helps Bo in amazing ways. He discovers the truth about the Joshua Covenant and battles evil forces that challenge his true identity. Will Bo survive the greatest threat ever to his career, his family, and his life? Bo risks it all to stop an enemy spy.